HENRIET

GOOD

VERNON LODER was a pseudonym for John George Haslette Vahey (1881-1938), an Anglo-Irish writer who also wrote as Henrietta Clandon, John Haslette, Anthony Lang, John Mowbray, Walter Proudfoot and George Varney. He was born in Belfast and educated at Ulster, Foyle College, and Hanover. Four years after he graduated college he was apprenticed to an architect and later tried his hand at accounting before turning to fiction writing full time.

According to the copy of Loder's *Two Dead* (1934): "He once wrote a novel in twenty days on a boarding-house table, and had it serialised in U.S.A. and England under another name . . . He works very quickly and thinks two hours a day in the morning quite enough for any one. He composes direct on a machine and does not re-write." While perhaps this is an exaggeration, Vahey was highly prolific, author of at least forty-four novels between 1926 and 1938.

Vahey's series characters were Inspector Brews, Chief Inspector R.J. "Terry" Chace, Donald Cairn (as Loder) and William Power, Penny & Vincent Mercer (as Henrietta Clandon).

With a solid reputation for witty characterisation and "the effortless telling of a good story" (*Observer*), Vahey's popularity was later summed up in the *Sunday Mercury*: "We have no better writer of thrill mystery in England."

Henrietta Clandon Mysteries
Available from Dean Street Press

Inquest

Good by Stealth

This Delicate Murder

Power on the Scent

HENRIETTA CLANDON

GOOD BY STEALTH

With an introduction by Curtis Evans

DEAN STREET PRESS

Published by Dean Street Press 2020

First published in 1936 by Geoffrey Bles

Cover by DSP

ISBN 978 1 913054 87 8

www.deanstreetpress.co.uk

STRING PUZZLES BY THE
COZY FIRESIDE

The Mysteries of Henrietta Clandon

Who is "Henrietta Clandon"? We don't know—we wish
we did!" Anyhow, "she" has written one of the best
murder novels we have read in a long time.

--newspaper advertisement by Geoffrey Bles,
publisher of the Henrietta Clandon detective novels

TODAY we know, as the coy "she" above hinted, that Golden Age
mystery writer Henrietta Clandon, author of seven detective
novels between 1933 and 1938, was in fact a man: John George
Haslette Vahey (1881-1938). Women mystery writers adopt-
ing the guise of masculine or sexually ambiguous pseudonyms
was a common enough practice during the Golden Age of detective fiction, as it had been with their Victorian and Edwardian
sisters. Margery Allingham wrote a trio of mysteries as Maxwell
March, Americans Dorothy Blair and Evelyn Page five as Roger
Scarlett and Lucy Beatrice Malleson over three score as Anthony
Gilbert, while the names Ngaio Marsh, Moray Dalton, E.C.R.
Lorac and E.X. Ferrars--the latter three respectively pseudonyms of Katherine Mary Dalton Renoir, Edith Caroline Rivett
and Morna Doris MacTaggart, aka Elizabeth Ferrars--left readers in doubt as to the authors' actual genders and male book
reviewers often referring, in their early years, to the excellent
books by Messrs. Marsh, Dalton, Lorac and Ferrars. When in
doubt, assume it is male, so the thinking then seemed to go.
(More recently the late scholar and mystery fan Jacques Barzun
referred to Moray Dalton as a "neglected man" while another,
Jared Lobdell, speculated that "Moray Dalton" might have been
yet another pseudonym of prolific British Golden Age mystery
writer Cecil John Charles Street.)

It was commonly believed, in those days, that men were more credible to readers as writers of detective fiction. It also was presumed that readers of detective fiction were predominantly male as well. "[T]he detective story . . . is primarily a man's novel," emphatically declared a woman, American Marjorie Nicolson, then serving as dean of the English department at Smith College, in "The Professor and the Detective," an essay originally published in the *Atlantic Monthly* in 1929. "Many women dislike it heartily, or at best accept it as a device to while away hours on the train. And while we do all honor to the three or four women who have written surpassingly good detective stories of the purest type, we must grant candidly that the great bulk of our detective stories today are being written by men."

This was an attitude which began decidedly to change, however, with the rise of Britain's so-called four Queens of Crime in the 1930s: Agatha Christie (first mystery novel published in 1920), Dorothy L. Sayers (1923), Margery Allingham (1928) and Ngaio Marsh (1934), not to mention a slew of additional talented British women detective writers, such as the aforementioned Anthony Gilbert and others like Patricia Wentworth, Moray Dalton, Gladys Mitchell, Annie Haynes, E.C.R. Lorac, Joan Cowdroy, Molly Thynne, Helen Simpson, Ianthe Jerrold, Elizabeth Gill, Josephine Bell, Mary Fitt, Dorothy Bowers, Harriet Rutland and, coming along a bit later in the 1940s, Christianna Brand and Elizabeth Ferrars. (In the United States there were, aside from Roger Scarlett, an admittedly minor player in the world of Golden Age detective fiction, the hugely popular Mary Roberts Rinehart and Mignon Eberhart and their many followers.) By the late Thirties and early Forties readers and reviewers alike had concluded that classic detective fiction was a form of fiction at which women excelled as much as, if not more then, the male of the species. It was, indeed, the men who might have been well advised to watch their backs, for fear of fatal feminine thrusts from wicked-bladed letter openers or jewel-encrusted hatpins.

It is this altered environment which led to the appearance, with the novel *Inquest* in 1933, of another purported woman crime writer, one who was emphatically a lady in tone, if not in fact: Henrietta Clandon. In the hands of Dorothy L. Sayers and, I would argue, Agatha Christie, with such novels as *Strong Poison, Have His Carcase, The Murder of Roger of Ackroyd* and *The Murder at the Vicarage*, there had arisen so-called "manners mystery" murder fiction, filled not just with corpses, crimes and clues, but witty and sardonic observation of people and social mores. (Male authors Anthony Berkeley/Francis Iles and C.H.B. Kitchin were also signal contributors in this regard.) Margery Allingham would follow suit in 1934 with the marvelous *Death of a Ghost*, accompanied by Ngaio Marsh's debut novel *A Man Lay Dead*, but Henrietta Clandon actually had already anticipated the two younger Crime Queens with a fully developed manners mystery in 1933.

When he created Henrietta Clandon, John Haslette Vahey was no new hand at mystery mongering. Born on March 5, 1881 in Strandtown, a district of Belfast, Northern Ireland, Vahey was the middle son of Herbert Vahey, a superintendent of Inland Revenue (i.e., tax collector), and his wife Jane Lowry Vahey, a daughter of a wealthy Belfast watchmaker and jeweler. Like his contemporary, author and crime writer E.R. Punshon, "Jack" Vahey, as he was known, after walking away from careers in business around the turn of the century (in Vahey's case insurance and accountancy), had started writing fiction professionally. Vahey published his first novel in 1909, while residing at a Bournemouth boarding house with his elder brother, who also wrote fiction, and he began turning out mysteries in the classic mold by the late 1920s, primarily under the pen name Vernon Loder, whose work recently has been highly praised by vintage mystery authorities Nigel Moss and John Norris. (Moss calls Vernon Loder "a paradigm of the English Golden Age mystery writer.") Jack Vahey's other known pen names—those besides his two most notable ones, Vernon Loder and Henrietta Clandon--are John Haslette, Anthony Lang, John Mowbray and the hobbit-ish Walter Proudfoot; under the entire tribe, whose output included mysteries, mainstream, adventure and espionage novels, and school tales, he ultimately produced sixty-five books, making him a prolific author indeed. Vahey boasted that he once composed a novel over a span of twenty days at a table at the boarding house, afterward serializing it in both the United Kingdom and the United States under different pseudonyms.

By 1933, when Jack Vahey at the age of fifty-two created Henrietta Clandon, he had as Vernon Loder already published eight detective novels in five years, and no fewer than three additional Loder novels would appear in print in 1933. Many of the Vernon Loder titles were published in both the UK (with the prestigious Collins Crime Club) and the US (with Morrow, publisher of Christopher Bush and, shortly in the future, Erle Stanley Gardner and Carter Dickson.) Why, then, one might ask, did Vahey start publishing under yet another pseudonym?

When one reads the Clandons, the "why" becomes readily apparent, for Vahey with this new line clearly was attempting to do something different, and more ambitious, with his crime fiction than he had with Vernon Loder, et al., as pleasing as some of the Loder novels are. The Henrietta Clandon novels are the most carefully crafted mysteries that Vahey ever wrote, models of manners mystery which present to the reader wittily epigrammatic and cuttingly sardonic murder in its most deceptively cozy British guises of country houses and villages—quintessential malice domestic, as it were. Critics responded favorably to the Clandons, sensing an enticing new spice of mystery in the air, one which seemed exquisitely feminine.

Dorothy L. Sayers herself welcomed Henrietta Clandon's *Inquest* in the pages of the *Sunday Times*, where Sayers was the crime fiction reviewer from 1933 to 1935, as "an attractive and promising piece of puzzle making." She added that the "book is very well written, the dialogue being quite exceptionally fresh and well-managed, and the characterization good," before adding encouragingly: "This appears to be Miss Henrietta Clandon's first detective story; I hope we shall hear more from her again." Score one for the ladies!

Of a later Clandon novel, *Rope by Arrangement*, Sayers keenly pronounced, employing a most apt image, that the novel's merit lay "in a kind of quiet tortuousness; to read it is rather like working out an intricate little string puzzle by the fireside. . . . the tale makes very agreeable reading." Nor was Sayers alone in her praise of Clandon. Concerning *This Delicate Murder*, Torquemada (noted crossword puzzle designer Edward Powys Mathers) in the *London Observer* praised its "wit" and the "nearly watertight impeccability" of its puzzle. For his part crime writer Milward Kennedy, Sayers' successor at the *Sunday Times*, in reviewing the superb inverted poison pen mystery *Good by Stealth*, which recalls not only works by Francis Iles but ones by Anthony Rolls and Richard Hull, lauded the author's "gift for irony in the depiction of the criminal's mind." An able literary limner like Henrietta Clandon, observed Kennedy admiringly, "can suit style to subject, and even enable us to see character in its true colour though revealed by colour-blind eyes." Perhaps Anthony Berkeley, reviewing crime fiction as Francis Iles, summed up best when he declared that "Henrietta Clandon's novels are always welcome. She has developed a style of her own in crime fiction."

Sadly, the steady series of Clandon mysteries was abruptly halted after the appearance of the seventh Clandon novel, *Fog off Weymouth* ("quite charming narration," pronounced Torquemada), which was published in March 1938, just three months before Jack Vahey's death at age fifty-seven on June 15. I do not know what killed the author, but only three years before his death he had flippantly boasted, in a letter to the *London Observer* signed "Vernon Loder," that "I have not spent a day in bed in thirty-two years," despite the fact that "I add great quantities of salt to my food, and vast quantities of sugar to tea, coffee and lemonade." As a remedy against the chronic throat inflammation he had suffered between the ages of fourteen and twenty-one, he had taken up smoking eucalyptus cigarettes (forerunners of menthols, recently banned in the state of Massachusetts). Salt, sugar and cigarettes—perhaps Jack's death should not have come as a surprise. It will be recalled that thriller writer Edgar Wallace, who died from a diabetic coma and double pneumonia in 1932, consumed copious amounts of sugary tea.

At the time of his untimely demise Vahey resided with his wife, Gertrude Crowe Barendt, formerly a music teacher from Liverpool, at a flat in affluent Branksome Park in Bournemouth (today Poole). A final Vernon Loder, *Kill in the Ring*, a boxing murder tale far removed from the milieu of Henrietta Clandon, was published in October and, after that, Vahey, who left no children, was largely forgotten. His elder brother, Herbert Lowry Vahey, a more peripatetic author than Jack, survived him by two decades, but though he wed as well, he left no children. Jack's younger brother, Samuel Lowry Vahey, an insurance executive who migrated to Canada and later Houston, Texas, predeceased Jack by a decade.

Where did Jack Vahey get his mind for "delicate murder," his ability to compose a quietly tortuous mystery resembling "an intricate little string puzzle"? He was educated at Foyle College, Londonderry, Northern Ireland and in the city of Hanover in the state of Saxony, Germany (which perhaps helps explain his later marriage to an Anglo-German wife), and his favored hobbies were shooting and fishing, but perhaps he carried within himself something of his canny Scots-Irish maternal grandfather, John Lowry, who died in Belfast in 1886, when Vahey was five years old. Old John Lowry was a highly respected maker and retailer of watches and chronometers (a time measuring instrument used in marine navigation to determine longitude), who owned a big shop in the High Street and did regular business as well in London. Pieces which Lowry designed are highly sought collector's items today. (For example, the website of David Penney's Antique Watch Store offers an exquisite "top quality" nineteenth-century chronometer by Lowry with gold hands and a "very rare sapphire roller.") At the old man's death, he left an estate that was valued at, in modern worth, some 470,000 pounds (over 600,000 dollars), indicating that he was a top person in his field.

A well-plotted Golden Age mystery, after all, resembles not only a string puzzle or Rubik's Cube, but a clock--whether or not unbreakable alibis and railway timetables are involved. Vahey's grandfather John Lowry possessed more than the consummate skill to construct intricate mechanical devices, however; he had, as well, personal experience with criminals. In 1867 Lowry, sounding like detective writer R. Austin's Freeman famed medical jurist sleuth Dr. John Thorndyke, testified at the criminal prosecution of one Bernard O'Kane for allegedly passing counterfeit coins around Belfast. At the trial, it was reported, Lowry established that the coins at issue were fake, being made of "base metal." Eleven years earlier, burglars had daringly invaded Lowry's shop at 66 High Street. The watchmaker had spent the evening and early morning hours on the roof of his house, where he had been engaged in "comparing his time by transit observations of the stars" until one o'clock in the morning. During this time he heard noises on the roof, but took this to be merely the nocturnal perambulations of a cat. Later that morning, when the entire household had gone to bed, a felonious party took a pane of glass out of a skylight and with a rope descended into the house. Fortunately, "the shop being well secured, the goods locked in a large safe, a party well-armed sleeping in a room connected with the shop, and doors properly barred inside, the robber or robbers could get no farther than the kitchen and back room, from which they took several articles of dress and even some eatables," departing without detection. It is the sort of setting that with embellishment might have inspired Edgar Wallace's famous mystery *The Clue of the New Pin* (1923), in which a shady businessman who keeps all his spoils hidden away at his home in a massive basement vault, securely locked up at night to make it impregnable, is found shot to death, inside his own locked vault. There is no gun anywhere to be found, merely a single pin. . . .

Great outré stuff for a classic Golden Age mystery (though in violation of the rules of Father Ronald Knox and the Detection Club, a mysterious "Chinaman" lurks), which might have been just the thing for that earnest fellow Vernon Loder. In Jack Vahey's more up-to-date and sophisticated Henrietta Clandon tales, however, finical readers should rest assured that murder is something altogether more refined, a delicacy which can be served to polite society in the drawing room, along with buttered scones and tea. Just keep an eye out for arsenic and acid bon mots.

Good by Stealth

Across the transatlantic world in the second and third decades of the twentieth century a terrible wave of poison attacks took place, cruelly claiming hordes of human victims. In contrast with the toxic chlorine, phosgene and mustard gases which armies put to such ghastly and inhuman use during the First World War, however, these particular poisons were not delivered via canisters and shells. Rather, the instrument through which these poisons inflicted their damage was the pen—the so-called "poison pen" (a term which encompassed as well that click-clacking symbol of modern business efficiency, the typewriter). For these poisons were words—words which, like weapons of war, could not only hurt but in some cases kill.

Hostilities seem to have started in the American state of New Jersey. There in 1911 in the city of Elizabeth, located near New York City, a sneaking individual possessed of a "serpent typewriter," as the newspapers put it, launched a campaign of harassment against some of the city's "best people" with a series of anonymous letters, "some innocuous, some catlike, some downright indecent." The chief victim of this manic postal onslaught seems to have been Mrs. Florence Jones, wife of dentist Charles F. Jones, treasurer of the New Jersey State Dental Society, who lived on fashionable Madison Avenue. Shockingly in March 1914, it was the Jones' next door neighbor, Mrs. Anna Pollard, the forty-three year old wife of New Jersey Public Service Commission electrical engineer Nelson Pollard and mother of two young daughters, who was arrested and charged with the crime of sending the malicious letters. More astoundingly yet, Mrs. Pollard was president of the Elizabeth Ladies' Aid Society and a member of Christ Episcopal Church and the Boudinot chapter of the Daughters of the American Revolution (DAR). Famed handwriting expert William Kinsley testified that the same machine which had produced the type on letters Mrs. Pollard had indisputably typed had done so as well with the poison pen letters, yet the jury, perhaps disinclined to believe that a woman of such impeccable local standing as the defendant could do such things, voted to acquit.

After Mrs. Pollard went free the sending of poison pen letters soon recommenced, this time not in type but in the form of hand printed block letters and words cut and pasted from newspapers. Once again, the unfortunate Mrs. Jones stood at the head of the recipients. In October Mrs. Pollard, having fallen into a wily trap laid for her by the local Federal postal inspector, was again arrested and charged with the crime; and this time she confessed to having written the letters, her motivation for doing so evidently having been her keen social jealousy. (She desperately wanted to "keep up with the Joneses," as it were.) A lenient judge fined Mrs. Pollard only $200 (about $5000 today), with no jail time; but the disgraced New Jersey matron was expelled from the Boudinot chapter of the DAR after her conviction, which some may have felt was sufficient humiliation to someone as painfully conscious of social standing as Mrs. Pollard. She died in 1947, still residing at the same house in Elizabeth with her two unmarried daughters, one of whom ironically had become a dentist.

This vein of epistolary venom, once opened, proved impossible for Lady Justice to stanch. A few years after the contentious affair at Elizabeth, in 1917, someone across the Atlantic Ocean began inundating the small French provincial city of Tulle with malevolent screeds, which were left at mailboxes, doorsteps and windowsills, slipped into women's shopping baskets and even placed on church pews and in confessionals. In December 1922, Angèle Laval, the thirty-seven year old daughter of a comfortably circumstanced widow, was arrested for writing the letters and charged with defamation. Although Angèle denied guilt, she was convicted, fined and sentenced to a term of penal servitude. Several suicides had resulted from the letters, including that of Angèle's own mother, who had been mortified by the accusations against her daughter. After her release from prison, Angèle lived reclusively in Tulle until her death in 1967. French director Henri-Georges Clouzot's 1942 mystery film *Le Corbeau* (The Crow) was inspired by the dreadful events at Tulle.

Around the time that terror engulfed Tulle, a rash of spiteful and often profane anonymous letters, some of them melodramatically signed "by the unknown hand," began appearing across the pleasant and seemingly placid little seaside town of Sheringham in Norfolk, England. After five months of finger-pointing and recriminations, police in November 1923 arrested twenty-five year old Dorothy Myrtle Thurburn, daughter of artist Percy Cecil Thurburn and great-granddaughter of Roger Thurburn, who in the early Victorian era had been Her Britannic Majesty's Consul in Egypt. A former Girl Guides leader who had arrived in Sheringham with her mother in 1921 and received scores of poison pen letters herself, Dorothy was described in newspapers, appreciative of the seeming incongruity between her appearance and her alleged wrongdoing, as a "pretty, demure little miss, very girlish in her appearance." She categorically denied having written the anonymous letters.

These letters which Dorothy denied writing, some of the less explicit of which were read out in court, were anything but demure. In sometimes shockingly profane language they accused Sheringham citizens of everything from having had extra-marital affairs and out-of-wedlock children to being "badly made-up," "walking like a duck" and having "yellow-dyed hair" and "odd hips and twitching eyes." The brazen letter writer, who seemingly lacked any sense of self-awareness, denounced local women as spiteful, jealous old cats and she-devils. Her targets included even the local gentry, as embodied in Lady Brainbridge of nearby Haddon Lodge.

Dorothy Thurburn's trial saga dragged out into 1925, as juries twice were unable to reach verdicts. By her own admission Dorothy had drawn ironic caricatures of and written frank letters about Sheringham residents, but her attorney insisted that this was all done in jest and that she had sincerely apologized afterwards to anyone whom she might have offended. He also argued that the drawing ink used to compose the letters was readily obtainable by anyone at ordinary stationers' shops and that during the time the anonymous letters had been sent, Dorothy had innocently kept a mild diary which gave no inkling, if you will, of wicked activities. The prosecution insisted that Dorothy had left vicious letters to herself to avert suspicion and a police constable testified that he had actually witnessed the "demure little miss" posting correspondence at a pillar box in which poison pen letters were shortly afterward found.

At Dorothy's second trial, in June 1924, her attorney was no less than Edward Marshall Hall, England's "Great Defender," whose gallery of notorious clients included George Joseph Smith, the infamous Brides-in-the-Bath murderer. (He had also been briefed to defend Hawley Harvey Crippen, but they two men had a falling out.) The great man made headway in discrediting the police constable's claim that he had seen Dorothy posting letters at the telltale pillar box. In summing up, however, Mr. Justice Sankey suggestively asked of letters which Dorothy had admitted to writing, "They are very funny letters for a young lady to write. Do you not think you are dealing with rather a peculiar lady who writes letters of that character? You may put it rather higher. Do you not think you are dealing with an abnormal young lady?" Despite these damning queries from on high, the jury again deadlocked.

At Dorothy's third trial in early 1925, the prosecution declined to offer evidence and Sheringham's "demure little miss" at long last walked free in fact, if not free from suspicion. Dorothy and her mother, who always stood by her, left the county, Dorothy proclaiming, "I never wish to see Norfolk again as long as I live." Shortly before the outbreak of the Second World War, Dorothy lived alone on private means, still beside the seaside, in Eastbourne, Sussex, where she passed away, unmarried, in 1975, a half century after she had been acquitted of crime. Whether or not she really was the "unknown hand" who callously engineered one of the most paradigmatic of real life English poison pen mysteries still remains, well, unknown.

Given these prominent outbreaks of poison pen letters in the United States, France and England, which coincided with the onset of the Golden Age of detective fiction, it is only surprising that poison pen mysteries seemingly did not pop up sooner in British crime writing. The first poison pen mystery novel of which I am aware is Ethel Lina White's *Fear Stalks the Village* (1932), followed in the Thirties and early Forties by Dorothy L. Sayers's *Gaudy Night* (1935), Henrietta Clandon's *Good by Stealth* (1936), J. J. Connington's *For Murder Will Speak* (1938) and Agatha Christie's *The Moving Finger* (1942). In their inimitable authors' particular fashions both *Gaudy Night* and *The Moving Finger* set high standards in puzzle making, but Henrietta Clandon's *Good by Stealth* has merits which are emphatically all "her" own within this beguiling mystery subgenre. It is clear from a reading of the novel that the author made a close study of real life poison pen cases.

Good by Stealth is an inverted mystery, meaning that from the beginning of the story we know who the culprit is and watch as this person's crimes unfold. Purporting to be the actual manuscript of thirty-eight year old Miss Edna Alice, late of the once peaceful English village of Lush Mellish, it is an apologia in which Miss Alice divulges how she came to terrorize the village inhabitants--all for their own good of course--with scores of poisonous missives. The apologia follows a foreword by Henrietta Clandon herself, who somewhat diffidently explains that she has sponsored the book, in some cases replacing surnames with Christian names to protect the anonymity of the individuals in the account. (In the Clandon novels "Henrietta Clandon" is identified as fictional detective novelist Penny Mercer, who first appears in the 1935 Clandon mystery *Rope by Arrangement*, although in the real world Henrietta Clandon was Anglo-Irish mystery writer John George Haslette Vahey.)

Like Richard Hull's classic inverted mystery novel *The Murder of My Aunt* (1934), Henrietta Clandon's *Good by Stealth* is a superb satirical study of a deranged criminal mind, told in an ironically droll and penetrating first person narrative. (Among the droll pleasures is a parody of the poetry of Gertrude Stein.) Just how deranged this mind is, I leave for you to decide for yourselves in the pages which follow. . . .

Curtis Evans

If you understand yourself, it is as much as you can be expected to do."—

A favourite aphorism of Miss Alice's father.

FOREWORD

EVER since I undertook to sponsor the late Mr. Montgomery Brace's *apologia*, *Rope by Arrangement*, I have been inundated with MSS. from people whose desire to express themselves in print is all too often in inverse ratio to their means of expression.

Was it not Mr. St. John Ervine who wrote: "(1) Do not send me MSS. without stamps. (2) Do not send me MSS.!"? Well—don't!

I only consented to see the present novel through the press for two very relevant, if not very good, reasons. First, Miss Alice's offering contained an undoubted reference to Mr. Brace's old friend, Mr. Power; then Miss Alice expressed herself with facility, and, at times, force. I make no comment on the case she puts forward for herself. Perhaps heredity *had* something to do with it. But she has tried clearly—if somewhat bitterly—to show that good deeds done by stealth may really be good deeds, though, to the prejudiced eye of the outsider, they may appear both actionable and dangerous. I make no comment on that either. You must judge for yourself.

The story stands as it was written, save for one fact. I have given some of the characters Christian names, instead of surnames. This is an act of pure charity on my part. Miss Edna Alice wanted them to remain under their own. Her motive is obscure.

So here you are. And here is a story told from the inside; a story which has already been told from the outside by the newspapers.

I leave it to you.

HENRIETTA CLANDON.

CHAPTER I

I CAME out of jail ten months ago, and have been occupied since then in writing the story of the latter part of my life, before malicious people, and an absurd verdict, unjustly deprived me of my liberty.

Yes, for twelve long months. It was the Second Division, they said. If I have come through it unscathed, and am still able to hold my head high, it is not that I did not detest the place, and the people, where I was confined. The wardresses were common women, and the prisoners, with one exception, vulgar girls, with no sense of decency or respect.

I am not writing an attack on British law, or an apology for my life. I leave the latter to others, who cannot say to themselves that from first to last their conduct was governed by a desire to do the right thing, and—what is much harder—to make other people do the right thing.

Before I go any further, I wish to make it clear that I had no pious desires to make other people better. As you will see later, the local vicar and the Nonconformist minister gave assistance to the prosecution. So it was foolish for the incompetent man who defended me to plead at the end of the case that I was suffering from religious mania. But all my life I have demanded right and justice, with the result you see.

"What do you mean by right?" I remember the stuffy old judge said, when I made this remark in court. "Your rights, or what you conceive to be your rights, or something for the general good? I may remark, Miss Alice, that there is some confusion between right and rights."

Silly old man! How can I govern my life by what seems right to others? Extravagant as the claim sounds, one of the witnesses against me said he thought it quite right to hit my dog. And a boor in court called out: "Damn' well right!" I am glad to say that he was turned out. But I shall come to that later. My point is that each of us knows what he himself should do. Can he be blamed if he does it?

But to return to the prison where I spent an unhappy twelve months. Vulgar and ignorant as the bulk of my fellow prisoners were, I had thought—absurdly, of course, since they had obviously done wrong—that they would see that I, at least, was a victim of persecution, one born before her time.

Not a bit of it. They each and all assumed that I was there for a very good reason. Opportunities for talking are infrequent in prisons. I thought that a hardship at first, but not for long. To one particularly vicious young woman, who, I heard, had stolen from shops, I had to protest that I was the victim of popular malice. I remember to this day her nasty, sneering laugh.

"Then what did you write those dirty letters for?" she asked, and giggled again at my shocked expression.

It showed me clearly that the vulgar mind is incapable of understanding the refined one, or, to put it in the vernacular: "What can you expect of a pig but a grunt?"

Dirty letters! There showed the essential obscenity of the common mind. I never wrote a single letter which contained an expression calculated to bring a blush to the cheek of youth. I said so to the brute who prosecuted me. He tucked up the tail of his gown in the silly fashion barristers have, and said that I had still left myself considerable scope, as things went nowadays.

Between a prosecutor who made these would-be witty debating points, and the foolish old man on the Bench, who talked to me in an impertinently fatherly way, I had a most unpleasant time.

"Come, come, Miss Alice," the latter said once—my name is Edna Alice, by the way—"if your intentions were such as you suggest, would it not have been fairer and juster for you to append your signature to these communications?"

Now wasn't that an odd thing for an educated and apparently intelligent man to say? Either he was trying to trap me, or he was overlooking the fact that signing my name would have got me into trouble just the same. I mean to say, people resent being made to do the right thing, and the only way to escape their mean vengeance is to omit your name when you write.

They can't expect to have it both ways.

After the first month in prison I decided to keep to myself, and did so bravely. I noticed after that that neither the prisoners nor wardresses forced their presence or speech on me. Not directly, at least; though I heard one fair-minded girl say that it wasn't fair putting me in jail with them. She is the exception to the rule of which I wrote just now. She made the other women laugh, though I do not know why.

The real trouble was, as I see since, that people do not discriminate. They lump all cases of what they consider a like nature together, and to their ill-informed minds I was in the same category as a mentally unsound woman who posts disgusting anonymous letters to her neighbours.

"You were trying, in fact," said the prosecutor, with a sneer, "to do good by stealth?"

"Yes," I said cuttingly. "If you have any record, sir, of doing good, either openly or by stealth, I shall be glad to hear it. So far, I only know you as a so-called man who attacks defenceless women."

If he had been a man of decency and refinement, he would have felt crushed. But it was too much to expect. He had obviously been picked for his venom by the crowd of spiteful people who initiated the prosecution. He even dared to laugh.

"Indeed, madam," he said, "it strikes me that you were not only in the possession of a deadly and cutting weapon, but you also found occasion to use it behind other people's backs. It was not a duel, shall I suggest, but verbal murder."

The judge pulled him up for that. It was the only time when he showed a grain of sense, and I am sure that if the age of judges is ever put to the vote, I shall be all in favour of a retiring age of fifty-five.

"I suggest," I replied with spirit, in face of some disgusting laughter in court, "that whatever weapon I used, I had occasion to use it."

"And used it with force, if not discretion," he said.

Of the busybodies and officious witnesses, I am sure the vicar and the Nonconformist parson were the worst. I had never attended their places of worship. I had never tried to make either of them do right, though I am sure I might have tried. In spite of that, they both came forward and said I had sent them letters charging members of their congregations with various things.

But there you are. Officious people will not mind their own business. They seemed as angry as if I had written to their parishioners charging *them* with something. Frankly, I could not understand their conduct.

When I had heard the sentence, I was not as crushed as the people in court hoped. Technically, I knew myself to be at fault, but everything is in intention, and my intentions had been blameless from the start. I wish I could believe it of the motives of the two clergymen who came forward to help my persecutors.

The chief blow came later. I was not to be allowed to have my dear dog, Tiblits, accompany me.

If it were nothing else but that, the savagery and cruelty of British law was shown up to be what it was. To dog-lovers like myself (real dog-lovers; not those who keep dogs, and even beat them at times), to lack one's dog is to miss everything that makes life dear. But I find that only a few people, the richer, choicer souls, love dogs. Most people love their fellows better; which is an extraordinary thing to me.

I wasn't asking that Tiblits should be treated luxuriously, or expensively; only that he should share my prison cell and prison fare. He would have been happy, and so should I, so you can imagine my horror when that dreadful old man, the judge, remarked that prison was supposed to be a form of punishment. As if Tiblits had done anything to deserve it.

He hardly knew me when I came out and went to fetch him. He had been "boarded out" with a dreadful woman, and there was no doubt that she had done her best to take his affections from me.

But there is no use going back on all that. I have come to accept the fact that the majority of people are callous and unsympathetic when they come in contact with those more sensitive and subtle than themselves. I suppose they feel a kind of inferiority secretly, and express it by harshness and cruelty.

We who cultivate an inner life have to be studied in the surroundings of our youth to be understood. We grow so much in that formative period. We are formed characters at an age when the common herd is still unshapen clay, if you know what I mean.

So I hope you won't feel bored if I tell you something of my father and mother. I am rather like them, I think; a little bit of each, and I do fervently believe in heredity.

My father was originally a very considerable land-owner. When I was born he had a very large and profitable rent-roll. Generations of independence had made him conscious of his rights, and he had, like me, a strong sense of justice.

It was that, I may say, which led gradually to a decline in our fortunes. At thirteen, I was sent to an expensive boarding-school; at seventeen, I had to leave it. I was taken away for reasons of economy.

The longer I live the more I see that people with a strong sense of justice are like geniuses. They run, as dear father used to say, very few to the acre. So it was perhaps natural that, in the county where we lived, most of our neighbours were narrow-minded, one-sided folk. They only considered their own interests.

As these interests very often clashed with ours—or, I should say, with my father's—he was unfortunately compelled to consult his lawyer, and, often, to take action to bring them to their senses.

But law is expensive, and we seemed to have a knack (though my logical father persisted that it was just chance) of having our cases decided by pig-headed, or prejudiced, juries. But father would never give up. Strong in his sense of right, he would take a case from one court to another; never realising, poor dear, that he was dealing with the same type of people wherever he went.

"If you left it there, and let them off with it," I remember hearing him say to my mother, "there'd be no justice left in the land. Right's right, and wrong's wrong."

Bit by bit he had to sell our land, and when I came home from my school—where I had never been really happy, I may say—I found that our fifteen hundred acres had shrunk to a miserable four hundred. And even that was not the end, for, when *Alice v. Gushall* went to the Lords, and with it my childish respect for the aristocracy, father had to mortgage our remaining property. If it had not been for old Aunt Smith, who had quarrelled with my father over their father's will, some forty years before, I should have faced the world penniless, or almost so.

She left me her little fortune, bringing in some six hundred a year.

The thing I remember best about my mother, apart from her devotion to me, was her wonderful way of judging character. There were few people who could hide their true selves from her. Naturally acute, and a hater of shams, she could see below the surface, and detect the real nature of men and women who had been able to hide from less perceptive folk the low motives and mean instincts actuating them.

I always admired and wondered at this trait in her. How did she know? How could she know? But she *did*. Long before Squire Pyrtson got his deserts, for instance, she told my father that the man would come to no good. Yet she was quite upset when that dreadful case did come on.

"It's almost as if I knew," she said. "Not that I ever wished the man any harm."

Only my father and I knew what charity lay behind those words; for Squire Pyrtson had been rude to her more than once, particularly in connection with the committee for the flower show.

"It's just like the cat's whiskers," my father said once in his jocular way. "Mummy doesn't require to see them; even in the dark she knows what's there."

My mother died, poor dear, when *Alice v. Sprigge and Sonsy* had just gone before the Court of Appeal. A week before, I heard her tell father that he had been unwise: "Lord Chief Justice Polloren doesn't *look* the man for his position, dad!" she said.

He felt a sort of bitter pleasure perhaps when he saw how right she had been. Old Polloren did not seem to have even listened to our side of the case. His judgment [*sic*] was a masterpiece of prejudice, and bad law—or so dad said.

Well, dad did not survive that year. The lawyers killed him, as they were, later, almost to kill me. I had my own income by then, and twenty pounds a year left by my father. I travelled on the Continent for six months, and then tried living with a friend in a flat in London.

Children are notoriously grudging of praise for their parents nowadays. But I say thankfully that, whatever I am, I owe it to my father and mother.

CHAPTER II

I SOON found that you cannot live with a friend in a flat. You lose one, or leave the other; or both.

You see, friends are strangers that you meet oftener than strangers, and you have always an idea that they share your ideas and ideals. But they never do; only look and talk as if they did until you are a few months in the same rooms with them.

And their friends! It is extraordinary how undiscriminating one's friends are. They get to know the most appalling people. And they *don't see it*.

Lucille and I started with a house-warming; and, of course, I dared not suggest that my friends and hers should come on different days. In fact, I went quite innocently and happily into the arrangement. I do not say that my friends would not have been quite nice to at least two of Lucille's. But she had at least eight people who were, to put it mildly, odd.

One was a lawyer's wife, and she got quite nasty when I spoke of my experience of lawyers, and how they had killed poor father. Then there was a woman who had something to do with art. My own opinion is that it went no further than her complexion.

And the men! You meet lots of men in the country, but those were too definitely absurd. One had a laugh like a horse; and another insisted on getting up and dancing with Lucille. They had blank faces, like the white sides of country cottages, and their idea of humour was extremely weird.

My friends did their best for a time, but even they could not put up with such a collection. When Dora, who lived in France for a long time, said: *"Réunion magnifique!"* (not knowing that anyone knew French) that art woman was furious.

Lucille—I must say that for her—was never too bad. But she was noisy, and terribly full of good spirits, and finally tried my nerves so much that I decided to leave. She was rather stuffy about it, but people are when you don't see eye to eye with them. I find they think they are never in the wrong; which is silly and illogical, but one must put up with it.

I tried several things after that: women's clubs, where they were silly and cattish, or very earnest; then a cottage in the country, where no one calls unless you belong to about six families; then a hotel in London. This was full of people who were very old and grumpy, or very young and stupid. Then I went abroad again.

What weird people go abroad! You never see them in England, but they are English. Perhaps we keep them for export. But they have one thing in common with the people at home. They never think of anyone else's tastes or feelings. I began to despair of human nature, and simply fled home again.

My father once said: "If you understand yourself, it is as much as you can be expected to do." How true that is! Every day I live I realise what a fund of wisdom he had. It just poured from him as water pours from a spring, clear and hard, and just right.

For some years I moved from place to place, but found no real peace. Then I took a furnished flat in London for a month, while I looked about me, and considered where I should live next.

All my life I have had to discard friends. I try to be charitable; to be indulgent. I try to call their defects foibles, and their strange habits of thought and conduct idiosyncrasies. But there always comes a time when I see that it is no use shutting one's eyes any longer.

But I have one dear old friend, a second cousin of my mother's, who lives in Skye, and is seventy-seven years of age. I hadn't seen her for eleven years when I decided to pay her a visit. It was a short visit, and we got on famously. The people on the island struck me as odd, but people on islands are naturally insular, and, of course, these were Celts, or something, and not always intelligible. Still, I enjoyed my three days' stay with old Mrs. Dochart, and put my problem to her.

She admitted that it was a problem, but gave me what seemed at the time very sage advice.

"I mind when I was a bit lassie, dearie," she said, "taking a wee trip to the south. There was another lassie of my own age, daughter to a big man that came here for the shooting. And one year she asked me down to stay with them."

"Where was this, Mrs. Dochart?" I asked.

"Oh, well, it was a small town called Lush Mellish," she said. "They say small towns hae small minds, and they do make a story about the clashing and tale-bearing and the like that goes on in them. But Lush Mellish, if I mind it right, was not like that. I heard no tales while I was there, and the people I met were right good folk."

Lush Mellish! How right it sounded. How perfectly it expressed the sense of our English scene; cattle browsing in the meadows, and a hot summer afternoon, with the grass high about their hooves. It made me quite poetical to think of it. At that time I forgot that lush grass may conceal snakes. All I thought of was that charming south-country town, and verdant water-meadows and buttercups.

I went into it with Mrs. Dochart, and she advised me to take a little house of my own. It appeared that there were many—Elizabethan, and Queen Anne, and Georgian—and not dear. Then there was a good supply of maids. They were cheap and good. The people with whom she stayed had five; all perfect darlings.

Of course, it was my fault. I always admit when I am in fault. But I did forget that it is not much use looking for a day excursion to Brighton in a Bradshaw of the year 1876 or so. And I forgot that Mrs. Dochart was staying with one of the country magnates; so, of course, she only met people I never met all the time I was at Lush Mellish, and the family never talked scandal about the local residents, of whose existence they were hardly aware.

But there I was, in far-off Skye, feeling that not a moment must be lost before I descended on Lush Mellish, and engaged two maids, and took a Queen Anne house. For a few days I was happy just thinking about it.

When I reached London again I inquired about houses in Lush Mellish. I was given quite a list.

Then I went down to see them. The town was perfect; old and sedate, with lovely surroundings, and even the people looked bright and intelligent.

I had just bought my first dog.

He was a beautiful bull-terrier, with a very white coat, and a tail that came to a nice point. I called him Leander, for he did look so heroic. He was quite young.

Of course, we had always had dogs at home; but they were working dogs—sheep-dogs and so on, and dad's retriever—not pets. That was the one point on which I could never agree with dad. He said dogs were not parasites, and did not like to be treated as such. They must be kept in their place.

How can I imagine Leander being kept in his place! He loved bouncing all over you, with his sweet white legs, and licking your face with his darling red tongue. And all in the sweetest, funniest spirit. But, perhaps, I loved him most because, like me, he was misunderstood. If they had only realised what a compliment Leander was paying them, the stuffy people who are always so fussy about their clothes would have smiled rather than been angry, as they so often were.

But to get back to Lush Mellish. I spent three days there at an inn, looking over houses. Most of them were very old. But they were definitely not cheap, and most out of date in their equipment. At last I bought a sweet Tudor cottage, in a perfect little garden, just on the outskirts of the town. I got a local builder to modernise it a little for me, and went back to London while I waited for him to complete the work.

And then—three weeks of day-dreams. How often are our dearest day-dreams followed by nightmares!

I was going to the dream-cottage in the dream-town. I was going to form a little circle, and be happy.

Maids had changed since Mrs. Dochart's day. They were not cheap from any point of view. I interviewed at least twenty before I realised that what they asked was the usual wage there. I got two at last. Neither of them was unsatisfactory, and cook was a fat woman with a continuous smile.

The housemaid took my heart at once because she said she doted on dogs. While she was with me she treated Leander as if he were a child. I often caught her fondling him when she should have been using the Bissel. It was a good fault, to my mind.

I must say at once that I entered on life at Lush Mellish with no prejudices. I had heard it was all sweetness and light, and I regarded each and every inhabitant as a potential angel. So you will see that what happened later was not the result of anything I did.

On entering the usual poky country hole, where gossip is rife, you have to be on the defensive at once, otherwise you will be slandered and annoyed. But I gave Lush Mellish a clean sheet. If any mud appeared on it later, it was local grown, and local thrown.

I was not sure if I should call and leave cards. It is out of fashion in town, but possibly Lush Mellish adhered to the dear old ways. I rather hoped it did.

In the first week of my residence the vicar's wife called. I was very nice to her, but I was rather afraid that she was a domineering woman. Perhaps I should have been happier in life if I had not inherited my mother's keen intuition.

She told me that there were many charming people in her husband's church. I did not dissent from that. I had not been long enough there to know them.

After her I had a little flood of those people who are all over you from the start. Very often they are the misfits of the community, and hope to make a nice new friend before the stranger learns that they do not fit into any set. They want to take you into their circle, such as it is.

I was not taken in.

Then I had a call from the wife of the veterinary surgeon. I am never very sure what position they occupy. In my dear father's day they were not of much importance except to cattle. The one in Lush Mellish had a nice house, and did well. Still, I had to draw the line somewhere, and when she first came into my drawing-room, with a sort of smirk, and held out her hand, I knew there was something odd about that woman.

She was enthusiastic about Leander, but my intuition held, and of course her husband might have expected to run up a bill if Leander was ever in need of attention. Of course, I was quite polite, but I had to wait and see.

Two doctors' wives called on me. One was tall and thin, and wore mannish tweeds; the other was short and stout, and, as I suspected, a great scout for her husband.

I was thirty-eight at that time, and never ill, so I had little use for doctors in a professional way. I was, however, prepared to be quite friendly with these two women, though I had an inner feeling that the thin one was a snob, and the stout one inclined to carry stories from one house to another. But I gave them the benefit of the doubt, and returned their calls.

The thin one had a hard, dried-up looking husband, who would never allow any of his patients to use salt. He looked like that.

The stout one had a husband younger than herself, a fine-looking man who, at one time, was very attentive to me. Jealousy is an odious passion, and I am sure his wife disliked me cordially later on. I may have been an elegant contrast to his blowzy wife, but I am sure I never encouraged him in any way.

In about a month's time I knew a fair number of people, and thought that my choice of Lush Mellish for a residence had been a good one. The only thorn in my side then was my neighbour to the west.

She was an elderly widow of forbidding aspect, and lived in a gem of a cottage. Our gardens marched, and she kept a cat.

They make jokes about the old spinster's cat. This was the widow's cat. But how few people recognise that men are fonder of cats than women. We coined the term "cattish" to mean acidulated sharpness and meanness. Surely common sense should tell us that we do not talk of our pets in terms of opprobrium? Doggish means gay and lively and gallant. No; most women I know are *not* fond of cats.

Still, I tried to be charitable. My neighbour was entitled to keep a cat. What I objected to was her undiscriminating treatment of it. She was always fondling and cosseting it, and bought the best meat and calves' liver for it, also a little cream. It made me slightly sick to see all that silly affection lavished on a swollen black beast. I mean to say, she made a perfect idol of her pet. What she saw in it I do not know.

Of course, I got in a gardener to put the garden in good working order. Dear, playful Leander used to course about there at times, and I had to check the man once or twice for throwing clods of earth at him.

"He is full of life and spirits, Joe," I told him, "and he is young. I am sure your father never threw clods at you when your youthful exuberance caused you to jump and sing."

"No, mum, I don't mind that he did," Joe said. "It was generally a good-sized faggot he used."

I am afraid I smiled. Children, of course, have to be disciplined. If you chide a dog, you may break his spirit.

Next thing, he complained of my neighbour's cat. He said it scratched up the new beds and seedlings.

"Then, Joe," I told him good-naturedly, "I can excuse you using one of your favourite clods. Not too large a one, of course, and not too hard. I do not wish the animal injured, but it must be taught a lesson."

To my surprise he flatly refused, and would give no reason for it. I learned afterwards that the old woman was a perfect terror if she did not get her own way.

But I had not come to Lush Mellish to be dictated to by an ancient female who made a fetish of a miserable cat. I had no desire to make trouble, but there is a limit to one's endurance.

It came very soon. I rose one morning and had my breakfast, feeling very happy and cheerful. It was a perfect summer's day, and the garden looked so gay and bright that I felt I must take a stroll in it before I began to give the maids directions for their work.

Darling Leander was, of course, on his tiptoes. He nearly upset my teacup at breakfast, and playfully ate one of my letters before I had even time to open it. He was *such* a waggish creature.

When I opened the french window and stepped out on to the lawn, a sparrow was sitting in a corner of one of the beds, and not five yards from it, in some rough grass, crouched that fiendish black cat from next door.

I am not very fond of sparrows in a garden, but they are creatures which have a right to their lives, and I was about to clap my hands to frighten it away, when the monster dashed forward and caught the little bird. Leander had gone out ahead of me, and was playfully trying his teeth on a sapling, when he saw this. Of course, he dashed at the cat, and a fine chase began.

They went all round the bushes, and it was most amusing how Leander tried to cut the wretched cat off at the corners, but never succeeded. I had to laugh, and I did. Every time the cat tried to cross the fence clever Leander anticipated her, and she had to dodge round the bushes again.

To make a long story short, she had to rush up a tree in the end, and sat there spitting and swearing, as cats do, for she had dropped her prey after the first dash. Leander, in the merriest mood, sat under the tree, and barked and barked.

He had given the cat a good fright for killing the poor sparrow, and I was about to call him off, when the most surprising thing happened. I heard a whizzing sound, then a yelp. I ran to Leander. There was a nasty little cut on his nose, and beside him lay a portion of a brick.

I turned, dumbfounded. There, behind the fence, was the widow, her forbidding face red with rage. But even then I could not believe that she had wantonly and brutally thrown a missile at my dear dog. It was only when I saw her stoop and rise again, to poise another fragment of brick, that I realised what an evil woman she was.

"Take your dog inside, you beast," she almost shouted, "or I'll give that filthy cur another!"

I gasped. She had completely forgotten herself. She was ordering me in out of my own garden. And to call my sweet, spotless Leander a filthy cur!

"My dog is a pedigree dog," I said, restraining myself with difficulty. "He is the son of Champion Prenderguest."

"Son of the Devil, you mean!" she said. "Take that brute away, and take it away now, or I'll lame him for life, and that's not half he deserves."

I got between her and the dog, for it was obvious that she had a gift, unusual in women, for throwing hard and straight.

"How dare you!" I said. "How dare you! Your cat's trespassing in my garden. He had killed one of my dear little birds—"

"Stuff and nonsense!" said that dreadful creature. "Sparrows don't belong to anybody. But they're pert and silly, and may suit you. Now I am going to count ten."

I gaped, but she went on counting, and when she came to six, I got Leander by the collar and took him with dignity inside the house.

"You shall hear from me," I said, as I left the garden.

"The less the better," she said. "Not at all would please me best—Come down the tree, sweetikins, and I shan't let the dirty white cur touch you."

What are you to do with a selfish virago like that?

It upset me for the day, and it took me some time to bathe darling Leander's nose.

Not that it really affected the pet's spirits, for I took him for a walk that afternoon, and he killed two field mice, and a rat, and tossed them up near me in such a playful way.

CHAPTER III

In my endeavour to be charitable, even after this monstrous behaviour, I decided that my elderly neighbour must have been under the influence of drink or drugs. That would explain how she had come to make an unprovoked attack on my harmless dog.

I never heard it said locally that she was an addict to either, but from my observation, and I lived close enough to see what others did not, her eccentricity must have been the result of secret indulgence.

I should not have worried my readers with a mention of her but for the fact that she comes into my story at another point. If she seems there even more contemptible than she did at first, it is not my fault. I tell the truth, however painful it may be to others.

Naturally, my first action after that was to put up high wire to keep out the cat, and the next to apply for membership of the local Animals' Defence Association.

The vicar's wife was the treasurer, and I sent a subscription to her, and waited. I received no receipt and no reply for some days. Then I met her in the High Street. Of course, I know that the wives of the clergy have much to do—though I admit that some of them do not seem to do it. But you must have business organisation in any association if it is to flourish.

I remarked to her that I trusted I should soon have my membership card, and congratulated her (rather untruthfully, I fear) on the hybrid dog she kept. My second dog, Tinker, killed it later, but that is another story. It always appeared to me to be a nasty creature, of an aggressive nature. I dislike dogs or people who are aggressive.

But to return to my meeting with the vicar's wife. She turned very red when I spoke to her, and quite innocently I imagined that she had forgotten her duty in the matter, and overlooked my subscription. Before long I was to learn that in Lush Mellish they are not strictly addicted to the truth. That is to say, they excuse certain phrases which they do not consider to be lies.

"Oh, the committee are considering your application, Miss Alice," she mumbled. "You will hear from them, no doubt."

I laughed a little. "Of course," I said, "but I should have thought it a matter of form merely. I am a great friend to animals, and hope to be an acquisition to your association. I am quite willing to take the chair on occasion, for instance, and spend and be spent in the cause."

"Sweet of you," she said hastily. You will hardly believe me when I say that she had a certain letter in her bag at that moment, and had not the courage to post it. Indeed, a local canon, appearing from a cake shop near us at that juncture, gave her an excuse to run away.

For the committee had sat on my application, and decided that the membership list was already full.

It was the first time I had ever known any association to refuse a subscription. I could not understand it. I made inquiries, and then I saw! That dreadful woman next door, that drug addict, was their chief patron. She had attended the meeting. She had told a dreadful lying story of my having set my dog on her wretched cat, egging the dog on and positively laughing at her pet's misery as it clung to a dangerous branch. I did not blame the rest of the committee. I hear they went in fear of her, and no doubt she described my harmless mirth in such a way as to suggest that I was cruel and callous.

My poor Leander! He does not figure much more in my tale. But I have to comment on the fact that Lush Mellish was full of dogs, almost as wicked and treacherous as their unpleasant owners. There was a butcher's dog, for example, who never let Leander pass without snarling and barking at him. There was a collie at "The Limes," who also barked most aggressively, and an ugly terrier in the High Street that positively snapped at Leander when he playfully knocked it over.

Was it my fault if Leander felt it was necessary to teach them a lesson? No. A high-bred dog is temperamental. The butcher complained to me that Leander had bitten his cur so severely that he had to have the vet. I reminded him (quite mildly) that Leander was a most gentlemanly dog, who never fought, but would defend himself as a gentleman should.

If he had any further complaint, he should have sent it to me. You will hardly believe what that savage actually did.

A few days later I was in the town shopping when dear, playful Leander slipped away for a few moments. Later I heard dreadful sounds, and saw people running down an alley. I followed them, and came on the corpse of my faithful friend.

Yes. Two brutal dogs had set upon him, and killed him, and the crowd which had gathered was most unfeeling.

"Why did you not interfere and save him?" I asked a rough-looking man who stood near.

"Me?" he said, and laughed in a coarse way. "Blimey, I don't want me legs bit off because you keeps tigers, do I?"

"Whose are the dogs?" I said coldly, as those about laughed. "I shall take steps to have them destroyed by the police."

But no one seemed to know. The dogs crept away, and I heard later that they were strange dogs, brought there by that very man, who had been bribed by the disgusting butcher to set them on dear Leander. Two to one. Think of it! The butcher's own cowardly cur would have never dared to face my dead darling.

And the police would not, or could not, help. Would not, I say; for one of them, a fat, lazy constable, had complained a week before that Leander had torn the hem of his trousers. But one never expects the police to have any sense of humour—or the postmen. I had a lot of trouble with postmen, who never realise that you must not take any notice of dogs that bark at you or follow you. They kick out and provoke our dumb friends, who are really *warning*, not threatening them.

The doctor's blowzy wife met me shortly afterwards, and pretended to be sorry.

"So distressing for you," she said hypocritically, "but I do think, in a place where there are so many dogs, one would do better to keep quite a little one; a Peke or Pom, or one of those sweet cockers."

So that was it. These people imagined that they were going to bully me into keeping the kind of pet *they* liked.

"I am buying another pet," I told her, "but, though he can never take the place of dear Leander, he must be of equal mettle and high breed. I adore courage and strength."

I went up to town and bought a darling bull-dog. His loving ugliness was a constant joy to me, and as everyone knows, bull-dogs never fight unless they are wantonly provoked.

Here I must say one thing; or, rather, ask one question: Why is it that people are so terrified of ugly features in a dog? They never run away from a man who is ugly, or pick up a stone or a stick when they see one; but a bull-dog appears to frighten them into wanton cruelties, and quite unnecessary hysteria.

As I said to one man: "Surely you are aware that dogs love sniffing, and have an equal love for human beings? If Tinker is sniffing at your ankles, it is because he is summing you up. You need not be afraid that he will bite them."

"I'm not," he said with a foolish sneer. "I'm afraid what will happen to your dog if he does—that's what it is! And me with my new boots on, too!"

"What has that to do with it?" I asked him.

"'Cause I use 'Apple Blossom' for 'em, not dog's brains," was his bestial reply. "Next time I have my old ones on he can come up and see me any time."

I walked away without a further word, and dear Tinker waddled after me. How merciful it is that our dogs cannot understand what they hear—only, of course, what is said to them by the beloved voice. I do not believe that Tinker would have soiled his perfect white teeth on the brute if he had, but he was a sensitive creature, and would have *felt* it.

Still, things were quiet for a little after I got him, and I began to consider forming my little circle.

I am literary and artistic, and also quite a good tennis player. I have been complimented on my bridge. Of course, I would have to be careful whom I chose. For, already, I had begun to realise that Lush Mellish had its cliques and coteries, and a perfectly dreadful Literary Society, in which the members read out their own poems and short stories. Some of these afterwards appeared in the *Lush Mellish Chronicle*. You know the kind of thing I mean. But there was no reason why I should not start a society of my own.

Then I paint a little, in water-colours, rather in the French impressionist style. I do not mean the ugly grotesques of to-day, but after Monet and Pissarro, and that sort of thing. I might have a little "One-Man Show," perhaps, in the town, and let people see that more beauty pervading their lives would have a tremendous mental and moral effect.

I had already joined the tennis club and the musical society. I may admit at once that I am not a gifted player of the piano. I have not had time for much practice, but I know how it ought to be played, and my mother had a lovely voice. I remember to this day how moved I was when she sat down and sang *"Il balen del suo surriso."*

You will see that I was very enterprising. I intended to enter into every phase of the town's life, and make Lush Mellish a pattern to its neighbours.

But, alas! how easily, how contemptuously, people toss away golden and generously proffered gifts! From the start I hoped; from the start I was condemned to failure by a wicked conspiracy against me. The old judge never mentioned *my* sufferings.

I was the first to start the Book Press Reading Circle in Lush Mellish. A literary paper had begun it in London, and the idea was to have provincial branches, where one met and talked of books, and tried to improve one's mind.

The difficulty, as I soon found, was that no one who wrote—and it is surprising how many there were in the town who wrote, or thought they wrote, which is worse—wanted to talk about anyone's books except his own. As I had to point out to one member, you could not call a manuscript a book. She resigned. Most of the members' books were in manuscript, and I could see that there was going to be trouble.

By the way, I found the same sort of thing in the music society. The members did not compose, as a rule, but none of them was interested in anything but the songs they sang, or the music they played. In fact, some of them did not seem to know that there was any other music.

Now I did. I have never tried to write till now, and I have never composed. But I knew what was good in literature, and music, and art. Oh, the vanity of these amateurs! They never realised how little they knew, and were not prepared to admit that I was in any better case.

Then I made the mistake of admitting Miss Mary Pauline as a member. She was the secretary of the literary association, and, of course, she had always been used to reading her own effusions at their meetings, and criticising the others' efforts.

Miss Pauline was one of those thin women who look like wire, and have the same sort of hard efficiency. I mean as secretaries, of course; for her stories were too absurd. They were sentimental, and very long for short stories. One or two of her own members had remarked on this before they resigned, and Miss Pauline said they were the best saleable length—three thousand words. Since she never sold any, I do not see that that mattered. What did matter was the fact that the members said how strange it was. They thought they must be at least ten thousand.

One of these resigning members was a Miss Hetty Elsie, who was plump and humorous. At least, I thought so at first. She promised to be a great acquisition to my club, till she produced the manuscript of a novel called *Locust Tears*. She had sent it to a publisher, who told her it had great promise. I had to remind her that there was a rule about reading one's own work.

Don't you believe anyone who says that stout people are always good-natured. It's often camouflage. She left us, and I was to have trouble with her later. Even our first meeting was not a success. I gave them an excellent tea, and announced that three hundred literary circles all over the kingdom were that day to give their views on the same book. It was Deraby's *Cumberland Chronicles*, a novel which was very much talked about; very long, and rather pompous, I thought.

I am afraid we never got to the book. I made an opening speech, and suggested that we should decide on our monthly procedure. Miss Pauline got up and told us what the custom was in her circle. I had to remind her that time was getting on, and speeches were limited to three minutes.

She was absurdly offended, and rose to go, saying that she had never been treated with such discourtesy. Lush Mellish was a country town, but everyone knew that what the country said to-day London repeated to-morrow. Somehow I felt that she was misquoting, but I did not correct her. I remarked merely that my little meeting had the imprimatur of a great literary organisation.

But she is one of these people who will not argue when they are in the wrong. She went out, and I remarked that we had now a quiet moment in which to consider the *Cumberland Chronicles*.

"Shouldn't it be the *Cumbersome Chronicles*?" one girl asked, and laughed at her own feeble wit.

Miss Mary Pauline was our subject for the rest of that séance. Some attacked her vehemently, and some defended her. People with literary tastes are extraordinarily contentious. It was monstrous what they said about her, and each other. Spiteful is a mild word to describe it.

I hate throwing pearls before swine, and dropped the literary circle very soon afterwards. I never did much with the local musical society. They had an accompanist who simply thumped. My own technique is, as I have previously admitted, not perfect, but my touch is impeccable.

The way that girl insisted on sticking to her place was absurd.

"I am not a singer," I told the president, "and if I were, I should hate to have my voice drowned. So there seems no place for me."

He said the girl had been with them for years. That was Lush Mellish all over. "Be not the last by whom the new is tried," is a proverb they simply cannot understand.

CHAPTER IV

I DON'T want anyone to think that my first months in Lush Mellish were unhappy. Nothing of the kind. I was enjoying myself in my own way, feeling my feet, and already able to sort out the sheep from the goats. I went warily, and avoided trampling on anyone's corns, which makes it more surprising how, later on, I was the subject of local abuse and persecution. I mean to say, I was prepared to be nice to everyone. I wanted to be *one* of them.

But oil and vinegar will not mix, and my own efforts to smooth away any difficulties that confronted me were misinterpreted, or scoffed at.

I had noticed in my walks with dear Tinker that we had quite a number of local artists; women of various ages who could be seen sitting at easels in the water-meadows, or the quainter parts of the town, painting quietly, and harming nobody.

Has it ever struck you how harmless most artists look? Literary and musical people have what I call a militant expression, as if they dared you to criticise them, but were rather afraid you would.

I decided to form an art circle, and it occurred to me that each of the members could visit the houses of the others in turn, and discuss their work. I had learned from my first circle that, in Lush Mellish, everyone must have a turn, or there is trouble.

I approached Miss Barbara May one afternoon. She was the most assiduous artist of all, and I came on her by the bridge, where she was painting a delightful reach of the River Lush.

I greeted her, and had a glance at the picture on the easel. It struck me as rather crude, but I did not tell her so. After a few minutes' talk, I ventured to remark that the poplars farther down reminded me of Corot.

"It never struck me," she replied, "but you may be right."

I was unaware that she thought I was speaking of some place abroad, and felt that her mild reply was a charming contrast to the heated exchanges of my literary circle.

So I broached my new idea, and Miss May was most interested.

"So you paint, too?" she said. "Oils?"

"Water-colour," I said. "It is true my masters took oil-colour as their medium, but I have tried to follow them in my humble way in the less exacting medium."

"Your masters?" she said.

"Monet and Renoir, Pissarro, and their school," I said. "Light, you know; vibrationist, and so forth. Broken tones, if you know what I mean."

She looked at me more interestedly than ever. "I rarely go up to town," she said, "so I am rather out of it."

I explained to her who they were, and she seemed pleased to hear about them, though she did not agree with my views on the question of impasto, chiaroscuro, and that sort of thing.

"Ah, Epstein and that lot," she remarked, to my surprise; "but surely you do not admire them? Dear Mr. Leader is the idol I worship, and try to emulate."

I trust you will believe me when I say that I thought that woman a perfectly harmless person. I wanted someone, pleasant and not intrusive, to help me form my new circle. Obviously, she could not paint, but she would help others of similar calibre not to feel abashed in the presence of the work of more gifted members.

I am telling you now what I thought at the time. Actually, I discovered later that none of them was abashed. Each had the curious notion that she was the gifted member.

At any rate, Miss May promised to go round to her artist friends, and get my idea started. She felt sure they would all be delighted, and then we could take the Town Hall one day, and have an exhibition. I was so pleased with her good nature that I invited her to accompany me home to tea, and actually carried her easel.

Naturally, I had to show her my water-colours. Some of them were charming bits I had done abroad.

"I flatter myself," I said after tea, when showing her an orchard in Normandy, "that here I might even have hoped for the approval of dear, good Monet. The refraction of light on the blossoms in the corner seems to me exactly right."

"Oh, that's the blossom," Miss May said slowly, and I felt that she was too much impressed to venture on criticism. "Oh, yes. I see. I see."

"It composes best at about five yards," I reminded her, as she walked forward to look at it more closely. "You get what we call the *perspective aérienne*. Which is, as you know, different from the architect's aerial perspective."

"I am afraid I never use it," she replied, and I felt sure that we should get on well together.

You see, pretentious people are always hard to get on with, and there are none worse than those who pretend to knowledge that they do not possess. Another type of woman might have made a reply which was argumentative, or showed that she was trying to be clever.

The art master at the grammar school seemed quite taken with my idea of an art circle. I never realised, of course, that he was an ambitious man, and proposed to use my efforts to further his own ends. In fact, Lush Mellish was full of people like that in all walks of life, and I, who had come there prepared to believe in everybody—at least, in the purity of their intentions—was deceived for some time. But not for long, as you may discover by reading on.

He called to see me, and said Miss May had told him, and he was going to help all he could. He asked me if I should like to see his water-colours, and, of course, I said I would. He had rooms near the school, and what he called a studio.

My savage neighbour was walking past when we went in. She did not look at me. But she saw me! I had proof of that later.

I must say that I thought the art master's productions woolly and dull. There was no refracted light, there were no broken tones, and he used a great deal of Chinese white.

I asked him about it, and I thought he looked cross. In the light of subsequent events, I know he was cross, and it taught me again that people do not like to be helped, or even have their most flagrant defects pointed out.

We held our first meeting at my house the following week. There were eighteen foundation members; and that was nearly seventeen too many, as it turned out. I had meant to get people who could paint pretty well, Miss May being added because she was not troublesome, and had assisted me to get the thing known.

When I say paint pretty well, you will understand that not all those who win popular favour can paint. One of the earliest disagreements arose over Mrs. Joan Agatha. I admit I had never heard of the woman before I met her at my house, and I had to go by the specimens of the work she showed me.

There was no line about it, if you ask me. She couldn't draw, and her colours screamed at you, and as for representation— there was none. In the kindest way, I suggested that she should take some lessons, or get copies of the French impressionists if she could not afford a trip to Paris.

"You see," I told her—and to this day I feel I was right—"all this crude colouring can be toned down if you *try*. If you will look at some of my little efforts, you will see at once what I mean."

She stared at me, and then smiled. "Ah, you think so. You think that would help?" she asked.

I know now that she was a cunning woman, with a despicable nature.

"I am sure it would," I said. "One has a feeling that you have it in you. I mean to say, your composition is not bad, and here and there one sees quite tolerable passages. But there is nothing like emulation and comparison with the work of others to give one an insight, so to speak."

She smiled again. "I think you are quite right, Miss Alice. You will do us all good, I feel sure. I am looking forward to our first meeting. I wonder what you will think of our joint efforts?"

"I am not really critical," I said. "People who know what they can do, and what they cannot do, will always find sympathy in me, and help if it is needed."

"How sweet!" she said. "Let's hope the circle will be a great success."

I began to be afraid that it would not, when I visited the houses of our members and saw their work. It was almost uniformly dreadful, and the sad part of the whole affair was that each considered herself quite good at it. People positively revel in taking themselves in.

The day before our first meeting I was seized with doubts. When it came to our exhibition, I might feel flattered that my own work showed up the blatant weaknesses of the others. But that is not my temperament. How could I feel happy and pleased at the sight of unhappy faces about me? What pleasure could there be for a nice person in seeing crowds gathered before her own pictures, while the other well-meaning artists were almost neglected?

It would not do. I wanted to take only my proper rank. I wanted all to feel happy. What was I to do? I had it! There was a well-known artist, Mr. Leonard Vumer, who lived outside the town. I would ask him to be an honorary member, and honour us by exhibiting two or three of his works at our show. Then we should have something really to admire; something which would be at once pleasing and instructive.

I went at once to call on him. I admit that I was disappointed in his appearance. He looked rather like a small draper in the town, and spoke in a drawl, which I always find very irritating.

"But why do you want me for your collection?" he asked, when I had told him all about it.

I said that most of our members were amateurs, and amateurish at that.

"So you are a professional?" he asked.

"No," I said. "I have heard it said that I missed my vocation, but I am certainly an amateur—at present."

"A gifted amateur," he said.

I laughed. "One does not like to say these things of oneself," I told him, "but when I studied abroad, my master, Monsieur Dupont, often remarked that my work was 'Épatant.'"

"In what tone?" said Mr. Vumer.

"Tone?" I said. "I rather favour the impressionists—broken tones and that sort of thing; refraction of light, you know."

He waved his hand. "That's the whole secret put in a nutshell, Miss Alice. Broken tones and refracted light. Admirable! And the rest of your ga—your circle are not quite up to that, eh? Break, break, break, on refracted tones, eh? I should love to see your work."

I told him that he could come to the first meeting, and I would be pleased to show him what I had done. He laughed, and said he was very busy, and was afraid he could not join.

"The fact is," he added, "I should only make the other members uncomfortable. Have you ever thought what these ungifted amateurs would feel when they saw me hanging breathless over your water-colours, and turning with physical faintness from their dreadful attempts?"

"But you could improve them," I said. "There is Mrs. Agatha, who lives in a world of the most terrible greens and reds, but is really modest, and anxious to do better."

He raised his eyebrows. "So you've got her, eh? And you think I could help her to have a flutter among the pastel shades, eh?"

"I am sure she would not be angry if you did," I said.

"You're perfectly right," he told me. "She would smile, or laugh."

"Yes; she is good-humoured," I agreed. "On the other hand, I am not sure that people who smile when they are criticised are likely to improve. They don't take their art seriously enough."

He shook his head seriously. "How true! Obviously there is little hope for poor Mrs. Agatha, who will not be serious." He offered me a cigarette, lit one himself, and added: "Now, Miss Alice, I must really get on with a commission, and I must definitely, if with the greatest regret, say that I cannot join your circle. But this I will say; you have greatly entertained me. I have doubts at times of my own reds and greens, and your theory of broken tones intrigues me immensely. Your first meeting is sure to be a great, perhaps, I may say, a howling success."

"How nice of you to say so!" I replied. "I really do value your appreciation very much."

"Don't mention it, Miss Alice," he remarked, as he showed me to the door. "You have thrown a new light on art and artists. A dry, hard light, but illuminating—illuminating. I am sure your fellow members will feel that as I do—even the weaker vessels, the apostles of vivid red and green. I shall be interested to know particularly what Mrs. Agatha thinks of it. If you can improve her painting, you will be doing a great work."

Well, of course, that had been my idea from the first.

There was, as I have already hinted, a disagreement at our first meeting. It came about in this way.

Fortified by Mr. Vumer's sympathy and advice, I spoke to Mrs. Agatha again about her crude colouring, and she laughed, as he had said she would, and made me remark that art was a serious business.

"Isn't it?" she said, and beckoned to the art master, who was walking about looking at my work. "Oh, Mr. Dumbler, do you think that I really ought to tone down my stuff?"

Mr. Dumbler laughed, too. "I never meddle with perfection," he said.

Dreadful little sycophant! I turned to him with a smile. "But, seriously," I said, "don't you think she could improve quite a lot?"

He laughed. "My dear Miss Alice, you will have your joke."

They laughed together, and some of the other members gathered round.

"I am not joking," I said. "I mean it."

Mr. Dumbler started. "Why, is it possible you do not know that Mrs. Agatha here—"

"Please!" she said hastily, but he went on.

"Mrs. Agatha here is one of the most gifted artists in the country—in England."

I did not, I could not, believe it. I had seen her pictures, and knew that this was untrue.

"I was talking to Mr. Vumer about her work yesterday," I said, rather stiffly, I fear, "and he agreed with me."

"Vumer agreed with you?" He started again, and so did she. "Oh, I see. Vumer's a sad dog."

"I don't see what that has to do with it," I said.

And I don't to this day. But I do know that Mrs. Agatha is a niece of my horrible neighbour, and is said to be a great artist. One lunatic even told me that Mr. Vumer is not in the same street with her. If hers is art, it is not what *I* know as art. I may even say it is not what my dear Monet would have called art. And my *cher maître* Monsieur Dupont would assuredly never have paused before her pictures and murmured: *"Épatant."*

In my opinion, the whole thing was a put-up job. I did not care to go farther with the art circle, and I realised more than ever that people hate you if you wish to improve them, or do them good *in any way*. For some days I saw Lush Mellish as the inferno of scandal, ill-nature and intolerance it really was.

And then I forgot. I am like that. Forget the evil and remember only the good. The perennial spring of my faith in human nature welled up again. Your amateur artist, your amateur writer, is a mass of frenzied conceit, and better left alone. But there were others in Lush Mellish, and I was determined to carry on my good work.

CHAPTER V

AT THAT time I had not realised the depth and subtlety of the conspiracy against me. Indeed, I was unaware that there was any. I had joined the Lush Mellish Musical Society unaware of its narrow conservatism and parochial outlook, which demanded, as it seemed to me, that old members must keep their places, however inefficient they were.

I have remarked that I am not a singer. I may say that I do not play any orchestral instrument. My place had appeared to be at the piano, but the Lush Mellish thumper was still there.

All through my life I have tried to adapt myself to people and circumstances. Art and literature were obviously dead in the town, but I understood that the musical society gave quite competent concerts, and I determined to sacrifice my pride and join.

But with a difference. It should not be said that I was pushing for a place among the performers. I met a Miss Mabel Ornsby, a newcomer to the town, and found that she was devoted to music, while unable to play or sing a note. Newcomers stick together, and she asked me if I would join the society with her.

"Gladly, Miss Ornsby," I replied. "I understand that there are performing and non-performing members. Let us join the latter group, when our talents will not be compared with those of others, and perhaps give rise to jealousy."

"I don't play or sing," she told me then, "so my talents won't hurt anyone. I can only lend them my ears."

"I do play," I said gently, "but I have made up my mind not to compete. I shall be, as they say in France, *hors concours*."

It seemed to me that I had better be a patron; which meant ten guineas. I joined a week before Tinker killed the vicar's savage cur. He is, *ex officio*, a patron of the society, and his plain daughter is the principal contralto. I mean, of course, that the vicar is a patron.

I do not want to harp on these troubles, but I may say here that my poor Tinker was absolutely blameless. There were several other wicked dogs about at the time that had always made a set at him, and he would probably have been torn to pieces if he had not quickly made an end to the cur, which, I am sure, had attacked him first.

So Miss Ornsby and I joined as non-playing members, and I felt that I had made a friend. I should have realised the folly and danger of taking up strangers before you know them. I ought to have known that these little, neutral-looking women, with pale-grey eyes, are thoroughly untrustworthy, and even venomous. And never more so than when you have befriended them. But I never go through life looking for unpleasantness; which accounts, perhaps, for my greater disillusionment when my trust is betrayed.

The first meeting which we attended was held at the Women's Institute. There were about a hundred and ten members present, but I soon saw that the driving force was in a group of about ten women who sat on the platform, among them the vicar's ugly daughter, and a fat woman with a square face, who, I learned, was Mrs. William Ella.

When the minutes had been read the question of the first autumn concert came up. Suggestions were invited, and I was rather amused to find that most of those present wanted to do the most familiar of Handel's oratorios.

But there were some dissentients even among those on the platform. It was some time before I realised the meaning of this. The fat Mrs. Ella was in favour of Coleridge-Taylor's "Hiawatha"; so was a thin woman at her side. One of the group wanted "The Golden Legend."

"Because she'll get the chief part," said a woman next to me. "I know they won't have her in 'Hiawatha'."

"Then me for 'Hiawatha' every time, my dear," said her companion, in a noisy whisper. "But we're safe on that. Minnie Ella always gets what she wants."

"What Eric and Nedda want," was the reply. "Last time neither of them turned up, just because it was 'Saul.' Too simply peevish."

The meaning of this escaped me till I remembered that Mrs. Ella had a son and daughter, who had apparently staked a claim to "Hiawatha" and "Minnehaha."

For quite a little time I thought these remarks simply spiteful, but I was to have my eyes opened before it ended.

In every meeting of the kind there are fifty per cent of those present who are afraid of the leading spirit, and vote with her to save trouble. I must admit that I am not a fervent Handelian. Again, I did not like Mrs. Ella's square face. Faces of that shape are no index to character.

I was, too (if newly joined), one of the twenty patrons, and when the conquering mien of that good lady suggested that she was about to take a vote, and get her son and daughter into Indian feathers again, I decided to take a hand.

I rose, caught her eye, and suggested that a very limited choice of works had been put before the meeting.

"Handel writes for a humane race," I said, and the foolish person at my side said she imagined he was an angel. "The Red Indians, whatever may be their condition now, were not the sentimental race Mr. Cowan—"

"Mr. Coleridge-Taylor," someone said near me.

"Mr. Coleridge-Taylor imagined," I corrected, bowing ironically to the interrupter. "But need we think that there are only three oratorios, or musical works to be sung by a gifted choir like that of Lush Mellish?"

One or two intelligent members said "Hear, hear." But Mrs. Ella's face grew even more square, and she stared at me as if I were a sort of beetle.

"Miss Alice," she said, in what she thought a sarcastic voice, "is flattering us, but she is not here long enough to know that we love our dear 'Hiawatha,' and no strange work has the same appeal to us."

"Question!" said a woman in the background, but I could not see who she was.

"There is no question about it," Mrs. Ella replied majestically. "I am sure we might do some new work at some other time, but this year we cannot do better than rely on our old favourite, which is always superbly done."

"If that is the case," I said, seeing that the others were cowed, and irritated, by her superior manner and domineering airs, "I for one shall do my best to make it a success."

Mrs. Ella was rather taken aback. "Thank you, Miss Alice," she said more graciously.

"Yes," I went on, "I would like to see it the talk of the country. I have not yet heard your choir, but I am sure it is most competent and well drilled. The presence here of Dr. Henty, the organist, assures me of that. But, as we all know, the commonest defect in performances given by amateur societies lies in the principals."

You could have heard a pin drop when I paused. Even Mrs. Ella had her breath taken away, and struggled to recover herself.

"If you had attended our last performance of the work," she said in a choked voice, "you would have known that my son and daughter sang delightfully. The *Chronicle—*"

"Excuse me," I said, "I was speaking generally. Naturally, most of the solo parts have to be taken by local amateurs, but it is usual, and, I think, most valuable, to have at least one professional to give a lead; to inspire the other soloists."

"We do not do it here," said Mrs. Ella, and her face was red as well as square then.

"You must try it," I said. "The part of Hiawatha is an exacting one. I am sure, for a fee of ten guineas, you could get a professional tenor to sing that part."

"Preposterous," she gasped.

"Well, an artiste from town to sing Minnehaha, then," I suggested. "Minnehaha really requires a good voice."

Two or three people giggled, and Mrs. Ella glared at me, and made several attempts to speak before she actually did.

"You are unaware that my son and daughter took those parts the last time we did 'Hiawatha', or else you are endeavouring to be insulting," she hissed. "I never heard such a thing in my life."

"I am afraid I have never heard your son and daughter sing," I said, quite calmly. "As to insulting them, I had no idea of it. How could I? Everyone knows that in musical societies fresh members take the parts in turn."

Quite a babel broke out. Some members plucked up courage, when I sat down, and suggested that they should do "The Golden Legend" after all, while the Ella party switched over to Handel, and the vicar's wife came over to whisper to me that Mrs. Ella was a charming woman, and the backbone of the society.

"Eric and Miss Ella are very promising singers," she added, "but I am afraid you have rather upset the poor dear. She is very sensitive to criticism, and I don't want her made unhappy."

I agreed that it would be a pity, and decided to rise again, and calm the troubled waters.

My getting up caused an extraordinary silence.

"Ladies and gentlemen," I began. "I am a newcomer, and a new patron of your society, and I am most anxious to convince you that my intervention just now was not intended in a personal sense."

"Hear, hear!" said someone behind me.

"Every society has its rules and customs," I went on, "and I forgot that, while it is a general rule that any good singing part is taken in turns, so as to give every soloist a chance, you think young Mr. and Miss Ella so promising that you call on them every year to take the principal parts in 'Hiawatha'."

"We do not do it every year," the organist intervened.

"I am sorry. I mean that every time you do 'Hiawatha' you call on Mr. and Miss Ella," I said. "May I just say that I am greatly in favour of giving the young every chance. I am sure these two soloists do their best, and if they fail at any part, no doubt the faults of youth will be corrected in the years to come. In these circumstances, may I suggest that the society does 'Hiawatha.' It will give me an opportunity of hearing Mrs. Ella's promising children sing. I shall look forward to it with great pleasure. Sung as I have heard it sung by Mr. Edward Williams and Madame Alice Chase, with the London Orpheolus Choir, the oratorio or cantata made a great impression on my mind."

There was another silence, and Mrs. Ella was now the colour of a beetroot.

What had I said or done? What did the woman want? I had made the *amende honorable*; I had voted for her choice, and referred in encouraging terms to her vocal offspring. And still she seemed dissatisfied.

Then babel broke out again, and I saw her beckon to the organist, whisper to him, and then leave the platform.

A voice near me said: "Some people have a nerve!" And another, fainter, voice murmured: "Jack the Giant-Killer!" The organist went to the front of the platform and held up his hand for silence.

"Ladies and gentlemen," he said. "Mrs. Ella, who has had to leave us owing to an important engagement, has asked me to suggest that our society should do 'The Golden Legend' for our first concert this year. In the circumstances, I feel justified in putting it to the vote. All in favour please hold up their hands."

I was one of the few who did not hold up their hands. "Let us not take advantage of Mrs. Ella's generosity," I said. "I vote that 'Hiawatha' be done with the *usual* soloists."

The organist turned very red. He was, I am sure, in that square-faced woman's pocket, and, to my surprise, there was general applause when he remarked timidly that new members, or patrons, always welcomed to their society, had full voting rights with the oldest members. But the vote had been given for "The Golden Legend," and, if convenient, practice and rehearsals would begin at the usual dates.

"Mrs. Ella feels," he added, to a storm of applause, "that fresh talent should always get its chance, and has nobly announced that her talented son and daughter will take no part in the singing of the cantata."

I turned to my companion. "How typical of the herd instinct, Miss Ornsby!" I whispered to her. "It has no ear for insincerity."

To my surprise, she raised her rather inadequate eyebrows. "I think you were most unkind," she said. "Mrs. Ella is obviously a most popular woman; otherwise her suggestion would not have been so well received."

I turned from her in disgust. New as she was to Lush Mellish, she had already become a sycophant; running after popularity, and determined to be in the ruling set, however petty and silly that set might be.

But is it not strange how often my efforts to help people, and give them a lift, led to ingratitude and offensiveness? For the hundredth time I made up my mind that afternoon to count on no friendship or support from the time-serving residents of Lush Mellish. And, for the hundredth time, my natural kindliness and lack of cynicism made me forget my promise, with the usual result.

It was the rule that patrons might attend practice and rehearsals, and I availed myself of the privilege, if privilege it can be called, of listening to the vocal efforts of the performing members. The standard, as I soon realised, was very low, and, as is so often the case, the members resented any criticism or attempt to improve them.

Many had never attended a London concert, or heard the great stars of whom I told them. Worse than that, they had the provincial habit of thinking, or pretending to think, that London is quite unmusical. One pert young woman indeed remarked that she had heard the famous Signora Battico sing sharp.

"It seems most unlikely," I told her, "and you do not allow for *ear*. Just as some people cannot distinguish red from green, others are *tone-blind*."

She was furious. But why? Surely it was more likely that she could not distinguish between one tone and another than that the famous Diva had sung sharp?

You will see that I found myself in a bewildering world at Lush Mellish. Whatever I said was wrong, and when I tried to make amends, that was wrong too. They did not want to be improved, *or* helped, or have kindnesses done to them. They were case-bound in the delusion that they were always right. They had no idea of give and take.

From my first coming I had spent time and money to make myself pleasant to everyone.

Jealousy? Perhaps.

Parochialism? Certainly.

But there must have been more than that; some *kink*, some sourness in the nature of the Lush Mellish people which made them (perhaps even against their wills) present a stony and harsh front to the kindliness and goodwill of the innocent stranger.

CHAPTER VI

MAIDS, they often say, are the greatest disseminators of gossip and secrets. If they are, it is in part due to their mistresses, who do not check them, or are even anxious to know what is going on in the houses of their neighbours.

I have always set a stern face against this. My cook and housemaid are as garrulous as most, but if I listen to them on occasion, it is to put an end to stories and rumours which are manifestly untrue, and to warn them that the matter must not be carried farther.

To turn a completely deaf ear to them is, of course, almost as harmful as encouraging them to gossip. There are some things one must hear, or they will be passed on recklessly, and do a great deal of harm. Again, there are occasions when one hears of an indiscretion which might be corrected in future. In other words, a wise mistress has to discriminate. She will know when to hear, and when to stop her ears; when to realise that her maids are moved by righteous indignation, and when they are only anxious to betray what they consider a spicy piece of news.

"Now," I said to my housemaid once, "do not let me hear you speak like that again, please. I am quite sure that you are misinformed, and those two young people are perfectly harmless, if somewhat reckless."

After that, she knew very well not to bring any idle tales to me.

But, of course, certain things were told me, for which I could not blame my maids. Venomous tongues had commented on me and my affairs after the first trouble with dear Leander. There was a recrudescence of this when the literary society was started, and again when I had that passage of arms with Mrs. Ella.

But these things did me no harm, the more so as cook knew a great deal about the slanderers and backbiters, and as good as told me that some of them were determined to drive me out of the town. Can you imagine people so lost to any sense of decency? In the end they had their wicked will, and so contrived it that I appeared technically to be at fault. But *was* it my fault if I had not their cunning and lack of principle?

In those later, dark days I often thought of my father, and his fight against lawlessness and unrighteousness. "As long as you feel sure that you are right, let nothing stop you," he used to say. "I have never begun an action until I was sure beyond a peradventure that my case was just." A saying like that buoys one up when assailed from all sides.

It was only my determination not to encourage gossip, or believe too much in what I heard, that prevented me from seeing in Lush Mellish a sink of iniquity. But I never failed to check any exaggeration, and must have stopped a hundred stories from getting into circulation. In this way, I did good by stealth, and did not expect to wake and find it fame.

Naturally, I could not truthfully have blamed my maids for some of the stories they told. You see, I knew something then of the people concerned, and I should have been blind indeed if I had protested their innocence. What I did do was to remark that this was to go no further, and, as far as I know, they obeyed me.

Still, the whole thing became depressing. There is a limit to charity and tolerance, and it was sad to think that my dream-town was really such as it was. Here, in the sweet air, among the meads and the flowers, the innocent trees, the crystal river, there was a great deal of wicked conspiracy, evil doing, and hidden vice.

Who would have believed, for instance, that Miss X., who lived in a tiny house on the Boster Road, was really a married woman who had run away from her husband? Or that Mr. Y., who was prolific in good works, had once been in prison for embezzling a client's funds? It was even wickedly hinted that he was now living on the proceeds, which he had hidden away somewhere until he was released.

"But can you be sure of this?" I asked cook sternly, when she told me. "It would be a dreadful thing to say if it were untrue."

"Not half it isn't, mum!" she said to me earnestly. "My half-sister, that I used to live with, married a man from the town where he came from, and she sent me on a photo. It was him all right, mum, if the name was different."

"The name would be different," I said, "but I want to hear no more about it, and I trust you will keep it to yourself."

So it remained a secret, and I think I am entitled to some credit for killing the story at its inception.

But I must return to the vicar's cur. Having, no doubt, goaded darling Tinker to frenzy, and been slain by one snap of those valiant jaws, it became, miraculously, a most valuable dog of pedigree!

"It was a Corgi, a great pet, and most valuable companion," the vicar complained to me, and I felt that he showed more heat than was becoming in a man of his profession. "That brute of yours attacked it in the most savage and unprovoked manner. It's a disgrace! I am sorry to have to say so, but I do think you have no right to import savage and dangerous dogs into our peaceful town."

"Excuse me, vicar," I said, with a calm which was in commendable contrast to his excited nonsense, "I really must refuse to believe that your dog was a valuable specimen. You will not think me rude, I hope, if I remark that Corgi sounds like a made-up name."

Even that seemed to annoy the irresponsible man. "Are you suggesting that I am not speaking the truth, Miss Alice?"

"Certainly not, vicar, but really, the name does sound absurd. Or perhaps I misunderstood you."

"A Corgi is a Welsh dog," he said; "a Welsh breed."

"Oh, the Welsh!" I told him. "I cannot say anything about that, and I am, of course, ready to admit that your dog may have been a Corgi. But I cannot believe that a Welsh dog with a name like that was valuable."

How was I to know that his mother was Welsh? And even had I known, it did not affect the point.

A hunched-up ugly thing like that could not represent "breed" to any dog lover.

"In future," he said coldly, running away from my logic, as I feared he would, "you will keep that dog under control, or I shall be forced to take some action to have it restrained. And that is a thing I am loth to do."

"Pray do not refrain on my account," I told him. "One of my pets has already been torn to pieces by savage dogs here, and injured by an ancient harridan with a missile. Any action you may take can only result in proving that Tinker only slew in self-defence."

I may just remark that Tinker was not chained or tied up, and the vicar took no action; no overt action, that is. But you will see, later on, that he and the Noncomformist minister were at the head of my accusers in the culmination of the great conspiracy to make me leave Lush Mellish.

The minister had even less provocation. Tinker killed his wife's cat. But the cat had spat at him, and arched her back in the most spiteful manner. I must also say that he behaved in the most ungentlemanly way, calling, and showing me a heavy stick he carried.

"Terriers can defend themselves," he said viciously, "but a cat is no match for a brutal bull-dog. I am buying my wife another pet, and if that beast of yours even shows his nose near my gate, I'll make sure that he has had his last cat-hunt."

I have rarely heard a more ruffianly threat, and said so plainly.

"I have nothing to say against your wife, whom I do not know," I said indignantly, "but your conduct is disgraceful, and would make you a pariah in any civilised community."

"Though perhaps not in a Moslem one, where dogs are regarded as unclean animals," he retorted. "Well, I have said my say. I like a nice dog myself, but, though I do not claim to be another St. George, I will have a cut at any monster I see on the roads."

All this may seem of little moment to you who read this. Dogs and cats are killed every day in one way or another. Yes; but a subtle eye will see in this the genesis of a campaign to wound and hurt me, and bring my name down into the dust.

Dishonest people are ashamed in the presence of the honest, and the good are a standing reproach to the wicked. I believe the vicar preached once on that text. Had I heard him, I might have been compelled to protest, for I had written to a friend of mine in town, and asked her if she had ever heard of a Welsh Corgi. She replied that there was no such thing. I must mean a Welsh collie; a species with wall-eyes. Obviously, if this was what the vicar meant—for the Welsh are quite likely to call a collie a Corgi—it proved that he was not accurate in calling it a pedigree dog. I do know a collie when I see it.

At last I began to turn from the spiteful bourgeois of Lush Mellish to thoughts of the better-class folk who lived outside. There, at least, one would find no snobbery, and no hatred of our dumb friends.

I remembered the family with whom my dear old Scottish friend had stayed as a girl. And, one afternoon, I hired a motor and called. I had rather a difficulty in seeing the member of the family who had originally invited old Mrs. Dochart to stay. She was a widow; and very old, and very forgetful, it seemed. She would insist that I had come for a subscription. When I reminded her of Mrs. Dochart, she did not seem to remember her at all.

"She was a girl in the Highlands at the time," I said.

"Oh, yes; a girl on a farm," she said after some time. "Quite a respectable young person, of course. And now, my dear, perhaps you will tell me why you came to see me? I mean to say, if it is one of the charities to which I usually give, I will write you a cheque."

I need not say that I was indignant, but I was saved the trouble of convincing the snobbish old woman by a noise outside. It appeared that Tinker, whom I had left to run about and play, had chased a cock pheasant, and was the mark for a garden boy who, afraid to approach him, was throwing stones and shouting.

It was absurd to imagine that a bulldog can catch a cock pheasant, as these birds run like race-horses, but the boy averred that my dog ran over the flowerbed, and damaged some of the blooms.

I had run out, to see what was happening, and assured him that the pheasants should not be allowed to infest the garden, where they would do more damage than my dog. At that moment the old woman came to a window, and, evidently overhearing the boy's loud, and one-sided, version of the business, called out to him.

"Tell that young woman to take her dog away at once! At once, do you hear!"

"My dear madam—" I began, but she cut me short.

"Remove that hideous animal, or I shall send for one of the gamekeepers! Stray dogs are shot here."

I may say that I went away at once. There is no use stopping to argue with a mad, old woman, and I have had experience of gamekeepers, who consider that their wretched game is more important than dogs' happiness. It was evident to me that the old lady was not in her right senses. She could never have been the charming girl Mrs. Dochart imagined.

So I was thrown back on the evil humours of Lush Mellish, and again made an attempt to establish a friendship with some of the more promising people.

There was the tennis club, and here one found the younger people. The so-called literary set, the pseudo-musical set, and the self-styled artists, revolved in their own little orbits. Probably they called the tennis players "Philistines," or something like that.

Now, I have always been fond of lawn-tennis, and played regularly when a girl at home. I met a Miss Betty once, and she seemed quite pleased at the idea of my joining the club.

"Glad you tired of the mouldy old book-worms," she said to me. "I think everyone does."

"Yours is an excellent phrase," I said. "They are book-worms; creatures that are parasitic on books, but know very little of their contents."

She grinned. "I say, you're hot stuff! Let's have your angle on the musicians."

Of course it never occurred to me that my little *espiègleries* would be passed on. "Most amateurs ought to confine their singing to their bathrooms," I said. "The running water does help."

"I like that," she said. "Garages would be helpful too, when the engine was warming up. Didn't they rope you in for their fusty old painting, too?"

I nodded. "Yes, that was rather a joy. I am not fond of people who paint their faces, but that picture does at least have a background."

"Quite some background sometimes!" she agreed.

I paid my subscription, and joined the tennis club. It was some time later that I heard how my comments—which were quite harmlessly witty—had been repeated and exaggerated, causing great offence. It was no good trying to prove that, and in the end I decided that the truth still remains the truth, even if embroidered. But people hate to recognise themselves in what they take to be a faulty mirror.

My first afternoon at the ground passed pleasantly enough. I met members and had tea, finding them a very merry crowd. Miss Betty asked me to have a knock-up afterwards. I was very much out of practice, but think I held my own pretty well.

In fact, I was really pleased to meet so many pleasant young people, and see them take such an interest in me. At one time I had quite a group round me, laughing uproariously at my little verbal portraits of some of the odder people of the town. I felt that I rather sparkled, and was at my best.

It was during the next week that I wondered if I had been wise to join the club. All the members seemed to make up their single and double engagements long in advance, so that one could hardly get a game. Then I had an unpleasant letter from Mrs. Ella, saying that she would be glad if I would refrain from making offensive comments on her, and almost threatening me at the end. Someone in the club must have been carrying stories; which I consider very bad form, and extremely unprincipled.

Still, I had joined to play tennis, and when I could get hardly any practice, I began to have suspicions, which were fully justified, as it turned out. Some of the members were relatives of the enemies who had pursued me since my arrival, and the idea was to make me look small.

Now that I am in possession of all the facts (cook has a niece in one of the member's houses), I can see that it was no place for me. They did not play the game as I knew it, but made it a rapid competitive business, slashing and jumping like maniacs; many of the girls wearing what were nothing better than disguised undies. In other words, I had joined a crowd of hoydens and louts, who called real lawn-tennis players "rabbits," and managed to reduce themselves at the end of an afternoon to flushed, perspiring and uncomely *beefsteaks*.

I did not resign at once, as I should have done. For something tragic occurred which put tennis out of my mind for a season.

CHAPTER VII

TINKER was dead!

I came down to breakfast one morning to find cook and the housemaid in a terrible state. They had not dared to tell me before, but a scullery window had been opened, they said, in the night, and the body of my darling pet was lying there stiff and cold.

He had his basket in the drawing-room, but I left all the doors open so that he could take exercise if he felt restless. He must have wandered (or been lured) to the scullery, where the fiend in human form had wantonly murdered him.

I telephoned at once for the veterinary surgeon, but he said he had to visit a sick cow first. Imagine it! There was my dear dog, and that brute must first attend a ridiculous cow. As there was no other vet near, I rang up the doctor, who came at once.

This was the man who had the blowzy and disagreeable wife. But he was most kind; told me that Tinker had probably been poisoned with strychnine and suggested that I should have that investigated by the county analyst. He also said I should inform the police.

The superintendent said he would send a man round, and he sent a fat, beefy constable, who was most unsympathetic and examined the window of the scullery instead of Tinker's corpse.

The man, I am sure, was a lunatic, for he came to me and said that I must examine the house to see what, if anything, had been stolen! He had not the faintest inkling of the *truth*.

Of course, I had to do it, and, of course, nothing was missing.

"Which just shows how absurd it is for you to suggest that it was the work of a burglar," I told him.

"Liver's what they generally uses, mum," he said, in his fat-headed way. "I dessay he heard some noise and hopped it before he took anything."

"So you think that is it?" I said ironically.

"Of course it is, mum, and we may lay him by the heels yet," he said.

I sent him away. He was worse than useless, and his superintendent was quite as silly. When the analyst discovered that Tinker had been poisoned by a piece of liver impregnated with strychnine, Superintendent Beever told me that proved it. As if no one in Lush Mellish ever bought liver! As if that wicked old woman next door did not buy liver for her foul cat!

I said no more. It was obvious that all Lush Mellish was in a plot to hush up the black deed. They never caught the "burglar," of course. No one could.

In justice to them both, for I want to be fair, I may say that neither the vicar nor the Nonconformist minister poisoned my dog. I made private inquiries, and satisfied myself that the one was in bed with a chill, and the other had gone to see his mother in Norfolk.

Of course, I cannot absolutely say that neither had anything to do with it indirectly. Only I have no proof even of their complicity, and must give them the benefit of the doubt.

But now I knew! Lush Mellish had determined to get rid of me by killing my dear pets, and I became the more determined to stay and fight them; to show them that right and justice must prevail over their slimy ways.

And I soon had something to fight for: two tombstones in my garden. Two days later I saw the old woman next door feeding her nasty cat. She was doling out pieces of calves' liver to it, and talking to it in the most absurd way.

They say that people with failing minds talk to themselves, and I decided to make sure that she was really mad. I was quite close to the fence, and presently she raised her voice a little, so that I could hear what she said.

"Tootsy poosums then!" (I shuddered at the absurd phrases.) "Did it like ums liver den?"

Liver! I pricked up my ears.

"Nice liver," the old fool went on. "Tootsy poosums wouldn't eat bad liver like silly cur; no, indeed she wouldn't!"

Bad liver! She knew. She was laughing at my brave, confiding dog! She might even yet say something to incriminate herself.

"Tootsy poosums is too wise to eat poison," she went on, with a chuckle. "Looks as if it was providential, doesn't it, my lamb pet!"

I was so indignant that I instinctively straightened myself, and met the eyes of that old woman, who was staring over the fence in my direction and grinning diabolically.

As I walked away with dignity, I wondered if it was senility, or drugs. Baby-talk to a cat suggested a failing brain. But poisoning was more like the deed of one whose moral sense had been perverted by drugs. I dare not say anything about that outside, but I owed a duty to my darling dog, and went at once to see the superintendent.

Realising how things were developing, I did not expect to get justice in Lush Mellish. Still, I paid my share of the police rate, and was as much entitled to protection as anybody else.

The superintendent seemed to me rather strange. "You say you were in your garden, and heard this, madam?" he asked.

I explained. "She grinned at me in a most marked way afterwards," I added.

"Then she may have known you were there," he remarked. "But what do you wish us to do?"

"I want you to investigate the matter," I told him. "And may I say, the woman would hardly be likely to incriminate herself if she had known that I was the other side of the fence."

"So I thought," he returned irrelevantly. "But just how did she incriminate herself?"

"She referred to the poisoned liver, and said the death of my dog seemed providential."

He stroked his silly moustache. "I see. But why tell the cat?"

"She was angry with me about a former dog, which, quite rightly, endeavoured to keep her cat from trespassing," I said.

"Do you allege, madam, that she poisoned your dog out of spite?"

"I am merely asking you to make inquiries."

"I don't see how we can. It is incredible that an elderly lady should, or could, break open a scullery window by night."

I made a gesture with a finger to my forehead.

"In certain circumstances—" I began.

"My dear madam, she is as sane as you are. If you wish to lay a charge, we shall have to consider it, but the fact that she seems pleased that there is no dog next door does not constitute proof."

"But are not your people employed to get proof?"

"If a charge is laid, yes. But everyone knows now that your dog was poisoned with strychnine, and that is a poison it is not easy to procure. It would not be sent by post, for example, and your neighbour never leaves Lush Mellish."

"Have you inquired at the chemists'?"

"We have. None of them has sold strychnine lately, and we have traced earlier buyers. There is no doubt that a burglar was to blame, and if I may advise you, madam, you will drop this idea."

"I shall get another dog," I said furiously. "If that is poisoned, too, in the same way, I shall know how to act."

He bowed in his hatefully complacent way. "Of course, that is a matter for you to judge, madam, but I suggest that you buy a quiet dog—"

"My dogs have been quiet dogs."

"Then, let me say, a dog which will appear as quiet to other people as it does to you, madam. We had some complaints about the last two, but managed to get them withdrawn."

The impertinence of it! He was not going to do anything, but read me a lesson on the kind of dogs the town wanted me to keep. He also pretended that he had helped me before.

"My dogs were the most intelligent, *and* quiet, *and* harmless creatures in this town," I observed coldly. "I mean of all the living creatures in it, without exception. It seems to me a most extraordinary place."

I decided to go up to town to buy a typewriter. I had an idea of trying to write some sketches or stories, and so fill up my spare time. I was certainly not prepared to waste my leisure on the savages at Lush Mellish. When in town I could buy a dog from a man who kept an animal shop in Soho.

I might also order a tombstone for Tinker from a place where they keep the most tasteful memorials.

At Harrows' I saw a second-hand typewriter of a well-known make. I bought it, and some carbons, and paper. Then I selected a stone with a charming line on it in memory of my dead pet, and finally went to see about a new dog.

I saw a dozen, but finally fixed on a sweet Irish terrier.

"A splendid guard, madam," I was told, "and a great ratter."

"Is he quite safe with cats?" I asked ironically.

After a moment's pause, he assured me that "Buffer" was very fond of cats.

So I would now be able to reassure that ridiculous policeman.

"And children?" I said.

"Dotes on them, madam. There were five where he came from."

"Over distemper?"

"Eighteen months ago, madam. One of the nicest dogs we've had for years."

When I took out the licence for "Buffer" I told the policeman what I had heard.

"Glad to hear it, madam," he said. "Other people are funny about their pets too."

The man was offensive. But I was not going to argue with him. What the Lush Mellish folk thought of the degraded and unpleasant beasts they kept had nothing to do with me.

I must say that I was delighted with Buffer. He was most affectionate and friendly, and I took to him at once. So did my maids.

It would be false to say that there was no unpleasantness after that. There was, but it was obviously vamped up; part of the campaign, now in full swing, to find fault with everything I did, and everything I loved.

Buffer was fond of cats, as I had been assured. But even the best-behaved and most kindly dog cannot be fond of savage and unfriendly cats. When we say that we are fond of birds, it does not, and is not meant to, mean that we cherish vultures, or eagles, or like to be pecked by parrots; even apart from the question of acquiring psittacosis.

There were cats that resented Buffer's friendly advances and the intelligent curiosity he displayed when they were near him. But why should I expect him to have his nose scratched, or his dear brown eyes threatened, and not resent it in the only way he knew?

I should hate to keep a grovelling dog, or a cowardly one.

The same applies to children. There had been five where he came from, but no doubt they were nice, well-brought up children, who respected our dumb friends.

Respect a dog, and he will respect you and show himself the innate gentleman he is. Treat him as a mere animal, or tease him, or show signs of fear, when he comes forward to caress you, and you at once unnerve him, and bring out his primitive qualities.

One could not expect, really, to see many nice children in Lush Mellish, when their elders and parents had so little idea of conducting themselves properly; and indeed, one did not see them.

As for the hordes of poor children, they were little better than Red Indians. Only Indians would have known that terriers are not wild beasts, to be screamed at, or have stones thrown at them.

I remember once dear Buffer dashing forward in his playful way to romp with some street children who were playing hop-scotch. You would have imagined a lion had attacked them, and one boy yelled murder when he ran off, and Buffer wanted to race him.

As I told his mother that evening: "Buffer likes to play. He came from a home where there were five children, and they all loved him."

"And funny kids they must've bin," she said, most raucously. "Wot their father says is that 'e'll give that narsty dog 'opscotch, next time he see 'im interfering with ours!"

And, of course, there was the fiend next door! I am not superstitious. If I had been, the conjunction of that woman and her black cat would have hinted that she was a witch. In spite of the wire, her cat still got into my garden, and Buffer, of course, walked over to look at it, and wanted to play. She scratched his nose, and bounced up and over the wire-netting, swearing as cats do, and the old woman was convinced that it was *his* fault. She wrote:

> "Mrs. W. presents her compliments to Miss Alice, and begs that she will dispose of her latest wild beast before Providence interposes.
>
> "Mrs. W. will, on application, supply Miss Alice with the name and address of a qualified chemist who undertakes to dispose (quietly and painlessly) of any animals whose offensive habits render their destruction necessary."

I replied at once:

> "Miss Alice presents her compliments to Mrs. W., and acknowledges receipt of her extraordinary letter.
>
> "A hater of all cruelty, she is moved to astonished anger by the suggestion that her harmless pet should be destroyed.
>
> "She wishes no harm to the marauder from next door, *which* is unlovely in its deeds as in its looks. If it cannot be kept within bounds, Miss Alice suggests that it be presented to the Zoological Society of London, who will

make provision for its comfort and safety with its kinsfolk: tigers, leopards, lynxes, ocelots, pumas, and jaguars.

"I think I am correct in saying that this is the tribe to which your pet belongs."

Now wasn't that much more dignified and witty than the foolish and venomous scrawl she sent me?

Further, that cat continued to trespass.

And, of course, Buffer took my part.

Just one more story of that woman's malignity.

A week after that, Buffer must have seen the cat in the garden, and followed it into its own demesne.

He came rushing in, making appealing noises, and his dear nose and head was concealed under a large cardboard cone. It does seem incredible, but that woman had smeared the inside of the cone with fish-glue (which smelt!) and laid a trap for him.

She was putting down other cones in her garden when I spoke to her about it.

"It's disgraceful!" I told her. "It took me two hours to get the vile stuff off, and the dog was almost blinded."

She peered at me with her grotesque smile. "I put them down to catch bats," she said softly. "Blind bats! I put them down in my own garden. I do not put them in the belfry. I know no law against catching bats."

Obviously mad! "Well," I said patiently, "when your cat gets stuck in one of them you may change your mind."

"Tootsy poosums won't," she said. "Cats aren't such damn' fools!"

The reference to bats was illuminating. Somehow, the old woman recognised her mental disability, I expect, and was letting me know tactfully that I must be tolerant with her.

CHAPTER VIII

IN THE law—if nowhere else—sauce for the goose is sauce for the gander.

If she had a legal right to protect her garden, I had an equal right to ensure that her horrid cat did not invade mine.

But, when I went indoors again, I sat down and thought it over. I was quite sure that the old woman, like all fanatics, grossly exaggerated the intelligence of her cat.

No one need tell me that cats are as brainy as dogs. They don't look like it; they have never been known to save a drowning person, as dogs have done, or to rescue a farmer from a mad bull. Both these feats have been performed time and again by dogs, which shows their ready wit by understanding that there was danger to master or mistress.

What had happened in the next garden was not obvious to me, but it was very likely that the old woman had actually *thrust* that cone on Buffer's head when he came up to talk to her in his doggy way. It was inconceivable that he should have run into a trap that a cat avoided.

I determined to put my theory to the proof, and ordered kippers that day.

Both my maids were fond of them, and also quite on my side as regards the intrusions of the black cat. They had already expressed indignation at the beastly trick played on Buffer, and were quite amused and interested when they heard what I proposed to do.

"That'll show her, ma'am," cook said, smiling. "It will indeed."

"But you must bone the kipper, cook," I told her. "I am not anxious that the cat should choke. Merely to teach it, and her, a lesson is what I want to do."

I made a cone, a smaller one, of course, and as I did not wish to buy nasty fish-glue, I bought some of the bird-lime they use for trapping birds, and thoroughly smeared the inside of the cone with it.

I knew by now where that wretched cat used to cross the wire, and when I had placed the boned kipper in the end of the cone, I went indoors again, leaving the cone ready for my test.

I was, of course, within my rights, and everything would have gone well, but for one thing. All of us have the defects of our qualities, and dogs are such intelligent animals because they have developed the faculty of observation, and with it that necessary curiosity which is vital if an animal is to co-ordinate the use of all his senses.

A cat will steal and devour a kipper out of sheer greed. If the kipper was not a food favoured by the cat, it would not even look at it. Anyone who is not foolishly prejudiced must recognise that. She must also see that a dog will investigate anything strange, so that, in future, he will know what to approach, or to avoid.

It was in the early mornings, usually, that the beast from next door invaded my garden, and at about half-past seven next morning I heard the most extraordinary sound of rushing and snuffling, mingled with a series of extraordinary hooting noises.

Unable to repress a smile, I got hastily out of bed, and raised the window-blind to look out. "The cat and the kipper!" I said to myself, though I was unable to recognise the hoots, which were not really animal sounds at all.

I had hardly glanced from the window when I saw what had happened, and rushed downstairs to help cook, who was already in the garden trying to stop poor Buffer, who was dashing blindly to and fro. Even while I looked, I had seen him cannon into the summer-house, and then charge a tree, poor darling.

When I was outside, I realised what the hooting meant. It had now turned to a sort of screech, mingled with choking.

That woman next door stood near the fence, her cat in her arms, and indulged in unholy laughter; even when I made my appearance, and gave her a look that would have made any sensitive person shrivel up.

But her laughter—if you can call that vulgar and almost maniacal glee laughter—became louder than ever, and she made silly remarks to her cat.

I determined to ignore her, and the housemaid now having come out to help, we did our best to corner Buffer, and take the cone from his head.

The fruit trees and flower-beds hampered us in our chase, but in the end he fell into the sunk water-butt, and we were able to rescue the poor darling, and take him indoors.

It struck me then how right was the law when it made it illegal to trap birds in this way. The bird-lime, if not so smelly, was even worse than fish-glue to remove, and the best part of the morning was spent taking it off, and cleaning Buffer's coat.

"It was entirely my fault," I told cook, who had tears in her eyes, which she tried to hide. "I might have known that dear, clever Buffer would try to see what it was that worried him last time."

Naturally, neither of my maids would carry the story farther, but the old woman must have done, for it ran over the town, and some ill-natured people even sent a message to the inspector of the R.S.P.C.A., who called to inquire.

He was a dense man, and did not seem to understand that I had not put down the cone to catch Buffer. He said that people might take measures, if not cruel ones, to protect their gardens, but ill-treatment of one's own animals was an offence.

"I understand, ma'am," he said, quite civilly, "that your dog did something you didn't like, and you stuck the cone on his head for a punishment like."

"A punishment for my darling dog?" I said indignantly. "It was a trap for—for mosquitoes, which are very numerous. Who informed you?"

"We are not at liberty to give the names of our informants, ma'am," he said, "but I see it was all right."

The hypocrisy of Lush Mellish! People were at liberty to slander one to the R.S.P.C.A., but unless you signed your name to a letter, giving information of a real and grave abuse, they put you in jail!

The incident really ended then, but, for some time after, the ruder children of the town (encouraged, I am afraid, by their elders) played a game they called "Cones." One child wore a conical cap over his eyes, and dashed about wildly, while the other ragamuffins chased him, and *barked*.

The police eventually put an end to this game, for an urchin, wearing a cap, ran into the way of a passing car, and then there were howls instead of barks. The boy broke his ankle, and I trusted it might be a lesson to him.

Yes, Lush Mellish was hypocritically shocked at the idea of anonymous letters later on, but in the next month I received two. "We damn the sins we have a mind to," is my truer version of the old saw.

Naturally, having been encouraged to make game of my poor dog's accident, the children began to think they could torment the dog himself. That is the only explanation of the fact that there were several young ruffians scratched by Buffer's playful teeth, and absurdly exaggerated complaints made to the police about it.

I paid compensation under protest on two occasions, and then, one day, I received a letter, in a cheap-looking envelope, printed in Roman capitals.

It contained part of a doggerel poem ending with:

"We ain't given our kids for yer dog to tear!"

For some time I tried to trace an association of ideas, and then it came to me. The line was a parody of a beautiful and tender poem, by Mr. Lucas or someone, about a spaniel, and giving your *"heart* to a dog to tear."

One can imagine the brutal mentality of a person who dared to parody that heart-rending poem. It gave me a clue, not only to the bestial character of the sender, but also to the class from which she came.

My father was a man who had keen deductive ability, and I flatter myself that my own essays in detection have not been fruitless. I am fond of reading detective fiction, and at once sat down to consider this insulting epistle as if I had been a C.I.D. man.

First, the content of the letter. The children who had tormented my dog were all of the poorer classes.

Poems of any kind, and most of all subtle poems about dogs, are not the favourite reading of the poor. Imagine a bricklayer confronted with the last line in its original state! He would be distressingly literal about it. How could a dog tear your heart? How could you give your heart for a dog to tear, while you were still alive?

No. It was not one of the proletariat who had sent me that anonymous letter. It was one of his "betters"; an ironical word in this connection. I had preserved both letter and envelope, and decided to set out to trace (1) the seller of the envelope; (2) of the paper. It was probable that they had been bought at different shops.

Reversing the sheet, so that the writing should not be seen, I took it to the best stationer's, and asked him if he sold that sort of paper.

"Only for school-children, madam," he said. "Do you wish to buy some?"

"Do they come in here for it?" I asked, ordering a quire.

"No, madam. It's generally the teachers who buy it for them. They get a discount."

"What about these envelopes?" I said, showing part of the torn one.

"Everyone sells them, madam. Of course, they are cheap, but lots of customers buy them in quantity."

I went to all the places where they sold stationery, but met with the same answer everywhere, and did not think it wise to ask too personal questions. I returned home with a great deal of paper and envelopes that I did not require.

I am relating this because, incredible as it seems, this buying of stationery, as a cover for my justifiable enquiries, was brought up against me at the trial!

The scoundrelly prosecutor insisted that I had asked what kind of paper was in the greatest request, and purchased absurd supplies of it.

"Miss Alice, you will note," he said, in his smarmy voice, "made sure that this paper was of a type not easily associated with its user, by reason of the fact that it was used by half the town."

I told him at once that not even the unscrupulous prosecution had alleged that I used the paper in question.

"You are perfectly correct," he said with a faint sneer, "but we may be justified in assuming that a clever woman might realise afterwards that her enquiries would cause talk, and abandon any idea she had of making use of that paper for the purpose specified."

You see, the man had an answer to everything; as unscrupulous people have. They always say that a truthful witness is more easily trapped than a lying one.

But I did not give up hope yet. I went to the superintendent, and laid the matter before him. This also I told counsel later, but he tried to make out that I was safeguarding myself in advance.

"How can I tell who wrote it?" the superintendent said.

"Is Lush Mellish so backward that it does not know how to develop fingerprints?" I asked.

It appeared that they did, and I admit that I was quite excited when I heard next day from the superintendent that fingerprints had been found on the envelope and letter.

"Some may be yours, madam," he said when I hurried round to see him.

I was, of course, quite ready to give him my prints for comparison, and when those were eliminated, there were still some on the envelope and the anonymous letter.

"Now we are getting warmer," I told him. "I hope you will lose no time in getting the rascal."

But it seemed that he was not yet content. I had to get my housemaid's fingerprints, and she made a fuss about it, since she read a great many cheap thrillers, and understood that this was the preliminary to making an arrest.

Yes, she had brought the letter to me, and her fingerprints were on the envelope. "And the postman evidently left his," the superintendent told me with a faint smile. "I've checked that."

I was disappointed. It seemed to me that these people were really glad to get out of the necessity for prosecuting anyone. There was something behind it all.

I have tried to present what I may call my day-to-day frame of mind as I recount this, and you cannot fail to see that I was gradually unravelling, thread by thread, the skein of conspiracy against me. I was beginning to see that there were no isolated instances of affront, injury and impertinence, but a dreadful scheme to hound me down, in which every person in the town, almost, took part.

"So I suppose you have nothing to go on?" I said, looking at him hard.

"There are still the prints of a finger and thumb, madam," he told me. "They may be difficult to trace, but we shall do our best."

That was something, and while he tried to discover the owner of the fingerprints, I made some inquiries about the local school-teachers, and particularly one young headmistress, a member of the tennis club, who was very rude, and kept a marmoset.

Cats are bad enough, but this impudent monkey was worse than a cat. And it always pretended to be terrified when I turned up at the club with my dog, and jumped on its mistress's shoulder, jibbering as these silly animals do.

I had also heard something about this young woman from cook, and, if it was true, she was very much out of place as mistress to innocent children, though "engaged" to a fat, red-faced young man in the bank.

One of my few sympathisers in Lush Mellish came to me soon after the first anonymous letter arrived, and told me that the woman had said I must be "batty," a word which is highly offensive, when you remember my education, and the culture the wretched town despised.

"But you mustn't mind her, dear," said my informant. "If that pompous young man of hers knew the truth, Humpty-Dumpty would have a great fall."

The superintendent was still investigating the fingerprints, or pretending to, when a second communication came to me, also printed, and extremely offensive, not only to me but to dear, dead Tinker's memory.

I was furious when I opened the dirty envelope and read the line inside:

"FOR SALE: BULLDOG. EAT ANYTHING.
VERY FOND OF CHILDREN."

As a joke that had been a passable one in its day, but applied to my old pet, and directed to me, it was disgusting and almost criminal.

I took it at once to the superintendent, and made him read it.

"Now what do you propose to do?" I asked indignantly.

"I don't see that we can do anything, madam," he said, to my astonishment.

"You do not propose to do anything?"

"Certainly not. I do not even think you have the substance of a charge, granting that you knew the sender," he replied. "This may be malicious, but it is neither criminal nor libellous."

"It is a libel on my dear dog that died," I said.

"Possibly, madam, but no prosecutions are carried on with dogs as complainants, and, if I were you, I should treat this as a rather poor joke."

"I am not asking for your advice as to how I should treat it," I said ironically. "Your failure in the last case would not justify me in doing so."

"Oh, the last case," he said. "We cleared that up this morning. It seems that the remaining fingerprints were those of Mr. Brown, the stationer, to whom you showed the sheet."

A most offensive person!

CHAPTER IX

BUFFER was run over.

Yes, the campaign of persecution had gone a step farther, and when I threatened to report the superintendent to the Watch Committee, and the Chief Constable, for slackness, he was positively rude.

"I am a busy man, madam," he said. "Your dog was killed last night by a car which failed to stop."

"How do you know that it failed to stop?"

"The driver did not report the accident, as he was bound to do. I shall take steps to investigate the matter, but I am not responsible for the deaths of straying dogs."

"He has as much right on the roads as the motorists," I said.

"And is as liable to be run down," he said impatiently. "Good morning, madam."

"You'll hear more about this, superintendent," I said angrily.

"I hope not, madam," he said rudely. "There seems to be some fatality about your dogs. You would have more peace of mind if you did not keep any."

The cloven hoof was peeping out now. "You almost suggest that you were going to say that you would, too," I said scornfully.

"Since you put the words in my mouth, madam, I'll accept them," he replied impudently. "I hardly knew there were dogs in this town until—"

Here he stopped wisely, seeing that he had gone too far.

"I shall inform the Chief Constable of what you say," I told him.

The Chief Constable is one of those superannuated army men who must be in the limelight somehow, and prevent the professional police from getting their proper promotion. I am speaking generally, of course, for the local superintendent would have made an incompetent sergeant and, if he had been in the army, would have been properly and frequently punished for silent insolence.

The major—I spell it with a small "m"—lived about half a mile outside the town. He has a caddish son, who has a considerable reputation as a Lothario, and is the ringleader of the male louts at the tennis club.

His wife is a quiet sort of woman, but quite negligible, and very dowdy. They say the major spends most of his income on sport and she has to make her own clothes. I have great sympathy for her, but, of course, she is brainless, and under the thumb of her martinet husband.

However, I went to see the major, and told him what had happened.

"So my three pets are dead," I ended. "They were quiet, valuable animals, and have fallen victims to spite."

"To what?" he snorted, and I began to see the type of man he was.

"Spite, major."

"That's not what I heard."

I stared at him. "May one ask what you have heard?"

"Well, you had a fighting bull-terrier that played hell—"

"You are not in the barracks now, major," I interrupted.

"That's obvious enough," he grunted. "Anyway, your dog thought himself such a h—such a champion that he tackled two devils worse than himself and got laid out."

"That is a lie," I said coldly.

"Well, you may as well hear the other two lies," he said. "A burglar poisoned the bull-dog, and your last child-chewer—"

I held up my hand. "My last what?"

He looked a little disconcerted. "We had a good many complaints from parents—"

"Lush Mellish parents," I interjected.

"Anyway," he went on, backing down, "your last dog was run over after dark by a passing car."

"That's the question," I said.

"How is it the question?" he demanded.

"It is possible that the thing was planned and arranged," I told him. "I don't believe for a moment that it was accidental. And that brings me to the reason for my coming to you. I wish to report your superintendent for being slack and impudent."

"Anything else?" grunted that offensive, barrack-room bully.

"Nothing," I said calmly. "I should think it was enough."

"Quite enough, if not more," he snorted. "And now just a hint from me, madam. If we have any more complaints about your dogs, we shall have to take action. *Good* morning."

I think it was then that I got my first idea about joining the town council, and heard more of the civic as well as the moral corruption that crept like an ill-weed near the flowery meads of Lush Mellish.

Sometimes one hears of a friend or acquaintance stricken down by a disease unheard of before. Afterwards one is constantly hearing of this complaint. And so it was with the affairs of the town. Once I had begun to keep my ears open for rumours of what the Americans call graft, I was surprised to discover that the place was rotten with it.

My visit to the Chief Constable was my last attempt to get evils officially remedied. I now saw that it was hopeless. Possibly he, like the other residents, did not wish to have among them one who had such a keen flair for abuses, coupled with a determination to right the wrong. It was this, and nothing but this, which was at the bottom of my campaign to make Lush Mellish as fragrant in fact as it was in name.

Just one word more about poor Buffer, before I relate the story of a visitor, and the incidents surrounding my nomination to the town council. Even if you are as hard to convince as a Lush Mellish jury, you cannot fail to gather from it an idea of the malicious character of many of the residents.

When I returned to my home, and was about to enter my gate, after my interview with the barrack-bully, I saw that a small car had stopped by the kerb.

I have keen eyes, and probably my thoughts were centred on my dead pet. At any rate, I saw, in the middle of the front tyre, near the road, a patch of dark reddish hair! What would you have thought in my place? I am sure you would have felt the same as I did.

I examined the patch, and also some hairs which still adhered to the mudguard in front. I had combed poor Buffer many hundreds of times, and knew if anyone did what the hair from an Irish terrier was like. And can I be blamed if I saw in this car the vehicle which had brutally struck Buffer down?

I felt rather sick as I looked, and saw that there was a reddish patch on the tyre. But I intended to make the brutal owner even more sick when I caught him.

I entered the garden and hid behind the macrocarpus hedge to wait. Five minutes passed, and then I heard the door of the wicked old woman's house open, and her voice, and that of a man.

I was sure now that I had got to the bottom of the plot. I heard them both come together to the gate, and slipping through mine, stood before the car as they came out. The man I now recognised. He was a nephew of the woman's, who came from Long Moleby.

"Excuse me," I said, going straight up to him as he opened the door of the car, "I shall be glad to have your name and address, sir."

He was more or less a lad, but tall and sardonic-looking. "What for?" he demanded, staring at me, and for once the old woman did not interfere.

"You know very well," I said indignantly. "My Irish terrier was run over and killed by a car after dark, and I have reason to believe you did it."

He looked at the old woman, who glanced at me. "Rubbish. I never ran over any dog."

"I cannot take your word for it," I said. "You will be good enough to wait here till I get a policeman to examine your car."

He looked rather sick, I imagined, and his aunt was unusually quiet. "What is the matter with my car?" he said.

Now I was afraid that if I told him and then went for the police he would remove the incriminating evidence before I could get back. At that moment, luckily, or unluckily, as it turned out, the beefy constable turned the corner and came walking down the road.

I called to him, and he came forward.

"Officer," I said, "I charge this young man with having run over and killed my dog."

"What, another dog, mum?" he asked stupidly.

"My Irish terrier."

"Have you any evidence of it, mum?"

I went to the front of the car, and pointed dramatically. "Here is his hair adhering to the tyre, officer, and there is a small patch on the mudguard. And look at this reddish stain."

The old woman came round too, and gasped. The policeman took his notebook from his pocket, and even the youth seemed crestfallen.

"So it looks, mum," the constable said, bending down to look. "Now, sir, what have you to say about that?"

"I wasn't in town at the time."

"How do you know, sir, what time the dog was killed?"

"Not here that night, I mean. I heard about the dog from my aunt."

"Has he any proof of that?" I asked coldly.

But the constable meant business this time. "Do you deny that those are dog's hair, sir?"

"No, I can't. I think they do look like Irish terrier's hairs, but I swear I never killed anyone's dog."

"I am afraid we'll need to know more about it than that, sir. The lady and you had better accompany me to the station if she is prepared to lay a charge. Also I may warn you, sir, that your duty was to report the accident, which you didn't do."

"But I never had an accident."

The constable made a note. "On your unsupported word, sir. Now just have a squin—a look at the stain here. Isn't that dried blood?"

"Can't be. I didn't hit anything."

"Doesn't it look like it?"

"It does, but I can't help that."

"My nephew wasn't here, and he wouldn't run over a dog," said my evil neighbour.

"I'm sorry, mum," said the constable, "but mere saying so doesn't help matters. If this gentleman can't bring some proof that he wasn't here, and ran over this lady's dog, failing to stop and report as he should, according to the Traffic Act, I shall have to ask you—"

"Wait a moment, wait a moment!" said the young man. "This lady has seen the patch, and my aunt's seen it, and you've seen it, so it's a fact of sorts, isn't it?"

"A damning fact," I said.

"I didn't like to use that word in your presence," he said impudently. "I meant to say that if I drive the car off now to try an experiment—"

"You mustn't do that, sir."

"Why not?"

The constable weakened and I frowned at him.

"What sort of an experiment, sir?"

"Well, I have driven sixty-two miles this morning, and it is some time since the dog was killed."

"What's that got to do with it?" I demanded.

"Only that I contend that the dog's hairs wouldn't stick on all that way," he said, more impudently now. "Gosh! Why, they aren't even dusty or smeared!" If I had been wise I would have looked at his aunt's face, which would at once have betrayed the dastardly plot. But I stared hard at him.

"I presume then that an Irish terrier dog, of which there happen to be no specimens in this road, came up casually since the car stood here, and happened to be bleeding as well?"

"Ah, that's just the point, mum," said my constable, making another note in his book. "What have you to say to that, young man?"

I did notice now that the aunt was grinning, but I am too innocent to suspect people of utter vileness. The youth looked at the patch again.

"I don't believe it is blood, now I come to look at it, constable. No, I'm sure it's not. Looks to me like red stain of some sort."

"Couldn't be Dermatinge, Herbert, could it?" said his aunt.

"Blessed if I don't think you're right," he said.

The constable glanced at him suspiciously. "What's Dermatinge?"

"Don't you know it?"

"Never heard of it, sir."

"Nor I," I said.

"It's a cure for mange and troubles with dogs' coats," said the youth. "Sort of reddish colour, don't you know." He paused suddenly and then laughed in a loutish way. "I say, aunt, I quite forgot Bowser!"

I felt that he was trying to sneak out of it in some way, but I was determined that he should not escape.

"That is not good enough," I remarked. "Officer, if you will see that he drives to the police station, I will be prepared to charge him."

"What about that, sir?" the constable asked.

I noticed then that his aunt had scuttled away in alarm, and gone into her garden.

"Not on your life," said the youth. "I wouldn't have got a hundred yards before that stuff was rubbed out, and then how could I prove it was Dermatinge?"

The constable scratched his head and reflected; then he said we must scrape off the patch, and it could be analysed, and the matter soon decided. I agreed that that was the wisest procedure, and was about to set off for the station—not being willing to travel in that young brute's car, even if he offered me a lift—when his aunt appeared again.

"Here's Bowser!" she said. "And how funny you forgot, Herbert! I see you have rubbed Dermatinge into his coat."

She had an Irish terrier under her arm, and its likeness to Buffer showed me how easy it was for me to be deceived. She exhibited the dog to the constable, and while they were looking at it, I withdrew to my own home with dignity.

Peals of laughter—some of the maniacal character I knew so well—came later to me from the roadway. Then the car drove off.

Such diabolical ingenuity, such pleasure in torment, such vile practical joking, told me that Long Moleby could not be a whit behind Lush Mellish itself. Unless, indeed, the whole disgusting plot had been evolved by the harridan next door.

If so, she must have summoned her nephew, waited till she saw me leave to visit the Chief Constable, and then assisted the lout in his fell work.

But that was not all. There was a preposterous account in the local paper, not mentioning my name, but headed:

"TRAGI-COMEDY OF DERMATINGE!
"AFFLICTED DOG USES TYRE AS COAT-SCRAPER.
"AMUSING COMEDY OF ERRORS."

Very well. I had given Lush Mellish its *last* chance.

CHAPTER X

OLD friends are certainly best. If it were nothing else, the fact that you have known them so long proves that you have something in common.

Queenie Bostarby was about my age. I had been her dear friend at school, and she had lived in Rhodesia ever since she left it, being taken there by her father, who had delicate lungs.

A month after the death of Buffer, and when I was really getting attached to my spaniel Tiblits, I had a letter from her from a London hotel, and promptly invited her to stay with me for a fortnight.

There are some people who can be quite entertaining for a week. They are not the majority, of course. But Queenie had been such a cheerful soul that I decided to chance a fortnight. After all, if it was not a success, no harm would be done, for she was going back to Rhodesia at the end of the month.

She was as cheerful as ever, when I met her at the station, but fat. Yes, the slim girl I had known had grown into a very plump woman.

"It's the mealies do it, darling," she assured me, when I ventured to comment on it.

"What are mealies?" I said, as I poured out the tea. "Meals?"

"Meals of mealies," she said. "Indian corn, you know—maize."

"But I thought only the negroes lived on maize?" I said in surprise.

"Oh, we pioneers," she smiled. "Maize for breakfast; mealie pap for lunch; perhaps the same, with a lion steak, for dinner."

I started. Lush Mellish was bad enough, but curs were our worst danger—and cats, of course. "Then you have lions?" I said.

"When we can get them," she said, reaching for a cake. "The trouble is that those over a year old are apt to be tough. Give me a cut off a juicy six-months-old, and you can have your barbecued leopard, or fricassied locust."

I learned later that this was a form of humour which she thought amusing. Naturally, never having been in Africa, I was not to know.

"Have you never read of locusts and wild honey?" she asked, when I seemed surprised. "Oh, I see. You mean the locust-bean. Well, we have to tell strangers that they are eating locust-beans, for fear they would be sick. Afterwards, they go out like the rest of us."

I have always been interested in travel and the strange customs of savage countries. "Extraordinary!" I gasped. "But what do you all go out for? I thought locusts were a pest."

"Wait till you have picked the wing of one," she said and smacked her lips in a way that suggested how easily she would grow fat. "Luscious!"

"But don't they eat every green thing?"

"So do cows here," said Queenie, passing her cup. "And that's how they have rich milk."

"You mean?" I said.

"Well, our locusts eat all the rich green vitamins, darling," she explained, "and we wait till they have assimilated them, and are what we call protein-rich."

"Oh, I see. Yes, they would be."

She nodded and tackled another cake. "Then we all rush out and catch them in our hats," she said. "You'll notice that most colonials wear large hats."

"I thought that was for the sun?"

She laughed. "We have to excuse our greediness somehow, darling. You're not out there very long before you become a locust fan. I knew one man who was quite disgusted at the idea when he came out first, and later he used to spend half his time on the stoep with a spy-glass."

"Doing what?" I demanded, much interested now.

"Watching for the first signs of the locust clouds," said Queenie. "You had to keep your eye on him, which rather muddled up the housework."

This was indeed strange. "But why?"

"My dear, he would get off first on his horse, and take the cream off the first crop," she assured me. "You see, the farther they fly, the tougher they get. Young ones are the rage. The last I heard of that man he was running a locust ranch, so that he could taste 'em quite fresh."

"How little we know of what goes on abroad," I said. "How did you first manage to try them?"

"Well, I was out one day, soon after I came, and met a negress with a native basket full of what looked like green vegetables. Greens are very scarce, so I ran over, hoping to be able to buy some. But what was it? A basket full of big green caterpillars."

"How filthy!" I said, with a shudder.

"So I thought then, darling. I asked her what she wanted them for, and she popped a big one in her mouth and said it was delicious."

"The brute!" I said.

"Me too," said Queenie. "No, I don't mean to say I ever ate them *au naturel*, my sweet. But fried—exquisite is the only word for them."

"You ate some?"

"I eat some. It's my one consolation about having to go back. That, and the thought of a locust pupa in aspic."

I hastened to change the subject. "But, my dear, are you not afraid of wild animals?"

She smiled. "Why, the place is lousy with them. They get used to us, and we get used to them. Take the lion. He's not such a bad chap. Buffaloes are bad—never seem to like petting, some-how—and leopards are too fond of dogs for my liking."

"Don't you like dogs?" I asked, glancing at dear Tiblits.

"That's why," she said. "Leopards are as crazy about dogs as we are about locusts and caterpillars for tea."

I shivered again. Why could she not stop talking about those loathsome insects?

"Then I suppose you have snakes too?" I said.

"They have their uses," she replied. "Eat up the scorpions and so forth, but I admit they are a bit thick in the spring, when their nests are in all the bushes."

"In the bushes, Queenie?" I asked.

"To keep their young out of the way of the soldier ants," she said, and took a third cake, to my horror. "Don't blame them myself."

"I have heard of soldier ants," I said. "Are they dangerous?"

"They do our spring cleaning," she said. "When an army comes along we clear out for the day—perhaps go for a locust drive—and they eat up every speck of life in the place. Some life, I can tell you. Or perhaps I had better not. I never got a greater laugh in my life than I did watching a mamba, which is the most dangerous snake in the world, trying to butt a column of soldier ants. In about two ticks you couldn't see the mamba, but you did see thousands of ants running about with scales in their teeth. I simply screamed when one young ant started to choke. He looked so human."

"You're joking," I said.

"Ask anyone who knows," she said. "Write to the man at the Zoo, and ask him about the green caterpillars. That's true enough."

"Does your father like the country, too, at his age?" I asked.

Her fingers were reaching out for a fourth cake, and she passed her cup again. But I remembered that she was dependent on mealies at home, and said nothing.

"He likes it," she said. "He's wonderful at taming things, even reptiles. At home he was afraid of grass snakes, but on my last birthday I came home to find Jan and Jean lying on the lawn forming the letters Q.B. I did think it sweet of dad."

He must be an astounding man, I thought, but she had not told me anything previously about her pets.

"I don't see how a dog could form the letter Q, darling," I protested. "You are drawing the long bow there, aren't you? I do know something about dogs."

She laughed again. "My dear! I shouldn't expect you to swallow that, of course. Jan and Jean are pythons. Dad caught them when they were young, at the bottom of the garden, and they are perfect loves."

"Nonsense! Pythons bite," I said.

"All snakes bite if they are annoyed," she said. "None of them go about biting at random; except the mamba, of course. The fact was that an elephant had taken a fancy to our mealie patch."

"An elephant in your garden?"

"My sweet, have you never read anything about Africa? Don't you know that elephants damage most of the natives' crops?"

"I think I have read that, Queenie."

"Well then, the natives grow mealies, and so do we. But, as I was saying, this elephant got a bit noisy, as well as thievish, bellowing and hooting in the night, you know, and dad was fed up. He took his elephant-gun, and laid out for the brute."

"In the garden?"

"At the bottom of it. Just when it was getting light, Edna, he saw the old monster, who had just scooped out a rhubarb frame, and was walking forward to have a nibble at my favourite fig tree. 'Ha, ha!' said dad, getting a bead on old Methuselah's one vital spot, 'here's where we try the new lead cure.' So he popped off the gun, and down came behemoth."

I was interested in her anecdote, but thought it irrelevant. "Yes, but where do the pythons come in?" I asked.

"Just there," she replied. "Jan and Jean had just crawled out to have a spot of sunbathing, when the old donkey of an elephant came pounding on his big flat feet. Another yard and he would have made snake pie of the two young dears. Luckily the rogue elephant toppled clear of them, and they have been pally with Dad ever since."

"But, Queenie," I protested, "how could they know that he had saved their lives?"

"Ask me another," she said. "These are lovely cakes of yours, by the way. Cakes of this quality are rarer than whales with us."

"I'll ring for some more," I said. "But *how* could they know?"

"Instinct, of course," she replied. "I don't think you know much about natural history, my dear. How do birds and fishes come back to their native lands after migration? How do eels swim here from the Caribbean Sea? Instinct, of course. It's a cheap snake that isn't hoots ahead of an eel when it comes to brains."

"Well, I can only say that I have no wish to live there," I said, when fresh cakes had been brought. "The local fauna is quite enough for me."

"Are they?" said Queenie. "I quite forgot to ask how you were getting on—loving this place I expect. It looks quite an Eden, if you ask me."

"Complete with serpents," I said. "Almost as many as you have."

"Even if they do not crawl on their bellies," said Queenie.

Native life had made her speech rather coarse, I noticed.

"I have had my own struggles with wild beasts," I agreed. "Not at Ephesus, but in this so-called Eden."

She helped herself to a cigarette from the box I had put beside her, and grinned. "Bad as that?"

"Really terrible," I told her. "They have already destroyed three of my dogs, but they are so cunning that they make it appear accident."

She looked earnestly at me. "What was the idea?"

"I don't know," I said. "Nominally, of course (for they have an answer to everything here), it was made out that my dogs were dangerous. But I have a shrewd suspicion there was something behind it."

I must say that she gave me her attention then; indeed, seemed quite concerned about my affairs. "I wonder what it was, darling."

"I saw through them," I told her. "My mother was gifted in that way. I expect it is very uncomfortable for people when they realise that you can penetrate behind the mask."

"It must be," she said slowly. "Darned uncomfortable, I should say! Do you mean that you can really tell when people are not what they seem?"

"Always," I said.

"Nearly read their thoughts?" she murmured. "Tell, I suppose, if they are speaking the truth or not?"

"Oh, yes," I replied, "I can do that."

She smiled a little. "I do wish you would tell me all about it," she begged. "It sounds most interesting. Where every prospect pleases and only man is vile. And one thought the hymn rather a generalisation."

"There is a conspiracy," I said. "I did not realise it at first. But bit by bit—there were various incidents—I understood. At first there were minor unpleasantnesses; later they began to come out in their true colours."

"So injudicious too—with your *gift*!" she said.

I told her about my first encounter with the fiend who owns the black cat, and she was forced to smile at my picture of that beastly animal perched in a tree while Leander barked below.

"What a silly old woman!" she remarked. "I mean to say, no sense of humour, had she? I always think people with no sense of humour are likely to become thoroughly dangerous."

"I agree with you absolutely," I said, and went on to tell her of the vicar's cur, and what the man had called it.

"He meant Curgi, of course," she laughed. "With an obvious derivation, my dear. But surely an educated man should have realised that your pure-bred dog would resent the existence of a—well, canine commoner."

"That is what I thought, Queenie," I told her. "But the whole thing is explained when you realise that that was only a *pretext*. It was part of the facade behind which this conspiracy to drive me out of the town was going on."

Queenie pursed her lips. "You are sure there is no mistake?"

"None whatever. My dear Tinker was poisoned and I am sure it was done by the savage next door."

When she had heard about the opened window, and the rest of it, she shook her head in a bewildered way. "You say there was a third dog?"

I told her all about poor Buffer, and the trick the ruffians had played on me. "That in itself gives them away," I said, when I had finished the story. "How did they know that I suspected someone of having run over the dog on purpose? It was given out as an accident."

"How indeed?" she murmured. "I should leave the place if I were you."

"Never!" I said. "I have inherited my father's spirit. He fought his enemies to the last. When you have the right on your side, you must go on."

"I do agree there," she said, lighting a fresh cigarette. "But what can you do against all these people?"

"I know something about them," I said. "My dear, it is not only vice but corruption that reigns here. If I were on the town council, I might do something to clean the Augean stables."

"Why not put up for it?" she asked, smiling.

"If I could!" I said, and a new idea came to me. "Queenie, you have given me a new hope. There must be some, even in this town, who long for clean, decent government. Not many, but *some*."

She clapped her hands. "Splendid! It will give you something to do, and think about, darling. How does one go about it?"

"I don't know, but I'll enquire," I said. "What a triumph it would be for the forces of right!"

CHAPTER XI

"Did you ever know, dear, that I had visions of becoming an author?" Queenie asked me next morning at breakfast.

I had provided a sippet of toast and a grapefruit as an alternative, since it was obvious that she was badly in need of a slimming diet, but she was tackling her second egg (after bacon and kidney) as she spoke.

"No, dear, had you?" I said.

"Yes. I have a teeny little second-hand typewriter in my big trunk upstairs, and a heap of lovely ivory paper, darling. It would be a positive joy to write on that beautiful surface, only I can't think of a word to write."

"Did you intend to write a novel?" I asked.

"Absolutely. It was to be a saga in four volumes. I have started each volume twice, and in different order. Now I am fed up. If I take it home, and I haven't time left here to make a proper start, the ants and other fauna will have a lovely time. But I shall have no paper."

"They eat paper?"

"Eat anything," she said. "At any rate, after much pain, I have decided to resign my position as potential author. Do you write?"

"Sketches, and so on," I said modestly.

"Splendid," she cried. "My dear, the dying author makes you her sole legatee. Eight reams of beautiful, ivory-surfaced paper at ten-and-six a ream; one second-hand Cremona typewriter, guaranteed to fold away, and go in your hand-bag. You write as you travel—by road, train or coach. You fill your mind with lovely images, and forget the hags and horrors of Lush Mellish."

"Terribly kind of you," I said, "but I have a full-sized type-writer already."

"Full-sized?" she said, laughing. "Oh, that won't do at all. You want a woman-sized one. I mean to say, you can't jot down your impressions when you travel, on a huge lump like that, can you?"

"But you may want to write when you get home," I said.

"Never!" she cried dramatically. "So many distractions, you know. I sit down, have a beautiful thought, and then there is a cry from someone: *'Locusts, ho!'* or *'Queenie, mind that mamba!'* Why life's too full of excitements over there."

"Well, it is extremely kind of you, and I shall treasure it as a memento of your visit," I said. "And I do hope you will take care of yourself when you return. I know you laugh about it very bravely, but lions in the garden are no joke."

"You're quite right, my dear," she said gratefully. "They even get on *my* nerves in time. I am going to ask dad to put up some wire just as soon as I reach home. Then, if the elephants keep away, I shall be much less disturbed."

As I have said, she had a queer sense of humour, but I did not understand it or, I am afraid, appreciate it.

Still, I did look up the encyclopedia about African tribes, and saw that they not only ate caterpillars but earth-worms, on occasion. So I suppose she was not romancing.

"Where did you get the paper?" I asked. "London?"

"In a sale, my dear. It was ten and sixpence, reduced to three shillings. I hope it will bring you luck."

I accepted both gifts gratefully, and put them away. But I do not think they brought me luck.

There were a few people with whom I still had tea or a chat. Queenie became rather tiresome at the end of the week, with her stories of native and animal habits. They were no doubt intensely interesting to an anthropologist, or a natural history person, but I felt at last that I had to share my responsibility, and took her out with me when I called. She had two independent invitations to tea after that, and I heard some months later that she had mentioned my anxiety to become a town councillor.

Mercifully, on the eleventh day, she had a wire recalling her to town. I must say she left me rather fatigued. I still think that old friends are best, but naturally they think one can stand anything, and are inclined to be too familiar.

However, Queenie left, and I had settled down to my routine, and was pondering the question of selling my house (that was in a moment of depression), when something happened.

There was a horsy-looking woman who was a town councillor, and also a Justice of the Peace. She died suddenly, and there was a vacancy on the council.

If I had toyed with the idea of joining this body, and trying, as the American films express it, "to clean up the town," I had done no more than toy. And in view of the local spite, and the conspiracy which was now gathering force and venom, I had practically abandoned the idea, when three women came to me on a deputation.

They were women I had seen, but did not know; young women, who said they knew that I was full of energy and good works, and so on, and not one to be put down or browbeaten by the prevailing clique. They wanted me to stand for the vacancy.

I admit that I was flattered, though, of course, I had just those qualities which are indispensable in a proper town councillor. I mean to say, energy, enterprise, a sense of right and justice, and a determination not to allow any underhand work to go on in the place.

"Mr. Krimson is standing," they said. "Everyone knows why."

"Not a word!" I intervened. "One has to be very tactful in these matters. Mr. Krimson's motives are probably no better and no worse than that of many already in office."

"You're so charitable," they said. "We are all burgesses, and if you care to have a shot at it, we will nominate you."

I told them I must think it over, and they left. But, of course, I saw that my chance had come, and spent the best part of the evening composing my address to the electors.

"THE TOWN WANTS CLEAN AND HONEST GOVERNMENT."

That was one of my inspirations, and another was:

"VOTE FOR ALICE AND AUSTERITY."

The last was an indirect allusion to vice, of course, but one ill-educated voter asked me if I thought there were two vacancies. He argued about it, too, and said he had never heard of the word, and was sure it would be misleading.

I was surprised and gratified, soon after I had agreed to stand, by the number of people, some of whom I hardly knew even by sight, who came up to congratulate me.

"You'll wipe the floor with this wicked lot, Miss Alice," one quiet young fellow said to me. "Krimson is already shaking in his shoes. You see if he isn't."

I met Mr. Krimson soon after that, and he looked at me very coldly. But I did not betray any triumph.

"It lies between you and me," I told him. "I am not afraid of the outcome."

"Well, madam," he said, "I can't say that I feel too happy about it, but the fight's not over yet."

I plunged into the fray with enthusiasm, and people who had not seemed at all kind to me before promised to send their cars for voters. At least nine had bills printed to put on their cars. Was right beginning to triumph? Was my struggle for it to be crowned by my election to the council? I asked myself those questions, and it did seem then that they must be answered in the affirmative.

When nomination day came, I had thirty names on my list. Mr. Krimson had ten!

That day I met two of the cars which had volunteered to show bills. One had a small placard: "Alice Also Ran." The other had quite a nice floral border round the words:

> "Red is no colour for Lush Mellish.
> Alice is our Darling."

I was told that the word "red" was a pun on my opponent's name. I am afraid it was a far-fetched one, since the word red (crimson) is not spelt with a "K."

We all have our weakness, even I, and for a day or two I believed that Lush Mellish had had a change of heart. People beamed at me, or smiled, and some laughed, with joy, I thought, at the idea of my purging the council of its baser elements.

The town seemed to be *en fête*, as the French express it, and many of the inhabitants *endimanchés*, on polling day. Wherever I went I was cheered, and greeted with great enthusiasm. Little boys ran beside the car I had hired for the day, and even the fat policeman on traffic duty at the Cornmarket greeted me with a broad smile.

The cars bringing voters for me tore about the streets, some of them full of laughing men and women, who waved their hats, and sang the tune of the famous Jacobite song to altered words:

> "Alice is our Darling!"

With my help, you are getting to know Lush Mellish by now; but I did not know it fully then.

You can imagine with what triumph and excitement I awaited the announcement of the figures late that night.

I took my stand at one side of the officer who was to make the announcement, and Mr. Krimson took the other. There was a roar of voices, and then the official held up his hand.

He read out the poll: "Mr. Krimson, nine hundred and seventy-three votes. Miss Alice, *three*."

I went home. I was stunned. I could not understand it. One moment so much enthusiasm; the next *this*.

It was from cook next day, an apologetic and sympathetic cook, that I learned the truth. It was all part of the conspiracy, part of the plan to drive me from my home in Lush Mellish. She had heard of it first from her brother-in-law's nephew, who was courting a local girl who sold programmes in the cinema.

She had been standing with her programmes, by the side of the last row of seats, looking at a film. She had heard voices mention my name, and then details of the plot, in which, it appeared, many were engaged. She told me the names of a dozen of them—I mean cook did, not the girl with the programmes.

I laughed bitterly at my own simple faith in the human decency of the inhabitants of Lush Mellish. Again my charitable habit of regarding everyone as good and agreeable, till I had proved the reverse, had let me down.

It was one of that scoundrel's points at my trial that I had tried to revenge myself for this affront. But I need not waste time on him. As you read on you will see that I disdained such petty motives.

Every effort I subsequently made was one to right a wrong, to improve someone, to ensure that Lush Mellish should presently be a place for respectable people to live in. I do not say "heroes." You will have realised by now that it was a place for heroes, and only heroes, to live in when I first came to it. If my own heroism was disregarded, even punished, it was not my fault.

As for the three women who had asked me to stand for the council, I had no quarrel with them. They must have been the three voters who stood out in contrast to the venal nine hundred and seventy-three.

For a while there was calm. I think the people must have realised that they had gone too far. I seized the opportunity to put in a little detective work for which I had discovered a sort of mild genius.

And I began a dossier of many people in Lush Mellish.

As I went on, I found my worst fears confirmed, and my mind saddened by proof of the town's depravity. Of course, it was not yet beyond hope of improvement. Many of its sinners, no doubt, just required to be pulled up sharply by those they had wronged or planned to wrong. In fact, I felt sure that they would come to thank me afterwards for having been shown the error of their ways.

Do not laugh! It may have been folly, but it was at least creditable folly. I do not set up to be a cynic, and to my charity I add reasonableness. They say it is not human nature to like being corrected. Well, if that is so, human nature has no reason in it. If that is so, then I am not a human being.

Show me where I am wrong, and I will thank you, and try to correct my error. All I ask is proof that I am at fault. Indeed, I welcome *just* criticism.

I well remember a high compliment paid me by my drawing master at school. "You are always right," he said. "Strange, isn't it?"

"I try to be," I told him. "Perhaps that's how it is."

He nodded his head twice, and smiled. "It must be that. It is an ideal that I have never claimed to touch, even to myself."

Nor did I claim it. I am sure I have made mistakes now and again, but they came from the heart, not the head.

I have always kept in good health, for good sense and good health go together, but after that disgusting incident, I confess that I felt like a little change. I put my servants on board-wages for three weeks, and went to London. There I saw an advertisement of a beautiful little cottage in the wilds of Cornwall.

It was furnished, and only ten shillings a week. I bought a tiny second-hand two-seater car, and learned to drive in a wonderfully short time, while I was negotiating with the owner of the cottage. It occurred to me that the place was cheap because it was far from civilisation. I might go down there and try to start a story of sorts.

I had brought my Cremona portable, and my reams of ivory paper, to London in my trunk. When I started off in my tiny car, I had these in a rumble built into the back of the car. There was also a luggage grid, on which I placed my trunk.

When I reached the cottage, which I had taken at that absurd rent for six months, I found it on the edge of a wild moor, about five miles from the nearest station. But it was a gem of a place, with just three small rooms, and flowering plants climbing over it. I had paid my rent in advance, and took the name I intended to use for my writing, "Babbie Thrums."

The owner met me, and showed me over it. She was an artist, and just off to paint for three months in the Alpes Maritimes. The furniture was just right, there was a very efficient oil cooking-stove, and, as she explained, the only snag was the lack of service.

No woman would come so far to work. Did I mind? Perhaps I enjoyed doing for myself?

"Cleaning lamps is rather a smelly job," she added, "but, of course, we are too far off for gas or electricity." I assured her that I had learned to cook at home, and we had had lamps in my earlier days.

"And the water is from a well," she said.

"I have come from more muddied pools," I said, thinking of Lush Mellish in an allegory. "Muddier pools and less transparent springs."

"Surely you write poetry?" she cried. "How very jolly! Well, if this place doesn't inspire you, nothing will."

A poetess? Yes, there had been a sort of *assonance*, if you know what I mean, in the phrase which had sprung to my lips. Why not? I might be a feminine Pope, and write a *Dunciad*—a *Roguead*, perhaps, bringing in the people of Lush Mellish, and scarifying in verse their ugly defects and smug complacency.

"Just now and again," I told her, "I might throw off a few cantos when I am here."

"Will you? So delightfully Scottian!" she cried. "'The moon was in her summer glow, and hoarse and high the breezes blow.' I do remember doing *Marmion* at school."

"But isn't that *The Lay of the Last Minstrel*?" I asked.

"Or *The Lady of the Lake*; one or the other," she agreed. "I must run now."

CHAPTER XII

I am not really a poetess. Or, perhaps, I should say that my Muse is incapable of long flights. I got out my dossiers, and made a brief résumé of each. But, when I came to translate it into verse, I found the rhyming and scansion a difficulty.

Of course, if I had wished to be a modern poet, I should have been untroubled. The dossiers themselves, put in broken form vertically, would have made a hit. At least I tried that way, and they looked as poetical as many poems do to-day.

But I have a fastidious taste in most things, and the first stanza I tried in this fashion looked modern but did not please me.

> "Mr. Brown, builder of jerry
> houses knows,
> A councillor, he will
> On occasion with money in hand
> Visit a certain
> Smith;
> No blacksmith but, as you
> May later see, a
> blackguard!"

There was a sort of snap about it, I admitted, but it was too blunt, though I had a witty word or two in it. I tried again with Mrs. Jones.

> "Mrs. Jones is
> Not married, but the prefix
> Is courtesy or
> Concealment, which?
> A husband gives a name to you and
> Is she Jones, Robinson, or
> No?"

That day I had read in my paper some verses by a woman who lives in Paris, and is very highly thought of. My verse would be too *direct* for publication. In her method it might pass. So I tried it.

"Mrs. Mrs. Mrs. Jones Jones not not
Not wed, married, wed, married married,
Which, concealment courtesy, courtesy,
Courtesy, which?
A husband a name a name a name to you
You you.
Jones Robinson, Robinson Jones, Jones
Which, which, which?"

On the whole, I felt justified in abandoning the attempt to write a long poem about Lush Mellish and its *aborigines*.

After that came the reaction which follows on all intensive work in the Arts. In this jaded state, there came up into my mind memories of the affronts and wrongs I had suffered ever since I went to live there. And consulting the dossiers had refreshed my memory.

Prosecuting counsel said that I was an egotist, a warped egotist. He seemed quite convinced that I was so centred in myself that my wrongs—purely imaginary wrongs, he called them—had turned my brain. If this book proves nothing else to you, it will prove that I am educated, in full possession of my faculties, and, above all, anxious that no newcomers to Lush Mellish should suffer as I had done. Where was the egotism in that?

Then I had been able to see that quite a good proportion of the residents lived distorted and narrow lives, because of the cruelty, the intolerance, and the vice of their neighbours. Would young M. X., for example, have sent in the wrong income tax returns for his employer, if his employer had not taken advantage of the fact that X was recently married, and had bought house and furniture on the instalment plan?

If I could effect any change in the lives of but half the inhabitants of the town, what a charming place it would be! If I could spare any new resident a dog-slaying campaign, a campaign of slander and conspiracy, how much I would have done towards improving the amenities of the town!

Lush Mellish was not used to altruism. No one appreciated my motives.

But, as I thought over the many abuses I had discovered, and finally decided that it would be both useless and dangerous to publish a satire in verse, I made up my mind that something must be done.

If it is the fact that "the greater the truth, the greater the libel" holds good in law, then, of course, my projected poem would give my enemies ground for action against me. I would pay, I would suffer. I would be in default. The moral value of that victory to my opponents would quite spoil the effect of my satire.

But I did nothing in haste. I left nothing undone to find an alternative before I finally decided on my course of action.

I could inform the police of the many grave errors I had unearthed. But the police require proof, which it is not always easy to give, and many of the offences were not of a kind punished in a court of law. Then I had had ample proof that, not only were the local police either too lazy, or too cowardly, to assist me, but that they were *in league* with the residents to hamper me at every turn.

The only other course was to write directly to those who had offended in one way or another, and warn them that trouble would follow if they did not amend their ways.

But here again was the chance of a libel action, and the certainty that you cannot threaten people with a big stick unless you have got one. Shorn of the aid of a venal constabulary, I had no big stick.

The painter's or potter's (or is it dyer's?) hand, says someone, is subdued to the stuff it works in. It was highly ironical that Lush Mellish, which had first pursued me with anonymous letters, objected strongly to my use of its own methods.

After all, everything lies in the intention. I had quite rid my mind of the idea of revenging myself, however justifiably, on those who had persecuted and mocked me. I was all out now for reform. I might not live long enough to be thanked. I was unselfish enough to do my good deed by stealth. I felt sure that it would never come to light who had morally and socially rejuvenated Lush Mellish. But a day would come when the very atmosphere of the town would so react on strangers that they would say: "Here is peace on earth!"

It was rather sad that I would have no share in that encomium. But it was not my aim to become famous as a reformer. If it had been so, the ferocious counsel might well have referred to me as a warped egotist.

Now that I had begun my work, I reflected with some satisfaction that I had the means to begin my campaign. No one knew that I was down in Cornwall. No one in Cornwall knew that I was Miss Edna Alice. No one in either Cornwall or Lush Mellish knew that I had a full-sized Imperial typewriter at home, with a supply of paper of a cheap kind, while I had also a portable Cremona, with a supply of expensive ivory paper in the concealed cupboard under the back seat of my car.

In Lush Mellish, I was Miss Edna Alice. In Cornwall, I was Miss Babbie Thrums, a poetess. Queenie Bostarby had gone to Rhodesia; the painter, my landlady, had gone to France.

I would not have been human, and the romantic creature I really am, if I had not found a good deal of secret pleasure in making my plans. It was essential that my name should not appear, for one thing. If it had, the recipients of the letters would have associated my action with the kind of beastly motives which were the mainsprings of their own.

One thing struck me at once. From time to time I had read cases bearing on anonymous letters. These letters had no good motive behind them. They were evil, and begotten of evil. The convictions of the senders had seemed to me right and just. Because, of course, they had tried to do wrong, or else they did not know the difference between right and wrong. They were, therefore, better away from contact with the world.

But in all these cases the senders of anonymous letters had directed letters to themselves!

It seemed to be the idea of these people with elementary brains and foolish minds that this was a precaution which was bound to save them from inquiry. In point of fact, it led to their discovery, and is said by detectives to be symptomatic of such people.

I was determined to act otherwise. For one thing, it was not safe. In the second place it would have proved the insincerity of my campaign to improve Lush Mellish. I could improve no one by writing letters to myself. It would have been hypocritical and, I contend, wrong.

The second weakness I detected in reading these cases was that the writers either spelled badly, when they could spell well, or used printing instead of script.

There was a third class, which used typewriters, and forgot that most machines have some slight difference in the type face, or that each manipulator has a different method of applying his finger-tips to the keys. In other words, the expert detective can decide on what machine, and by whose hand, a letter was typed.

There was another point that I did not overlook. It applied to those who wantonly mis-spelled. If they were educated people, they tried to ape the solecisms, the phrasing, and the simplicity of the poor. If you read any novel with characters drawn from the working classes, you will find that none of them speaks as poor people do. You will find the same sort of fault in novels written about the middle classes by people of position and wealth. They have the financial problems all wrong, and they give their middle-class characters the mentality of artisans. I remember one in which a man with eight hundred a year was unable to afford a car, and his wife used to buy cheap joints on Saturday! But that is beside the point here.

I made a resolution to avoid these things, and I decided that my Cremona portable should be kept in the car, and never used outside it. There were a dozen charming rural spots, on and near the moor, where I could draw up, place the typewriter on my knees and carry on the good work. Free from fear of discovery, free from distractions, with the heath blooming about me, and the birds singing, I could give myself to the composition of the Thrums letters.

I remember very well the first day I set out. I drove my dear little car, with Tiblits by my side, deep into the moor. There, beside a clear running stream, burbling in its rock pools, with a water-ousel to charm my eye, as it dived from a stone, I took out my Cremona, and a sheet of paper.

The sky was blue and cloudless, the air warm and pleasant. On just such a day I had come to Lush Mellish, and believed it to be my dream town.

I must say that I was rather a novice at this sort of composition, so my first effort was distinctly short, if to the point. But it took me much longer to phrase than you would have imagined, and I had done five sheets, torn them up and buried them under a rock, before I was satisfied.

It would be disingenuous for me to fail to say that I sent it to a young woman who had been very unpleasant to me. In any event, most of you will have read the details of that unjust trial. But you must remember that, if I decided not to write to those who were unpleasant to me in Lush Mellish, I could have had few to whom to write, and no hope of improving the town at large! It just happened so, that's all.

In case some of my readers have not read details of the trial, I am giving this letter in full.

> "If Miss W. will go any Thursday night, after dark, to the road-house at Wolleson, she will possibly have a surprise, but may yet effect a reformation of one dear to her."

I want you to study that letter, free from prejudice. What was there in it to offend anyone? If you saw a man about to fall over a cliff, and telephoned to his wife to save him, would she charge you with malice or wickedness? No.

I myself felt sure at the time that somewhere (hidden beneath, and deep down, but undoubtedly present) in Miss W's fiancé, was a streak of good. Few of us are wholly evil, and a word in time might save him from the abyss in which he threatened to fall.

That the letter should give Miss W. pain was unavoidable. But pain is the only warning of things gone wrong with us, doctors say, and so has its splendid uses—even if we fail to see them when racked by agony, bodily or mental.

I also typed an envelope, and was careful to wear thin gloves both while writing the letter and addressing the envelope. Counsel commented on this at the trial.

"So it seems that you took precautions which are taken by burglars," he said brutally.

"I have more regard for my hands, sir," I said, "than you appear to have." For he had big hands, and coarse skin, with, I thought, ill-cared-for nails. "Even if it had been as you suggest, the young woman bore me ill-will, and would have scouted my well-meant advice on that account."

I decided to go back to Lush Mellish, posting the letter on my way. I drove to London, starting very early, and going by way of Salisbury. Outside the town, I met a child on the way to school, and gave her a penny to put the letter in the nearest pillar-box. As this appeared to be only a hundred yards away, I was able to see her post it as I drove slowly on.

I turned down the road to Winchester after that, and went by way of Basingstoke to a garage at Ealing, where I decided to rent a lock-up for a year. Locking my precious Cremona and its supplies in the little hiding-place, I took train home.

I would not have been human if I had not been thrilled at the success of my ruse. It struck me then that that may account for the pertinacity with which some people stick to crime. But theirs is crime; not the same thing at all. *Finis coronat opus*, as the Romans used to say.

When I reached Lush Mellish again, it was assumed that I had been in London. I was eager to see if my first good deed had had its effect. In other words, had I saved that young woman—unpleasant as she was—from her foolish infatuation, or, better still, had I given the young man a sharp pull-up on his first venture on the primrose path? Of course, I dare not ask anyone, lest my motives should afterwards be misunderstood. But I had an ocular demonstration next day that my hint had taken effect.

I had just gone down the Cornmarket, shopping, when I saw the girl come from the confectioner's, and pause for a moment on the edge of the pavement. A young man, almost simultaneously, stopped his car near her. He smiled and raised his hat;

she turned her back on him, and left him there, very red in the face, and pretending that he had only taken off his hat to brush it.

I went homeward in two minds. Should I feel glad or sorry that the engagement had been broken off? I gave it a good deal of earnest thought, and finally came to the conclusion that both the girl and I could congratulate ourselves on the outcome of my intervention.

For when you come to think of it, it is not easy to reform a man of that type. He may be all right for a little while, and then he returns to his fatally easy and evil courses.

She would never know what I had done, perhaps never thank me, but it was all the more gratifying for me to realise that, in spite of my feelings, I had done her a good turn. It wasn't as if I had selected a personal friend, or one to whom I owed something, and helped her. She was a secret, if not an open, enemy, and I had saved her from a life of unhappiness. Did my persecutors later ever think of that side of it? No. They had no imagination. They were narrow, one-sided, prejudiced, blind to one of the basic facts of life: that everything has two sides.

I am honest enough to admit that the writing of those letters had a certain fascination that lifted it above the level of ordinary humdrum good works. I got no praise, I had no score of merit marked up for me, but, quietly and unostentatiously I went to work, and as the days went on, began to long to help some other person or cause.

Naturally, people one has seen come quickest into one's thoughts, and that was probably the reason why I remembered the young man who kept an Irish terrier. It was difficult to forget him, after my experience, and the constant presence next door of his aunt kept him in my memory.

Now, you have heard enough about that wicked old woman to realise that there was nothing even remotely agreeable or pleasant about her. She was cunning and cruel, addicted, I had no doubt, to drugs or drink, infatuated by a loathsome cat, and not even very hospitable.

I did not see that her nephew was an attractive young man. But that was not the point. She was his aunt, and the only time she had asked him to come to see her, as far as I knew, was when she concocted that vile plot to mock me and dear, dead Buffer. In other words, she was neither a nice woman nor a good aunt.

Then why had he consented to help her in this disgusting business? She had money and he was *after her money*. There seemed no other adequate explanation. He was a good amateur actor, as my experience showed, and quite capable of pretending affection for her.

Very well. My like, or dislike, of the old woman must not weigh in the balance. I must drop all that sort of feeling. I must say to myself that, whatever she was, my neighbour must be protected from the mercenary machinations of a scheming nephew. She was old; she was either senile, or a drug addict. But he was none of these things, and I must concentrate my mind on the protection of the weak against the strong.

That I made up my mind more quickly to act on this occasion shows how successfully I had conquered my personal pride, to sink my feelings in a desire for the common good. I even saw her in the garden in the morning with her hateful cat, and smiled at her.

"You hate me, poor woman!" I said to myself. "You would do me harm if you could. I am sorry for you. I will forget that, and do what I can for you."

Yet I was the "warped egotist" of that loathsome reptile's speech at the trial!

Of course, at that time, I knew nothing actually against the nephew. But people with intuition almost amounting to second sight (my mother's gift to me) do not require ocular or oral evidence in every case. I knew that the man was up to something, and what could it be in connection with that woman next door but lust for money—her money?

CHAPTER XIII

THE NEXT day I had something to go on. The man *came*. Was that not an extraordinary thing? He went out into the garden with her, and I saw him pick up that silly cat and stroke it. She walked at his side, evidently pleased, and thinking what a nice fellow he was.

Cook mentioned him when she came in for orders. As you know, I never encourage my servants to gossip, but I do not like to hurt their feelings by being too abrupt, and she remarked that the young man next door was mad about motors, and going to start an agency, before I checked her.

"Now, cook," I said gently, "how can you know that?"

"Well, ma'am," she said, "my aunt lives where he does, you know, and it is said he wants his aunt, the lady next door, to set him up."

"Pure speculation," I told her. "Do try to remember that idle gossip is not necessarily the truth."

Had I been harsh with her? Afterwards, I thought it might be so, for what she said fitted in very well with my estimate of that young hypocrite's character and sly ways.

Picking up and petting that cat; coming over to see her when he wanted money to throw away in some mad speculation! I had been harsh.

He might already be her heir, I reflected. But he would know that senile old women often change their wills at the last moment, and she was capable of leaving her money to a home for cats, or some mad institution of the kind. It would pay him, perhaps, to get some of the money in advance, before she dissipated it by will.

As I pondered the problem, I came on another and darker theory, which, I confess, filled me with horror. I could not believe it, even of him, yet; but it was logical, possible, and fitted the facts.

I had seen him arrive in his car; watched him enter the gate. He was carrying under his arm what looked very like a bottle in brown paper, and he took from his pocket as he went up the path one of those unmistakable white parcels with red seals which suggest a visit to the chemist.

Now I do not wish anyone to think that I accused the young man of murderous designs. Nothing of the kind. It never occurred to me that he might think of poison in its open form.

What did occur to me was the possibility that, anxious to shorten his period of waiting, or perhaps to break down her *resistance* to his demands, he was secretly supplying her with drink or drugs. She would naturally have to regulate her supplies of spirits from local sources, since Lush Mellish always thinks evil readily. But what was easier than for the scheming nephew to smuggle in fresh supplies?

That evening I went into it seriously, and felt sure that this accounted for her conduct to me. He was more to blame than she, playing on her weaknesses, and hoping soon to get her completely under his thumb. When he did, it would be more than motor agencies he would wish to finance.

There was nothing for it but to save her from herself and from him by taking action. It would be useless to write to her in my own name. She would not believe me, and she might drop a hint of it to her nephew, who would redouble his precautions.

But here I had to be exceedingly careful. Like many another in her condition, the old woman was possessed of a sort of low cunning. She might even suspect me, since she judged everyone by her own standards.

I could not always be running down to Cornwall to find inspiration. I was called up to town by my lawyer, which was almost providential, and when I had completed my small business with him, went by Tube to a northern suburb. I had seen an advertisement of an office where you could hire a machine to write your letters.

I had almost reached this office, when I stopped at a shop window. The shop was really a kind of store, and I saw second-hand typewriters (renovated) in a window. I went in.

The place was full of people, and understaffed. One young man seemed to have charge of the typewriters, and half another department as well. I asked him if I could try some of the machines, before thinking of buying one, and he said I could, and gave me a couple of sheets of paper.

At that moment, fortunately, he was called away by a fat woman with a string bag, and I sat down, and typed two lines of my letter on a portable Ganser; then did two more on a full-sized Imperial, one on the Ganser again, and wound up on a big Barlock.

Not only is understaffing a menace to the health of the assistants, but it is also unfair to customers. That young man was so long away that I had to leave before he came back. As payment for using the machines I was careful to buy something in another department.

I had had an envelope in my bag, and managed to address it as well. The completed letter I posted at the pillar-box in the station where I changed trains going home. I thought it better to miss the express, and take this later train, which only went a part of the way. I went to bed that night feeling sure that I had prevented my annoying neighbour from suffering what she deserved for her weakness and folly. Later I was to learn what naturalists call the folly of disturbing the balance of nature.

It appears that some birds, like hawks, have their uses in killing off other birds which threaten to be pests. If you kill the hawks, you let loose upon yourself a worse pest than any hawk can be.

Next morning I took my typewriter—at least cook carried it for me—to a table placed in the garden. I wanted to make the best use of the last of the warm autumn days.

There I sat and began my first attempt to write a novel. It was not to come to fruition, but it did give me practice in writing which has enabled me, I hope, to lay my case clearly before you.

I often wondered what was the urge which made great philanthropists go on without haste or rest. Florence Nightingale, Shaftesbury, and others, lived in a perfect fever of striving and working. Once started on their career of good works, nothing could stop them.

I do not claim to have their gifts, or do what they did, but in my humble way I began to feel the same sort of furious urge. At least I am sure it was the same. It made me exalted, excited, anxious to get the day over till I could begin my work anew.

I know my work on the novel suffered from this cause. How could I whole-heartedly absorb myself in the lives of my characters when my mind was concentrated on a cure for civic corruption and private wickedness? The human mind, to a certain extent, can occupy itself with two things at once, but one suffers. While I was trying to describe the first scene in my novel, my mind would fly to the new cottages of Lush Mellish, and the graft which had enabled their builder to secure the contract.

Graft should be the target for my next arrow. The builder was a sort of second cousin of one of the councillors, who was on the Building Committee of the council. His eldest daughter had driven one of the cars which had taken part in that scandalous election. Even had I wished to save her the unpleasantness of having her father exposed, I could not do so and still remove one of the cankering sores from which the town was suffering.

It might even do her good *indirectly*, for some of us need sobering down, if we are ever to be good citizens, but I am not going to suggest that I did what I did for her sake.

But to go back to my work in the garden. I had not been there long when my savage neighbour, scowling and evidently much perturbed, came to the fence, and actually stared at me over it. I took no notice of her, but went on with my typing.

Of course I knew what she was after. I could read her thoughts. I typed. She had received a typewritten letter. She felt sure that I had sent it!

Really, the serious side apart, I felt that I was to be a good deal amused by my new work. It was like hide-and-seek and blind man's buff combined. It was exciting and romantic, but had a substratum of serious purpose and high endeavour.

The next day, to my amusement, I was approached by a girl who had never taken any notice of me before.

"Oh, Miss Alice," she said with a sweet smile, "I am terribly sorry to trouble you, but I know you write, and I am an awful duffer at that sort of thing. I have to get out an appeal for the Cottage Homes Fund. I mean to say, would you have a shot at it for me."

The ordinary person would have felt flattered by this, but I was not only up in my Lush Mellish by now, but also had those gifts of psychological insight of which I have already told you. My neighbour was one of the committee!

So I smiled, and asked if she would be able to read my writing. "I am not terribly legible," I said. "Does that matter?"

"Not really," she said, "though, of course, it will have to be typed if approved."

I had seen that coming, and smiled still more broadly. "Not at all," I told her. "I shall be happy to do the appeal for you, and I shall type it myself."

She registered wonder, as the films say. "But how kind of you! Have you a machine?"

"You shall see," I told her. "I'll go home and do it now, and let you have it this evening."

Little hypocrite! She did not know how pleased I was to give that wretched woman next door a sample of my typing, though what they meant to do with it I was not quite sure.

I wrote out rather a moving appeal, and then typed it. So that I should lose no time, I sent it by my housemaid to the girl at once.

Then I awaited the next move. It was not long in coming. That evening, before dark, I sat upstairs in my bedroom, staring out along the road, admiring the growing autumn tints, when I saw a woman turn in at the gate next door. I watched her come out again half an hour later, and knew that my detective instinct had not played me false.

The grammar-school and the girls' high school at Lush Mellish are both old foundations, and specialise in old-fashioned education. Indeed, there was some reactionary irritation in the town when a modern school of commercial subjects was set up by a woman from Birmingham.

But the school flourished, and a very efficient Londoner came down to preside over the department where they taught shorthand and typewriting. She had attained some extraordinary speed in a competition, and could even take the machines to pieces and repair them. It was this woman I had seen going into my neighbour's house that evening.

I must say that I was greatly amused. My neighbour had no boys or girls to attend the school, and I know that she had written a letter to the local paper, when it was first set up, saying that the country was fast passing into the grip of the machines. As if a typewriter could grip a country!

I never asked cook what happened, but it came to me from another source that the nephew did not start that motor agency, and was going about scowling and angry, so that it did appear that my little effort had not been wholly in vain.

I met that girl three days afterwards, and asked if my appeal was to be printed soon, as I should like to have some copies for distribution. She seemed rather uncomfortable, as well she might, and told me that the committee had decided that it was, after all, not a good time to issue an appeal. As I knew the committee had not even *met*, I was now quite aware of the trickery my opponents adopted. They liked the darkness because it hid the blackness of their deeds.

Having given them a nasty set-back, I felt sure that this was a good opportunity to push on with my reforming campaign. They had tried to catch me out and failed. They would take their time before they suspected me again. I heard a story later to the effect that my neighbour had made inquiries of some, not too discreet, friends of her nephew, and heard from them of some, what one might call "anticipatory," remarks the young man had made. He had not been unkind about his aunt, but it is upsetting to hear that your kinsman has even alluded distantly to your demise, the more so when he has a chance of profiting by it.

Still, it was unforgivable for those so-called friends of his to carry stories to the aunt. Tactless, I call it.

I went to London again, and told cook to forward any letters to the little club to which I belonged. But I did not dally in town, going on straight to Ealing, and setting off in my car. In a lane on the borders of a Hertfordshire beech wood, where the glories of leaf and the rich hues about me would have distracted a less determined woman from her salutary task, I wrote a fresh letter.

It was directed to a rival builder, and very briefly suggested that he should see how often second cousins met after dark, and how careful they were not to display their intimacy. As the recipient was a very sharp man, and at feud with the grafting ruffian, he could not fail to understand my allusion.

I set out again in my car and took a run northwards for fifty miles. It was dark, of course, but I did not mind that, especially as I was able to post my letter in a box in a park wall miles from a village.

Then back to Ealing, where I stayed a night in a small hotel, put my car in another garage, and only drove it back to my lock-up next day at eleven.

On my way home, my mind was filled with ideas. Like a novelist who has had a fresh inspiration, my mind simply seethed with new projects. Still, I had better see if any good had come of my last effort before I tried again. It was a hardship, but I endured it.

I cannot say if any good came of it. The facts of the case were obscured by something that occurred two evenings later. This fortuitous happening prevented my letter from having its full effect. It put the man on his guard.

What took place was this: The recipient of my letter, perhaps more angry than judicious, had determined to act on my hint about his corrupt rival.

He was anxious to see if the venal councillor and his second cousin did actually meet, and concoct plans for fleecing the ratepayers, by giving and accepting tenders, not necessarily the lowest. Though, indeed, I hear that you may even profit by a low tender, if you supply materials of a low standard. I expect this scoundrel did *both*.

Seeing that his rival was setting off that evening in the direction of his cousin's villa outside the town, the man I had warned ran ahead. But he found it difficult to keep observation from the road.

In these circumstances, he rather lost his head, and walking quietly up the path to the back door, hid himself in an angle of the building near the sitting-room window. Justifiably enough, he imagined he might hear something on which he could take action.

Unfortunately, a maid-servant came out to post a letter to her sweetheart, and seeing a man hiding, set up a scream. The builder rushed out with a thick stick, and my man had to fly down the path towards the road. Unfortunately, the cousin just arrived then, saw what he took to be an escaping burglar, and having played rugby years before, brought him down on the pavement.

His captive received several blows from the builder's stick before he could get up and explain who he was. But he could not explain why he was hiding in the grounds, and the thing was only settled out of court because he threatened a counter-claim for injuries received.

And, naturally, his rival was not anxious that his surreptitious meetings with the councillor should be known!

CHAPTER XIV

THOUGH I have a good many accomplishments, and, what is rarer, a combination of common sense and intuition, I would not claim to have made a study of such difficult subjects as psychology.

So I cannot explain scientifically why, with my new joy in my work for the regeneration of Lush Mellish, I felt a sense of *power*. But I did feel it, and it made me more sympathetic with those European dictators who were once rather a source of amusement to me. When I came to the town first I was at everyone's mercy, the subject of scandal and persecution, and quite unable to protect myself against these venomous assaults. Now I knew that they were in my power, but, throughout my campaign I tempered justice with mercy, and did not act as an unscrupulous or cruel person would have done.

I never wrote a letter to anyone who, in my opinion, was not either doing evil to others, or the victim of the evil-doer whom I wished to save from harm.

But to return to this sense of power. It was at once a stimulus and a help. Powers, like talents, are not given us to be concealed or wasted. I cannot blame myself if I felt an acute pleasure in the exercise of my power. The normal man or woman enjoys his food. Short of gluttony, it is right that he should. While he is taking the nutriment requisite to keep up his bodily strength, he is also enjoying his meals. If a man give a subscription to a charitable object, he must and does feel a mild glow of satisfaction. All human motives are mixed, and I have never claimed to be more than human.

Very naturally too, I was keen to experience this pleasure again. After a decent interval the normal person looks forward to his next meal. If I use these simple, rather material, similes, it is just that you may understand my case.

Every day I realised what a lot of material I had to work on, and my fear was that I should not get the work done in the time allotted to me. "So little done, so much to do," as someone has very happily said.

Lush Mellish, having recovered from its idea that it had gone too far, now became offensive again. Several people cut me in the street. There were other incidents which I need not recount. Let us keep passion, resentment and revenge, out of my story. They had no part in my actions.

I wrote three more letters, soon after that. The ideas came to me in a flood. Again I exercised my ingenuity in the sending of the letters, and wondered to find how clever I was in these arts. I found this fascinating too, and spent a good deal of my time thinking out methods and ways of conveyance. And every day I sat for a short time in my garden, if it was fine, and worked openly on my novel.

I confess that at times I was rather like a doctor who prescribes for a patient, and sees no visible change in his condition. I could not see how my letters were received, or know if they brought terror to the heart of the wrongdoer, or comfort to those on whose behalf I was intervening. Watched and spied on as I was, I dare not make too open inquiries. But I had to check cook now and then for bringing gossip to me from which I gathered that I had not been wholly unsuccessful.

I was very indignant one day when the Chief Constable stopped me and remarked, with a false smile, that he heard I was writing a novel. Did I find it difficult? He was always interested in literature, and anxious to know how authors worked.

"I suppose you write it down first, and then have it typed?" he said, while I smiled to myself. "Jove! I think of having a stab at doin' my own reminiscences one day. You know of a good typing office, Miss Alice?"

Cunning old scoundrel! I began to wonder then if he had not been the head and front of the conspiracy against me. With the venal police at his back, he had a better chance than any of the others to drive me out of the town.

"I think you had better do as I do," I said coldly. "Purchase a machine and learn to type. I do all my novel on my own machine."

He went away rather crestfallen. I suppose he had fancied himself as a detective, but he had come up against someone who saw through him. In fact, he had given himself away, and it was now obvious that he was my chief enemy. If you doubt that, read the accounts of the trial. He did not admit that he had acted as what the French call an *agent provocateur*, but that is what I am sure he was.

Now, a bad man in a small position is not in a way to do much real harm. But it was a crying disgrace that so much power should be put into the hands of a man like the Chief Constable. Hiding behind his official position, like Caesar's wife, he was able to wreck and ruin the lives of harmless and justice-loving newcomers. Further, to protect himself, he *had* to do it. This may seem an extraordinary state of affairs, but then Lush Mellish was an extraordinary town.

Someone had talked, and like the girl sent by my evil neighbour, the Chief Constable was fishing for information. He did not get it; he would not get it. He was setting himself up against me. But I was not afraid of him. In the joy of my new sense of power, I felt invulnerable and ready to cope with the very police themselves.

They had the better of the combat later, I admit, but how? By cunning, by sneaking ways, by unfair use of their powers, and the collaboration of a ruffian, whose vile machinations turned the scale, a man whose evidence would not have been accepted by any judge of intelligence or honesty.

I went to London, and on to Cornwall. As I drove to my cottage, I asked myself what other vices the Chief Constable possessed, in addition to his passion for persecution, and his desire to suppress evidence against himself and his friends.

I had already passed Bodmin when I remembered a story told me by my housemaid. I had only listened to it because it concerned her brother's father-in-law, a labourer who lived five miles from Lush Mellish, on the edge of a wood.

He kept chickens; a laudable thing to do, now that we are told every attempt should be made to produce foodstuffs in and for our own country.

Unfortunately, certain foxes lived in the wood, the property of a country gentleman who was the Chief Constable's great friend. On one occasion the labourer, maddened by the killing of six fowls, killed a fox. That they both enjoyed killing foxes with the aid of a pack of hounds did not prevent those worthies from venting their fury on the unfortunate labourer.

But there was no legal remedy, and the man was employed by a farmer who put up wire on his farm, and was no friend to the hunt, largely because they never paid him sufficiently for the damage the "field" did when out.

But the resources of a wicked policeman are not easily exhausted. As my housemaid told me, they had the poor fellow arrested later on a charge of poaching, and sent him to jail. The landed proprietor's head keeper had been seen talking to the Chief Constable some days before, and I have no doubt that, between them, they arranged to fake a charge against the man. My housemaid said it was a common thing in that part, and her brother's father-in-law had only picked up a pheasant which had flown against some telegraph wires in the dark and been killed by the impact.

Of course, the wretched police had an answer to that, which caused some amusement among the callous spectators in court.

"I am afraid the pheasant is not such a fly-by-night as the prisoner," the sycophantic solicitor said, for he liked a day's shooting free. "I wonder what made this bird break his regular habits, as well as his neck?"

He thought that witty. Witty! I expect I shall pose as a wit next. I could certainly do better than that.

If I had been in the dock, I should have said that the bird had probably been wilfully disturbed by an accomplice keeper, who knew where the telegraph wires were, and had seen similar happenings by day.

I had it! For favour, to enjoy certain sporting amenities he could not enjoy on his official salary (if, indeed, he did not add to it by accepting gifts of money), the Chief Constable was willing to pervert the ends of justice. Surely that was an evil and an abuse that could, and must, be put right?

By the time I reached my pretty cottage, where all was serenity and placid joy, I knew what I must do.

I am not much in favour of Labour politics, but even they have their uses when it comes to righting a wrong of this kind. There was one Member of Parliament who was very much against country sports and county gentlemen. He was also fond of asking questions in the House suggesting that the police were not the allies of the poor, as they should be.

I sat down after supper to write a letter to him, in which I pointed out the injustices suffered by agricultural labourers who lived near game preserves. It was difficult enough for them to prove that they did not poach. But that difficulty was multiplied tenfold when the preservers were hand in glove with the local Chief Constable, and able to fake evidence, and send innocent men to prison.

"If these gentlemen do not take money," I added, "they take a good many days' shooting and fishing and hunting, and those, as we all know, cost money. A bribe is no less a bribe because it is taken in kind."

Of course, I was careful to see that, in general terms, I referred to the Lush Mellish district.

I drove back next day to London, very tired, but very excited. If they did not actually dismiss the Chief Constable, they would no doubt censure him, and make him more careful, when the truth came out.

One of the most foolish remarks made at the trial came from the judge. He said that I might have been saved from my follies if I had possessed any sense of humour.

Think of it! I, who have a keen sense of humour, even if I refuse to laugh at jests which have no *point*! It is not those who laugh constantly and heartily who have a sense of humour; merely those who are afraid they will be charged with not possessing it.

So it may not be amiss to show you where my sense of fun came in. You will realise then that the subtler forms alone have my approval.

The day after my return home, I went to the General Post Office in Lush Mellish, and bought ten-shillings' worth of postage stamps, all three-ha'pennies.

"I have a good deal of correspondence," I told the girl, "so I may as well get a supply."

She mumbled something, but people in the post office near me stared, and obviously knew what I had said. But they did not see the point of my joke, any more than my neighbour realised that I had a purpose in typing under her nose in my garden.

Still, my purchase got noised abroad, as most things did there, and evidently the local dullhead police had a brainy idea.

Quite a number of people in my road ran short of stamps then, and if I had not seen through them I might have wondered why; especially as none of them was normally friendly, and had to make insincere apologies.

They wanted to make me buy more stamps!

Of course, I obliged them; even one woman's servant who said she wanted two shillings' worth to put on a collecting card.

I had to refuse the last caller, and told her I had finished my stock of stamps.

I was amused to see the clerk looked startled for a moment when I visited the post office next day and asked for another ten shillings' worth of stamps. She found them for me in a drawer, after a little search, and apologised for them not being in a sheet.

"That does not matter," I said. "As long as they are good stamps, I don't mind."

She giggled at that, but, of course, did not understand my real meaning.

When I went home I put them in a drawer in my escritoire, and proposed to devote some time to them after lunch. I was never worried by callers now, and could examine the stamps at my leisure.

Among the things left to me by my father was a powerful watchmaker's lens. It was one of his pleasures to examine minute things, and I had kept it in a drawer without using it till now.

I took my coffee into the drawing-room, told the housemaid that I was not to be disturbed on any account, and settled myself with my chair in the window, to get a good light. I had also kept one stamp from the last purchase for purposes of comparison.

This stamp I studied very carefully for five minutes, before I took up some of the other specimens, and studied them even more carefully. It was thoroughly amusing to me to reflect that I could meet the challenge of that absurd Chief Constable on equal terms. His mind ran in ruts, and his methods were based on routine. Perhaps he imagined that I never read the newspapers!

Suddenly I laughed.

CHAPTER XV

I HAD good cause to laugh. On some part of every one of those eighty stamps was a tiny cross which the foolish operator had tried to mix up with the design!

Of course, I do not say that the ordinary person would have seen these crosses, or even guessed their meaning, but I knew at once. My intuition, aided by the magnifying glass, had detected the mean plot. To be correct, of course, I must say that most accounts I had read of investigations of the kind mentioned this crude plan.

But vainly is the net spread in the sight of any bird. I put the stamps away, had tea early, and then sat down to write letters. I wrote a great many, most of them short, and used other stamps in sending cheques to pay local bills. I think I paid fourteen that afternoon.

It was about dinner-time before I had finished the thirty-seven enclosures and prepared to address them. But my much maligned sense of humour did not allow me to stop there. I typed all the addresses.

The Chief Constable had insulted me by taking me for a fool. I intended to show him that I was not so brainless as he imagined. But I do not suppose he will take the lesson to himself.

Of course, he and his myrmidons will think the typing means something. I smiled to myself at the thought over dinner. I was sorry for them in a way, but if people try to trap you in these horrid, concealed ways, they deserve what they get. I have always understood that British law gave everyone a fair chance, and worked in the open. So much for our reputation for justice and fair play!

But a mind like mine could not be content long with a mere display of superior cleverness. There must be other, subtle little touches, which I alone could discover, to complete the discomfiture of our clumsy police force.

I had accepted their marked stamps; I had written five times more letters than even my best record. I had carefully typed the addresses, so that they might regard them as suspicious. For a little while I considered the question of placing a small red ink cross over each of their crosses, and thus showing them up to their silly selves for the noodles they were.

It was not the fact that it would take me some time that made me refrain. No. I realised that this would show them that I knew they suspected me.

I was sitting in the drawing-room after dinner, smoking a cigarette, and sipping my coffee, when the great idea came to me. I could have laughed aloud if I had not been afraid that it would be heard by cook and the housemaid.

Again I must admit my indebtedness to the newspapers. If I were the police, I would certainly ask the Press to refrain from mentioning the methods used for trapping.

There was a pillar-box at the end of my road, near a lamp, and opposite a garden with a ragged holly hedge.

I would not send the housemaid to post the letters. I would wait till it was dark, and then steal out myself!

For a woman who committed follies because she had "no sense of humour," it was not a bad little comedy I was staging for the benefit of those dunder-headed police.

Stifling my laughter, I left the house at ten, went very quickly and quietly with my letters in a bag to the pillar-box, and looked up and down the deserted pavements.

Did I hear a noise behind the holly hedge? Yes, I did, but I took no notice of it. It might be a rat. A rat behind the arras, such as Hamlet found! But I did not intend to spear it with a rapier. The weapon of irony I used would go deeper, and hurt more.

I posted those letters very quickly, hid my bag under my arm, and raced home. I wished afterwards that I had prolonged the fun by stealing into a neighbouring garden, and watching from there for the policeman to emerge from behind the hedge. But I decided that it would be unwise.

Among the letters I had written was one to Mrs. Ella, and two to others who had treated me shamefully on my arrival. I "saw" those seized with indecent avidity.

Actually, I sent small contributions, with my compliments, to charities with which my enemies were associated.

I went to bed that night feeling very happy. I would give the fools a few days in which to discover their mistake, then I could write some more letters which would help to reform Lush Mellish.

I met the Chief Constable two days later, and noticed that he did not stop me to ask how my literary work was getting on.

So I stopped him. "Really, I do think you should get a type-writer and begin your reminiscences right away," I said. "I find mine a tremendous help and joy."

"I must think about it," he growled, looking not too comfort-able.

"Do," I said, "and I hope you won't confine your book to telling us about your service abroad. I mean to say, everyone will be terribly interested to hear how you go about catching crim-inals at home. I don't know how you do it myself, but you must be very clever."

His face was a study, but he got away very soon, and I was able to smile to myself at the rank flattery I had used.

One thing I had learned lately, not so much from direct information as from putting two and two together, and collating various stories. There was a gambling-house in the neighbour-hood, and one of the *habituées* was a woman who painted. She was also treasurer to one of the local charities, and you know what happens when that sort of people take to gambling.

At first they only mean it as a loan, but they get deep in the grip of their fellow gamblers, and gradually go on until they are caught and sentenced. It would be a good deed to rescue at least one victim from the pit.

It would be more charitable to write to her at first. If she did not cease to frequent the place, other action could be taken. If she refused to be reformed, then, of course, the money of the charity must be saved.

I sat down, and considered what was the best thing to do.

I admit that, as I went on, the magnitude of my task began to bewilder me. At first I had imagined that here and there among the residents of Lush Mellish there were evil-doers, slanderers, and conscienceless people, to whom letters might usefully be directed. Then I began to see that practically the whole town was seething with venom and ill-doing, so that there was hardly a household which could not have been improved by my efforts.

"You seem to have ended by deluging the place with letters," the foul prosecutor remarked. "You developed a perfect mania for it!"

Was there ever anything more unjust? Not in the words, perhaps, but in the implication. "You might as well blame the law for convicting thousands of guilty people," I told him, "and forget that it did so because there were so many who deserved it."

Even in the antagonistic atmosphere of that court, I could see that my ruthless logic had made an impression. As I had to make my way against trained legal minds, you will see that I did not do badly.

It was now necessary to take a trip to London again to compose that letter, so I decided that I might as well try a couple more, and save time and expense.

When I was on the platform before the train started, I saw the Chief Constable come hurriedly on, and enter a carriage. I took my seat, and determined to look out for him at the terminus.

When I reached London, I thought I would try a little ruse, and walked up a poor street near the station, turned about, and down a side street, and came back to see a man hurrying away.

Smiling to myself, I took a taxi and went to my club. I am sure it was followed, and when I got down another taxi passed me slowly. The man in it was bending down to do something, but I recognised the Chief Constable's hat!

Fortunately, there is a back entrance to the club, which leads out to a Mews, and I walked right through, and travelled out to the suburbs to get my little car.

Three letters were the result of that inspiration.

The direct result that is, for I got ideas for at least four more. If you consider my position, in hostile country, with official and unofficial foes on every side, you will realise that I opened my campaign brilliantly. Whether, later, I was wise to try to reform too many people at once is another matter. I felt that I was called to do so, and there it is.

As you perhaps read in the accounts of the trial, those policemen had an account kept of the stamps I bought, and the number of letters I posted! They had the pillar-box cleared the moment I visited it, and perpetrated certain other absurdities of a like kind.

What did they think of me? They knew I had started a painting club and a literary circle, and made suggestions for improving the low standard of local music. They must have known of my gifts, and believed that I had, at least rudimentary, intelligence.

But they did not act as if they had, and I am quite convinced that they would never have been able to wreak their vengeance on me, if left to their own devices.

They made themselves the laughing-stock of at least one humble resident of Lush Mellish.

I had forgotten to tell you about my dog Tiblits. He had caused no trouble so far, probably because he is one of those who prefer (like myself when possible) to remain quiet and peaceable, even in the face of provocation.

He is a golden spaniel, one of those dogs with a beautiful coat and a temperament to match their name. A great comfort and joy to me, he liked nothing better than to lie on my lap in the teeny car, while I composed my letters, previous to typing them, and look up at me with his soft eyes in approval.

How the fiends used even my lovely pet to trap me is another story, of which you shall hear later. I do think that dogs should be left out of human quarrels. But there was no ruse too base or low to be used by my unscrupulous opponents.

I saw a good many policemen and plain-clothes men in my road after that, but no one had troubled me, and I was beginning to think that I was dealing with foemen quite unworthy of my steel, when I had a visit from a detective.

This was the solitary detective-inspector, a thin, lean man with a grave face and a treacly sort of voice. I never heard of him detecting anything or anybody, but they had to have a figure-head, and sent this fool to call on me.

His smile when I interviewed him sat ill on his grave face. It was obviously forced, and, like forced fruit and flowers, wilted too soon to be valuable.

I may say that neither then nor at any other time did he discover a single clue.

"I am sorry to trouble you, madam," he began, "but the Chief Constable has asked me to investigate a rather pressing business, and I am sure you will give me any information you can."

"Certainly," I said, with an ironical smile. "I expect he has now seen that it is wise to pay some attention to my complaints—"

"No, madam," he said; "it is quite another matter. It may have affected you, or it may not. I am anxious to hear."

"I have given up complaining, as I can get no redress," I said.

"I am sorry to hear that, madam. But what I am anxious to know is this. Several residents have been the recipients of anonymous letters. Not everyone similarly worried takes the matter to us."

"I don't wonder," I told him. "I have had three dogs killed, and I have had no help."

He bowed. "I am sorry you think so, madam, but in this matter we are anxious to do all we can to help you."

"Liar!" I said to myself, and added in a polite voice: "Do go on."

"As we are making general inquiries," he blundered on, "I wanted to ask you if you have had any anonymous letters."

Now it was out. I could hardly keep my face straight as I replied: "I am afraid so, inspector. But I hardly expect protection now from the powers that be."

"On the contrary," he said, with false warmth, "we are straining every nerve to find out the perpetrator of these outrages, and think we shall be able to do so."

"Splendid!" I said. "Well?"

"How many letters, may I ask?"

"I have received two anonymous letters, inspector."

"Two, madam? I wonder if you have any objection to showing them to me?"

"I destroyed them," I said.

"That is a pity, madam. You should have brought them to us to examine. They might have given us a clue to the writer."

"Really? Well, I cannot bring them back now."

"Perhaps you can tell me if they were typed, or written by hand, madam?"

I shook my head. "Neither. They were printed in capitals with a pen."

"Printed in capitals? May I ask what was their purport, also when you received them?"

"They contained vicious and foolish reference to my dear pets," I said, "and even if they did not come to your notice, they did to that of the Chief Constable and superintendent. If you are relying on them to deduce anything from anonymous letters, you are leaning on a broken reed."

His forced smile showed its first sign of wilting. "Oh, *those* letters," he said, not troubling to repress his disappointment. "I was referring to something more recent, madam."

I raised my eyebrows; for I can act, if he can't. "Indeed. Then I do not see how I can help you."

The donkey seemed rather at sea then. "Do you mean to say, madam, that you have not received any anonymous letters within the past ten days, say?"

"Certainly not. Why should I? Though I have no sympathy with the people who complained of my dead dogs, I can quite see that my present gentle darling, Tiblits here, could not provoke resentment in the basest breast. Spaniels are notoriously gentle, and even in this place, where dogs are regarded as pariahs, inspector, he has offended no one."

He wriggled nervously after I had made this speech. "These letters were typed, madam," he said. "So it may be that there is another hand behind them."

"Very likely," I agreed, "but I can't help you at all. I have not received a single anonymous letter since your superiors bungled the two I did receive, and I trust I never shall."

"I trust not," he said, with a puzzled look at me. "They are not very agreeable."

He went away, and I had a long silent laugh. Dear Lush Mellish! How it clung to the old ways, the old methods, already thoroughly ventilated by the newspapers. I would have faked letters to myself. They would know that I had sent them. I would be trapped! How silly it all was.

This was a good time to get off my other batch of letters. I did so, and then reflected that my frequent absences might lead to trouble. I would stay for a week in Cornwall, and there prepare a big batch of warnings. These I could send out as occasion offered. Meantime, I would sublet my Cornish cottage, and "Babbie Thrums" would be no more.

It occurred to me that I must limit my activities. If I managed to write, say, forty letters, I should have done what I could. It was obviously impossible to deal with all the rogues in the town.

I took Tiblits, went to London, and so to Ealing, and then off to my quiet retreat. No one followed me. The Chief Constable and his men had concluded that, as I had not followed the routine usual in these affairs, I had nothing to do with the business. In short, they treated me as if I were a stupid, dull-witted criminal, a fact which I much resented.

What fun we had in Cornwall, Tiblits and I! We walked over the moors, or sat in heathy corners, Tiblits on the corner of my skirt, my own fingers busy with the typewriter, or sorting the batches of envelopes into which my missives were to go. Those were halcyon days, when neither he nor I knew how soon we would be separated by the brutal processes and insensitive savagery of British "law"-givers.

In the first three days I wrote twenty-eight letters, some of them masterpieces of their kind. In the next three days I did nineteen. I found it rather a strain towards the end, and I did not care to make them repetitive, but had a thought for variety and style.

I had managed to get an offer for a sublet through the agent who had got the place for me, and the new tenant was to come in the day after I left. I smiled when I saw the agreement, where my name figured as "Miss Babbie Thrums."

I had now nearly put that phase of my life behind me. I completed it at Ealing, in the garage.

The little two-seater was a part of the machinery of my campaign. If it was ever traced, it would be as once the property of a poetess with a Scottish name. In other words, the garage proprietor had a buyer for just such a car, who had come from

Wales for a stay in London. He had also a new and charming little saloon, which would suit me admirably. I exchanged, paying the sum of one hundred and twenty pounds to balance the bargain.

Could I have done more?

CHAPTER XVI

So TIBLITS and I returned in state to Lush Mellish, and I was amused at the stares with which many people greeted me as I drove home through the town.

It was when I was having tea that I learned from my house-maid of a tragedy which had occurred near the town on the previous day.

A great deal of capital was made of this sad event at the trial, but most unjustly, I think. People who commit suicide are border-line cases. Sooner or later they kill themselves. Often they have no real motive. When they have a motive it is some-times that they have done wrong, and try to fly from the scene of their misdemeanours.

In this case a young woman had gassed herself. She left no explanation of her deed, but the opinion generally held was that, having discovered the character of her fiancé, she knew that she would not dare to marry him.

Now there is something to be said here which needs saying. If what she discovered proved that the man she loved was a bad character, then that discovery saved her from a life of unhappi-ness and misery. That is to say, if she *really* loved the man.

It was held at the inquest that she must have done so, or would not have committed suicide. She had before her the alternatives of a miserable death or a miserable life, and she chose her own way.

But how could it be argued that the way in which she made the discovery had anything to do with her death? If she blamed the man without any proof, she was not the wife for him. If she had proof, how she came by it had no relevance in the case.

But, as you know, I was long past seeking for relevance or logic in the legal proceedings of Lush Mellish. Everything was dragged in by the heels, and instead of sitting to decide how she came by her death—which was obvious enough, and their bounden duty—the police actually produced a letter found in the dead woman's room, and put it in.

I have never had much use for coroners, and most people agree that they are busybodies who would be better done away with. But the man we had at Lush Mellish was, perhaps, the worst specimen of his nasty type.

He was fond of hearing himself speak, a pleasure not shared by any of the residents, and he began with a wordy preliminary summary, and ended with a verbose summing-up which was a masterpiece of bad reasoning and spiteful abuse.

Instead of realising that a crazy woman's lack of balance had resulted in her death, he blamed the person who had warned her of the character of her lover! He did not even try to refute the statement that the man was a bad character. He concentrated his venom on the one who had done her best to help the victim.

The woman, he said in his turgid way, had been the victim of one of the foulest and most insidious crimes known to the law, the victim of an anonymous letter-writer. Living in the country as they did, where nature was at her purest and loveliest, they had not realised till now that there was a serpent in their meadows, a snake in the grass, which crept up to innocent souls and injected its venom into their veins.

He was informed that the police had been aware for some time of a campaign of calumny, and slander, and scandal, perpetrated by a fiend in human form. Letters had been received by many, reducing them to a state of misery and terror, poisoning the wells of faith, embittering the dearest relations, plunging Lush Mellish into a state of excitement and almost despair.

He said that the emitter of these poisonous epistles was known to be one in their midst, but one who, by cunning and a very serpent-like trickery, and slimy cleverness, had so far managed to escape detection. But he was informed that it would not be for long. The evil-doer would be laid by the heels, and suffer condign punishment. He counselled calm and hope for the present. Let those who were sent these disgusting letters take no notice of them.

Letters of this kind, he added absurdly, must be taken at their proper value. They could not be taken as proof of anything. If the sender had really any proof, he or she would have put it before the police, not thrown it about in this filthy fashion. He ended by saying that the girl was as much a victim of the letter-writer as if she had been taken by the throat and strangled.

Wild, whirling words; but with the whole point of the matter left out, the wrong things stressed, and a great deal of hysterical nonsense he should have been ashamed to utter.

As I felt as sorry for the young woman as he, but knew that hers had been, in one sense, a happy release, my withers were unwrung. And, of course, anyone can make a point by a partial statement of the truth. But a coroner should have some legal training, and not lump things together without discrimination.

When he spoke so harshly of the senders of anonymous letters, he was naturally speaking of those whose spite, or mental infirmity, leads them to make untruthful and sometimes obscene allegations against their fellows. And, of course, people like that can have no mercy shown them. They are real Ishmaelites.

But if authorities are going to act and talk as he did, they may as well begin at once by prosecuting the Salvation Army, with all reformers, and bodies of people who warn others in time that they are on the wrong road. It is true that none of those I have mentioned write anonymous letters. But they are allowed to carry on their work *openly*, while I was punished for doing what I had to do in the only way they left open to me.

In the end, of course, the silly man had to stop talking and accept the obvious verdict of suicide. The foreman of the jury, naturally, seized a chance to be listened to patiently for the first time in his life. He added a rider, as spiteful and foolish as that of the coroner. And so ended one of the most absurd inquiries I have ever read of.

I did not attend. The affair had nothing to do with me.

I do think hysteria is such a sign of weakness. And what they call mass-hysteria is worst of all. Lush Mellish got it badly after the inquest, and I do know that some people who had never had an anonymous letter complained to the police that they had.

But, of course, it was said that various vicious people paid off old scores when they heard of my campaign, and that may in part account for what was said to me in jail by those disgusting young women. My counsel, before he retreated on the absurd defence of insanity, made something of that. He did not succeed with that red herring, but then he was a vastly over-rated advocate.

I shall not weary you by mentioning all the clever ruses and devices I adopted to get rid of the rest of my letters. Besides, it might be harmful if I disclosed these secrets to people who would use them to forward some private end, or wantonly to injure innocent people.

I have an idea that the Chief Constable thought he was being very clever when he announced that all the letters had been typed. He expected, of course, that the writer would be afraid of discovery, and adopt some more easily traced method. Naturally I did nothing of the kind.

The ineffective inspector made a round of every house and shop in the place where a typewriter was kept. It took him weeks, and I believe an expert from Scotland Yard said that the letters had been typed on a portable Cremona.

But, though certain people in Lush Mellish had Cremonas, none of them reproduced the small defects looked for. My old machine was, of course, not to hand. I had placed it in a deep hole, under the bridge over a river I crossed coming to London from Cornwall.

The delightful ivory paper I burned when I made tea by the roadside on a tiny bonfire, just as the tramps do. But I was very careful to put out the fire afterwards, and bury the debris; in which I was an example to those careless campers who leave litter in the beautiful countryside.

Now that the hysterical and those with guilty consciences in Lush Mellish had realised that the police kept confidence, if requested, I think a great many did take their warnings to the police. Some did not. My shafts had gone home there. The others, with human inconsistency, could not believe that they had done the things with which I charged them. How easily we deceive ourselves!

When I heard that Scotland Yard had been asked to look at the letters I was sure that our Chief Constable would admit his inefficiency next, and call in the C.I.D.

It may seem strange to you, who are not in my then exalted mood, but I admit that this idea gave me pleasure rather than anxiety. I am casting no reflections on the C.I.D. when I say that they failed to do what the locals had failed to do. But they knew nothing of local conditions, which is a sort of excuse.

Then their training and experience of investigation were met by my clever brain, and that intuition which they could not be expected to possess. Again, they were used to dealing with mere criminals, dull, primitive minds. As well expect a man with a walking-stick to conquer a master of the rapier.

I bore them no ill-will and am, indeed, ready to give them a hint. They forget that servants hear much that their employers do not. When a big smiling man, calling himself Mr. Purkiss, came down in tweeds to stay at the Blue Boar, just outside, I soon heard from cook that he was supposed to be a chief inspector from Scotland Yard. Someone in the Blue Boar—the ostler, I think—said he had seen his picture in the paper the year before.

"You mustn't make these ridiculous guesses, cook," I told her. "And after all it has nothing to do with us. The police have a right to do what they wish in the matter, and you may hamper the poor man if you mention his being here incognito."

Of course, he was the man the ostler thought him to be, and the day after he arrived, he walked down my road, and glanced into several gardens. He did not look at mine, which was a foolish oversight. For I had begun to see lately that it is not only what people do, but what they fail to do that is informative.

He was very popular in the bar of the Blue Boar, and dozens of men gathered there in the evening, so that he heard a great deal about the people of Lush Mellish. For men love gossip, and the inn is a regular radio station.

There was also a smaller and thinner man who came down, and I knew from my reading that this must be the detective-sergeant who always accompanies his superior in country inquiries.

These two had hardly been in the place two days, when a man in the council offices ran away. I do not mean that their presence had anything to do with it. A warning and a guilty conscience were enough for him. Of course, he had taken some money and there was an inquiry, which led to a letter being found in an old jacket in his rooms.

At this point the local paper lost its head completely, and published a letter, most banally headed "The Poison Pen!" They did not see that medicine for the good of a patient is not necessarily poison; and why the town should be angry because I had driven away a peculator of the council's funds, I am unable to say.

But the leader gave the impression that hardly a resident was able to sleep soundly for fear this "dastardly" person should send him a venomous and libellous letter. London papers quoted this, and worked it up, and one of those foolish young men the newspapers love to call their crime specialist came down, and tried to open an inquiry on his own. Like all amateurs, he failed completely, but was kicked by a man whom he had plagued over the matter.

Most of his time was spent in bars, and his reports to his journal were the most mendacious things I have ever seen. He even visited my house, and wrote of me as "Lush Mellish Lady Laughs at the Libeller!"

Of course, he had heard something from the police, and was anxious to see if he could fix on me. I saw him, and gave him my impressions, as a budding novelist.

"I think," I said, "that the letters must have been done on a second-hand machine. I am not so sure if they were typed by anyone resident here, though the local knowledge they appear to display suggests that they were."

"Good!" he said. "Suggests? Rather a point that."

"I am glad to hear you say so," I replied, "but what exactly do you mean?"

He smiled smugly.

"It occurred to me at first that the writer might mug up all this information easily here. I've heard enough lately to blow up the place. This inner dope, you know, would make people imagine he was a local resident."

"Does it not occur to you that a woman might be at the back of it?" I said, for I was not anxious that he should father this idea on me. "It's more like a woman's work."

He put that in his paper, and carried on, until his editor got tired of hearing that his "crime specialist" had got a clue, and ordered him back to London.

Then Scotland Yard faded away. Mr. Purkiss and his tweeds vanished from the Blue Boar. His assistant followed him. Our Chief Constable went about like a bear with a sore head.

I had still three letters to send off, but their dispatch took me much longer than the ten before.

I posted the last in a pillar-box in the Cornmarket, while I was talking to the Chief Constable himself! Of course, they did not clear that box till the usual time. His presence was my safeguard. Another letter was posted in the inner box of the post office itself. I slipped the envelope among a pile of letters a lady was stamping, when she turned to the assistant to get some more stamps. I wrote a telegram till she had finished, and made sure that she had posted the lot before I went home.

She was a stranger to the place, so there was no danger of her being mistaken for the sender. Indeed, at the back of my mind all along was a determination not to let any outsider get the credit for my deeds. If everyone else showed a similar consideration, this would be a better world.

While I have deprecated the hysterical state into which Lush Mellish had worked itself, I do not say that some people had not justification of sorts for their terror. The guilty went about afraid of further discoveries, and those they had wronged, in certain cases, took action to revenge themselves, or refused to have anything further to do with the offenders.

I heard that two divorces were pending; but there again, it had nothing to do with me. Separated from their unpleasant partners, they could build up a new and more wholesome life alone.

I could not resist a last dig at my enemy, the Chief Constable.

"Why don't you call in Scotland Yard?" I asked him. "You must forgive me if I do think you stand on your dignity too much, or value your prestige too highly. It would be better to admit that your force is not an efficient one, on its detective side, and get the experienced aid of the C.I.D."

He looked furious, but what could he say?

CHAPTER XVII

You will have discovered by now that I am a very human person. I like society—fellowship—if you know what I mean, and naturally I want to be liked.

So I was hurt, and I think I had the right to be, when I found that most of the residents of Lush Mellish regarded me with suspicion, and showed it in unmistakable ways.

However the matter might have been twisted during the trial, at that time no one had an atom of evidence that I had written the letters. So what right had they to suspect me, or ostracise me? What is the use of saying one is innocent till proved guilty if people act like that? As you know, I am not without resources. I had my garden, my pet, my reading, and I am glad to say with the old poet: "My mind to me a kingdom is."

But none of those things can rob the truly human person of a wish to mingle on equal and pleasant terms with some at least of their fellows. In spite of all, there were times when I felt lonely, when I wished I could find someone to whom I could pour out my troubles; in other words, a friend and sympathiser.

If I am more sagacious and intelligent than most people of my class and age, I am still young, and was then (before the weight of that unjust sentence bore me down) not ill-looking. And now I was nearing the end of my campaign of reform. There was a certain reaction, common enough in such cases, I believe, and at times I felt depressed.

For I was not only suspected, but watched. The old woman next door was always in her garden when I was in mine. The woman at the other side peered over the fence at times in a most unpleasant fashion. This was specially the case when I was typing. When I went to the post in the evening I saw people stealing along near me, which was very disagreeable.

Then when I went shopping, groups would stare at me insolently, and make whispered remarks.

But what hurt me most was an occasion when I let Tiblits out for a few minutes at night, and he came in again, wagging his innocent tail. There was a small luggage label tied to his collar, and on it was printed:

"Whisper and I shall hear."

I took it round to the police station next day, and explained what had happened to the superintendent.

"But this isn't libellous or offensive, madam," he said at once. "It sounds to me like the name of an old song."

There again you see the persistent unfairness of these people. I could get no redress. What other people did *to me* was harmless!

Spaniels are very affectionate creatures, and have the defect of that virtue. Tiblits took to anyone, and I was always afraid he would be taken by someone who saw how quickly he responded to a word or look. He was not the dog for a jealous owner.

My last letter had gone, though I had yet to see how several of my warnings had taken effect. There were some hardened people in the town whom nothing would improve. And I was not content.

It did seem to me as if I had lost any possible friends I might have had in the town, without having the full consolation of knowing that I had really left the town better than I found it. Certain devils had been driven out, but in their place had come suspicion, spying, and a hundred mean vices dormant before. When I think of the misplaced ingenuity which finally led to my trial, I could cry.

I remember following the otter hounds when I was a girl, and seeing an otter slip quietly away downstream. He would have made his escape in spite of the hounds, had not some hideous busybody on the bank (not one of the "field" at all) given warning of the poor animal's presence.

It was just like that with me. Left to myself, all the horrible official and unofficial hounds in Lush Mellish could never have caught me. But they were not left to themselves. This is a sore subject with me, so I shall leave it for the present, and unfold my story as it befell, so that you may understand the palpable unfairness of it all.

My maids, as you will have seen, had stuck to me through thick and thin, and they were both as fond of Tiblits as of my former pets. It was carelessness, not evil-mindedness, which led the housemaid one night to forget to lock the french window of the room where Tiblits slept in his basket.

At any rate, when she woke me, next morning, to bring me my early tea, she was hardly able to speak for agitation, and broke the news to me that dear Tiblits was missing.

"The fiends!" I cried, as I jumped out of bed. "They have taken my last treasure from me. But this time I will see that someone is punished!" I refused breakfast, dressed hastily, and ran to the police station. The lazy superintendent had, of course, not turned up then, but I told my story to a sergeant, who was markedly unsympathetic.

"We'll look into it, of course, mum," he said, "but dogs do stray, and if he's got his collar on, as by rights he should have, someone'll bring him back."

"The someone who took him away!" I said scornfully.

"You never told me someone took him away," he said stupidly.

"Of course they did," I replied indignantly. "This is my fourth pet to be torn from me by spiteful people, who try to avenge their rancour by striking at me through my dogs. But this is the end of it! If you do not do something I shall complain to the highest authorities; to the Home Secretary, if need be. When a ratepayer is denied even elementary justice it is time that our so-called guardians of the peace had a rude shock."

I admit now that I was wrong in this solitary instance, but that does not invalidate my general charge. If the dog *had* been stolen, they would not have tried to help me.

Feeling perfectly furious, I returned home to organise some sort of search for dear Tiblits. To my surprise cook was waiting at the gate, her face beaming as she cried: "He's back, ma'am!"

I could hardly speak for a moment, then: "Tiblits back? Where is he?" I demanded. "Is he safe—unhurt?"

"A bit muddy, ma'am, but I'll soon clean that off," said kind cook. "It was a strange gentleman found and brought him, ma'am, and I made him sit down in the drawing-room, knowing you would like to hear about it."

"A strange gentleman?" I said.

"Not a gentleman what lives here," said cook.

"It would be hard to find one who lives here!" I said. "Where is Tiblits?"

"We have him in the scullery to wash, ma'am," she said, "but I think the gentleman was in a bit of a hurry."

Tiblits was in good, kind hands, so I went straight to the drawing-room to have a look at this new phoenix in Lush Mellish. I half feared that he was a detective in disguise.

I saw, instead, a handsome and personable young man of about thirty, wearing a smart blue serge suit, which had got rather dirty from carrying Tiblits, with fine dark eyes and fair wavy hair.

I took to him at once, for he was, I concluded, a great animal lover. The suit was practically new, and he had forgotten it, it seemed, in his desire to carry poor, weary Tiblits home.

I thanked him most gratefully, of course, and offered him a cigarette. He took it, smiling, and said he was very fond of dogs, but, being a stranger to the place, had not at first known where to return it.

"Such a jolly dog," he said. "I wish I had one like it."

"Are you staying with someone here," I said; "I mean, at a private house?"

"No," he said, "I'm putting up at a pub—hotel they call it. Good food, you know, but I like to call places and things by their proper names, don't you?"

This seemed to me a wonderful flash of insight, and I agreed. "Oh, I do," I cried. "But do let me get you a brush for your suit. I should hate to think it was spoiled in return for your kindness to Tiblits."

"What an awfully jolly name," he beamed. "But don't worry, Miss Alice, a man who thinks so much of his rotten suits when a dog is in trouble is no man at all."

How true that was, and how rarely said, or felt! I was flattered too, for cook had said my visitor was in a hurry, and here he sat, chatting and at ease, not at all anxious to be gone. I have met men like that before, but after the last weeks of neglect and ostracism, his presence and interest were like balm to my wounded spirit.

His name was Mower, William Mower, he gave me to understand, and he hoped to have a month in Lush Mellish. He had arrived the previous day, and was enthusiastic about the charms of the place, but very critical of the few people he had seen.

"Rather a stuffy, sniffy lot, I imagine," he told me. "And gloomy! My aunt! You'd think undertaking was the chief job here."

I knew he would hear sooner or later of the local trouble. "Quite," I told him. "There have been some anonymous letters received lately, and people here are suspicious and panicky. I have never received any, but then, I keep to myself and have nothing to fear."

He slapped his knees. "Golly! That must have been what a fellow was talking about in the pub last night. What's it all about?"

"I don't know the latest details," I said, "but you will hear all about it from the people you meet."

He offered me a cigarette now. "Shall I? Not much! I came down here to enjoy a hunt round the country, not to hear bits out of the police news. Anyway, wind-up in these little towns is a common affair. Where the country breezes blow, what?"

I must say that I liked his slangy, but rather fascinating way of talking, and I did like his detachment from the potty affairs of Lush Mellish.

"Very much so," I replied, laughing.

He suddenly looked at his watch, and jumped up. "Gosh! How time does fly. I meant to catch the train to Woolan, but here I've lost it. I'm afraid I'd lose oodles of trains, Miss Alice, if you kept me talking."

"Must you really go?" I asked, forgetting that I had had no breakfast in my pleasure at this new friend. "Of course, if you must—"

"Absolutely," he said, beaming at me. "But may I beg a favour?"

I repressed a start. "Perhaps you had better let me hear it."

"Well, if I might, I should love to have another look at your jolly little dog before I go," he said. "Delightful little chap; even if I have golden souvenirs of him all over me," he added, detaching a hair from his coat, and laughingly holding it up. "Kind of platinum blond, isn't he?"

"Perhaps that is why you took a fancy to him," I said.

He laughed again. "Blond, perhaps, but not platinum, surely? But do let us have a squint at the duck before I tear myself away."

We went into the kitchen, where cook and the housemaid had dear Tiblits nicely washed, and were drying him, and combing him, before the fire.

Can you wonder that I was rather fascinated by Mr. Mower? Even now I can understand his charm. And his manner with dogs was perfect.

For a few days after that we had quite a number of dogs straying into the garden, which rather puzzled me, but there was an explanation of it later.

Having seen Tiblits at his toilet, Mr. Mower went away. But I asked him if he would care to come in during the afternoon, and he accepted my invitation with apparent pleasure.

"Sure you want me?" he said before he left. "I mean to say, don't think you owe me anything. Nothing worth while, anyway."

"Oh, I should like you to come," I told him. "And Tiblits will be his own dear self by then. He has taken to you."

"I took—I took to him," said Mr. Mower, raised his hat, and went off.

Again you may smile at the idea of my gratification in finding that I was to have an attractive visitor. I forgive you, for you have not known what it is to be lonely, to feel yourself almost an outcast, without even the miserable consolation of knowing that you deserve it.

And dear Tiblits had been the indirect means of giving me a new friend, one who scoffed at the panic of Lush Mellish, and was not at all likely to be affected by its false mob-hysteria. Cook was quite lyrical in praise of the "strange gentleman"; who obviously was one, not like the "upstarts" in the town. Apparently, as the *Punch* joke said, he "rose his hat at her" physically and metaphorically, and took her by storm.

"Nearly spoiling his nice new suit, mum," she said to me. "It will be someone for company, mum."

Someone for company? Yes, that is what I thought. I gave cook a rise in wages, and also the housemaid, who had helped to make Tiblits presentable.

What a difference some little thing may make in one's mental atmosphere. When I went into town to shop, and to get some cakes for tea, I almost knew the meaning of the phrase walking on air. I forgot the petty insolence of those I passed; the stares of some, the whispered comments of others. When I came home, I was even able to smile at the antics of that beastly black cat next door, which tried to do a tight-rope stunt on top of the fence, and fell over. I smiled again at the absurd consolations offered to it by its hateful mistress.

It was now autumn, but it felt like spring. It promised to be one of those still, warm, autumn days, and I put on a charming little frock I had bought on my last visit to town, and arranged chairs and table under my copper beech.

My two maids were as anxious to shine as I. Cook made some little Italian pastries I had never seen before; delicious little flaky twists, dusted with castor sugar, that melted in the mouth.

The housemaid somehow contrived to make my tea-table look more inviting than ever before.

Tiblits was now dry, and his silky coat shone golden in the sun. He had an extra biscuit, and sat on a chair by the table on his favourite blue silk cushion, looking a perfect picture.

"There will be *two* gentlemen here to-day, Tiblits, precious!" I murmured to him. "Two! No cads in good clothes, no louts still perspiring from the game they call tennis. Just two *gentlemen*."

Tiblits languished up at me in his sweet way, and I knew that he understood.

In this softer mood, I even spared a thought for the woman next door. Her sole male belongings consisted in that unlicked, mercenary cub, the cadging nephew who had treated me so rudely. The cat was a male, but then it was only a cat. I have heard cat fanatics speak of a gentleman cat, but it is the sort of absurdity one would expect from such people.

Her disappointment over that young scoundrel did not seem to worry her that day, or else she hid it very well. I saw her look over into my garden once with a patently forced smile, and when Mr. Mower came at a quarter past four, she began to chuckle to her cat. I wished her luck of the silly beast.

It said a great deal for Mr. Mower's common sense, I thought, that the gossip and scandal about the letters had not only left him untouched, but did not seem to have interested him at all.

He described his doings of the early part of the day wittily and well, and when we were having tea, began to talk of books and authors. Not that he had met many authors, but he had known two, one quite well.

"The poor chap is dead now," he added. "Conked out after an accident. A funny fellow he was. T'other, a chap called Mercer, is still alive, I believe."

"Why don't you try to write?" I asked him. "You describe things so well, and have a racy way of talking."

"I used to do some engrossing," he said, with his sunny smile.

"Is that a sort of writing?" I asked.

"Yes, but it's a slow job. Now, I often wonder if I could write a novel. Don't laugh, please, Miss Alice! I know most people have that idea once in their lives."

"I certainly should not laugh at you, for people in glass houses must not throw stones," I told him.

He started. "Why, are you a novelist?"

"A budding one, perhaps."

"But how jolly! I wish you would give me a hint how to do one. How to start, for instance. I don't believe so much in really local colour, do you?"

"No," I said, "I don't. Mine is a sort of fantasy."

"Would you think me rude if I asked to have a look at it?" he said rather wistfully. "Might kind of inspire me, don't you know."

"After tea, if you are very good," I promised him.

"I will be good," he said and turned to tickle dear Tiblits. "Dog! we are going to have a lesson, and profit by it, just you and I. But this is a treat you often get, so you must excuse me if I am a little excited the first time."

At that moment the black cat tried its tight-rope walking again, and my visitor laughed and pointed to it.

"What-ho, a cat!"

"A cat," I said. "Yes, it's the sort of thing a foolish old woman would keep."

"You took the words out of my mouth," he said, and added:—"Scat! Get off it, you brute! Shissh!"

The cat "shisshed," almost falling off the fence, and my neighbour suddenly popped up, and glared at Mr. Mower.

"How dare you frighten my cat, you cad!"

"Is that a cat?" Mr. Mower asked her gravely.

"You know very well that it is a cat," she replied angrily.

"Pardon me, madam," he said, to my secret amusement, "when the—er—animal first appeared on the fence, I thought it was the top of an old mop which someone had used to mop up spilled ink with. I apologise to you, and to the cat."

He was such a funny fellow, and I had to repress a laugh as she retreated with the beast in her arms. An old mop used to mop up ink! It was really a most apt description.

But Mr. Mower did not let me forget that I had promised to show him my manuscript, so I had to bring out the first forty pages, and he sat and smoked, and skimmed, chuckling to himself, and sometimes making a flattering comment.

"This kills *my* young ambitions," he said, "stone dead, Miss Alice! I am a thoroughly impudent fellow to think that I could do this sort of thing."

"You think it good?" I said.

"Priceless," he replied. "Just the right mixture of—"

"Irony?" I said, as he paused.

"Absolutely. Irony and what-ye-may-call-it. Don't tell me this is your first effort."

"I am afraid it is," I said.

He stared at me. "Great Scott! And Lush Mellish inspired this? There must be something good in the town after all. Or can you only write in the country?"

"Well," I said, happy to find a twin soul, "there is incubation, you know, and then writing."

"What a donkey I am!" he laughed. "Of course. First hatch your chick, and then commit him to paper. But that's a rotten simile. You can't very well commit a chicken to paper. Now, this chap Mercer I told you about is a town-bird. Can't write a line except among the chimney-pots in the big smoke. Dries up absolutely, he told me, away from London."

"How odd that is!" I said.

"Crazy! Let a bird chirp, a nightingale sing, a cow low, and poor old Mercer sees his muse skipping for the nearest railhead."

"While I, on the contrary, like the serenity of the country for inspiration," I told him.

CHAPTER XVIII

"I SAY," Mr. Mower began, after a short pause, "did you say the 'serenity of the country'? That cat, and its attendant female, isn't going to help you much, I should imagine. A 'Miaow, miaow!' in the middle of the great thought rather puts the lid on the onions, doesn't it?"

"It is not conducive to poetical inspiration," I agreed, "but I am not confined to Lush Mellish, Mr. Mower. I can get away, you know."

"Got a car, eh?" he said. "Well, that does make a difference. I'm still a learner, but I expect you're the real goods at the wheel."

I smiled. "Not exactly a novice, of course, but not as expert as all that."

"It's going to be a great thing to me," he said, tickling Tiblits again. "I mean to say, seeing something of my own country, and all that. Blowed if I ever knew England was so big."

"Isn't it?" I said. "You travel miles and miles, and never cover even a fraction of the country. Do you know the south at all well?"

"No," he said, "not much of it. Cumberland I do know. I say, may I have a look at your jigger while I'm here? I am still motor-proud."

"Certainly, if you would like to," I assured him.

He showed the greatest interest in my new car, and wanted to know if my speedometer was accurate. Of course, I knew that the speed limit made that very necessary, but I was unaware that some were very flattering, and made the bright young driver think he was going much faster than he was.

"Though what satisfaction there can be in that," I said, "I do not understand."

"It's a mania," he replied. "But yours is a jolly car all right. Tip-top hill-climber, eh?"

"I don't know," I told him. "I think so. Aren't there some fearsome hills in Cumberland?"

"Oh, rather. Some of the passes are perfectly horrid. Well, I wish you luck of your little beauty, Miss Alice."

"You must let me show you some of the beauty spots while you are here," I suggested, and we went back to our seats under the copper beech.

"Ever been in Ireland?" he asked, after he had lit a cigarette.

"No," I replied, "never."

He smiled. "I went to Ulster last year. Surprised me, that did. Why, there were lots of spots they never advertise just as fine as anything I ever saw; moors, cliffs, rivers. Jove! bits reminded me of Scotland, and other bits of Devon. I give you my word, there were miles of moor just as attractive as Dartmoor, and no one seemed to know they were anything out of the way."

"Really?" I said. "But England's full of beauty, isn't it?"

"Topping, I admit. What county do you think the finest, Miss Alice?"

I smiled. "It's hard to say. How is one to compare, Mr. Mower?"

"There is that," he murmured. "Bits of South Wales take some beating—Pembroke, and so on. But, as you say, it all depends on what sort of scenery one likes. Now if I were able to retire and set up in a small way, me for a nice bit of river scenery in a valley, within touch of some spot where I could get a book, or do some shopping—not too near."

"You don't like real solitude?" I asked him.

"H'm, not quite. Rather a blue egg if you get the hump, and have to live on it too long. Do you?"

"Not for always, perhaps," I said, "but for a holiday it seems to me so refreshing; such a change."

"And then there are the ribbon builders in your way. Where are you going to get a nice lonely place to live? Cumberland, of course, gives you a chance. Mr. Jerry Builder can't get his free roadway among the heather."

"I must try it," I told him. "I confess to having a partiality for heather."

"The moorland; what better!" he cried enthusiastically. "I mean, if you like that sort of thing. You adore Yorkshire and Derbyshire, I expect."

I shook my head. "I am afraid I have never visited either. I must go."

"Ah, you like something wilder; Northumberland or Durham," he murmured. "Have you ever driven across from—"

"No," I laughed. "You see, I have never been there either. Your heart seems to be in the north, Mr. Mower."

He smiled at that. "Well, when you ask for moors, your choice is somewhat limited. Scotland and Ireland are richer that way."

"I must go to Scotland," I told him. "I know one of the islands, but not much about the mainland."

"Pretty hilly," he said. "But perhaps you don't mind that. I know a chap who absolutely *chooses* routes where he can buzz up the sides of mountains."

"It is rather thrilling," I admitted. "I have gone up some pretty steep places, and just loved it. Specially coming down the other side."

"Risky, unless you have decent brakes," he said. "Personally I don't like the feeling that one might slip back suddenly. But I expect you have more nerve than I."

"I am sure you are quite mistaken," I told him. "Probably I never thought of the risk, that's all."

He nodded. "Maybe so, though I bet you are very plucky. I know I did one hill that was said to be one in six, and I felt as if the blessed jigger was hitting the stars—standing on end, if you know what I mean."

I felt sure that he was exaggerating his sensations, for he looked a healthy, courageous young man, and modest with it.

"Then I can beat you," I said. "I did one that is said to be one in five. I had to creep up on first gear, of course, and the hill seemed miles long, though I don't suppose it was."

"They never are," he assured me. "I can see you love the country. I expect I might even put up with the solitary places if I knew a bit more about the birds and flowers, and so on. I'm a perfect dud at that. Hardly know a hawk from an owl."

"I was brought up in the country," I said. "I think observing Nature is one of my chief joys. I am very observant."

"Lucky you!" he moaned. "Now me; I've eaten oodles of grouse, but I doubt if I would recognise one in the air."

"Nor I," I admitted. "I have never seen one in flight. But grouse are confined to a few counties, aren't they?"

"Like nightingales," he said. "Ever see any rare birds on your wanderings?"

It was pleasant to feel that he wanted to linger in my garden, for I had a shrewd suspicion that he was making conversation so that he would not have to leave.

"Not very rare," I said, "but I have seen buzzards—"

"Just a sec.," he said, reaching his cigarette-case to me. "I do know they're jolly rare, if not extinct. They used to catch 'em on Salisbury Plain. I got that from a book once. Fine eating, it said they were."

I smiled. "Not bustards; buzzards—a kind of hawk," I corrected him. "You find them where you find ravens, you know."

He appeared enlightened. "I read about one in *Barnaby Rudge*. Like a kind of crow," he said. "And you've seen one?"

"Not very long ago," I assured him. "A pair. But they aren't pretty. And I like the prettier birds. Know what a water-ousel is?"

He scratched his head. "Gosh, no! Heard of the River Ouse, that's all. 'Ousels on the Ouse' sounds a good headline."

"It may be, but they generally frequent little moorland rills," I informed him. "They perch on rocks and stones in the stream, and dive down to get insects under water. That's why they are commonly called dippers."

"You seem to know a bit about everything," he said admiringly. "I hope you will show me some birds one day."

"What about to-morrow?" I asked. "I know a sweet spot on the river ten miles away where you may see a kingfisher, perhaps two. Would you care to come. We can take a picnic tea in the car."

He got up. "Would I care to come! Why, I should simply love to get on the track of a rare, shy bird, Miss Alice. But you're sure I won't bore you?"

"If you do, I shall simply drop you, and let you walk home," I told him, "but somehow I don't think you will."

"I know I shall never get home if I dally like this," he said very gallantly. "You'll think me a perfect pig to have taken up so much of your time."

Before he left we had arranged that I should pick him up at the town bridge at half-past three next day. He said good-bye to Tiblits in his inimitable way, and then I saw him to the gate.

I must say that that was the happiest day I had spent that year. I knew nothing of what was to come after, but I did feel that I had at last chanced on a kind, reasonable being; so different from the riff-raff of Lush Mellish.

My two maids did not say much, but I knew that they were as much impressed as I had been by the visitor's charm. When cook heard of the picnic tea she promised to make more of the little Italian pastries, and took the greatest interest in the preparation of our little al fresco feast.

Even Tiblits was excited that day.

Now I must confess to one of my little weaknesses. At least, it was a weakness then, and a not unnatural one.

There are a good many more women than men in Lush Mellish, and as a considerable proportion of the majority are not very well favoured, or attractively feminine, a nice man is an acquisition. When he is handsome as well, then one has reason to be proud. I admit at once that I was pleased and excited at the idea of driving Mr. Mower in my car, and hoped that people would see that I did not require their patronage or countenance, but was able to do very well without it. I knew that hundreds of local young women would give their eyes to be in my place.

The town bridge is just at the entry to the town, and when I drove up next afternoon, with the picnic basket in the back seat, I noticed that there were a number of people about, some going to the last tennis tournament of the season. Of course, I took no notice of them, but drove up to the bridge, where I saw Mr. Mower leaning against the parapet waiting for me. Yes, *waiting*. And he gave me such a charming smile as I drew up and opened the door for him.

I was not unconscious of dozens of eyes watching me, as I smiled at him in greeting. At least five women I had reason to object to saw our meeting, and tried to look superior and unimpressed. They failed, of course. Sour grapes do set the teeth on edge, and that alters the set of your face, giving it a disappointed look.

"But how nice of you to be early!" I said, as we moved off.

"How silly of me if I had been late!" he replied. "I have been looking forward to this since I saw you last. Which way do we go?"

"To the little valley near Ribsole," I told him, purposely just swerving round the wretched Mrs. Ella, tennis racket in hand, who gave me a fierce look. "You'll love it."

We chatted as we drove, and he complimented me on my skill. Indeed, it only seemed a few minutes before I pulled up the car in the sweet little valley, and showed him that rare thing nowadays, a farrier's at the side of the road.

"By Jove!" he cried delightedly. "It just reminds me of Cockington Forge, Miss Alice. Doesn't it you?"

"Where is that?" I asked.

"Devonshire, near Torquay," he replied. "It's rather a show place."

"I have passed through Devon, but know very little about it," I said. "If you will get out, we can have a little walk along the stream before it is time for tea."

"The very goat's toe!" he cried, racy as usual. "You have topping ideas for a nice afternoon, I must say. And aren't the trees gorgeous? No mistake about the autumn tints here."

CHAPTER XIX

"ARE you never lonely here?" Mr. Mower asked, when we had returned from a delightful ramble along the banks of the stream, and he was seeing to my Sirram kettle, while I put out the sandwiches and cakes.

"Oh, I am, at times," I admitted. "I have two very good maids, and dear Tiblits here is a host in himself, but I might be happier if I had a friend with kindred tastes."

"Literary and artistic?" he said, as he got to his feet again. "I know. It must be dull at times in a one-horse show like this, but why don't you get someone to share—another writer, I mean?"

I smiled at his innocence. "My dear Mr. Mower, you evidently haven't come much in contact with the artistic temperament; even if you did know two novelists!" I murmured. "Writing people are too troublesome to live with long. Then it isn't easy even for two friends to live together, unless they have everything in common."

He grinned. "Really? I never tried it, but you seem to speak from sad experience, Miss Alice," he said. "What a good wheeze this little muslin bag full of tea is, by the way. Take it out and throw it away after—isn't that the idea?"

"It is," I said; "but don't you believe what I have said about friends? I was thinking of two women friends, of course."

That seemed to amuse him mightily. "Makes all that difference, does it? Being a man I shouldn't have dared to say that. But what, actually, is the difficulty?"

I poured him out a cup of tea. "Well, one woman can never be really friends with another," I told him. "I suppose we know too much about each other. At any rate, I had a visitor once, and if you had asked me beforehand I should have said her visit would be a delight. As it was, she proved a bore—I hadn't met her for years—and I was terribly disappointed."

"A bore?" He nibbled a cake, and looked at me speculatively. "Will you believe me when I say I have never been bored in my life? It's true. It may be that little things interest me. Of course, I can imagine cases—your friend, for example, may have talked dress all the time, and, of course, you would want to discuss books and art."

I laughed. "Indeed, no; she was not at all dressy. She was just full of stories about natives and animals. At first I thought it all most quaint and amusing, but when you get natives and animals from breakfast to dinner you do get fed up."

"I like animal stories myself, but then I don't read 'em all day," he said. "I wish you would let me hear one."

So I told him about the locusts, and he laughed a great deal, and said he would be eternally grateful to me for telling him that one.

"If the lady could discover a new use for wasps," he said, "it would be great. I nearly swallowed one on my cake just now—a beastly, belated insect."

"Perhaps they don't have wasps in Rhodesia," I said. "She never mentioned them. Elephants seemed just as troublesome."

He smiled. "From the sublime to the irritating. I suppose Rhodesia is all right for women? Not like the Gold Coast, for example?"

"If there were no elephants or lions, it would be a delightful place," I told him. "At any rate, she did not seem, to me, afraid to go back."

"I was wondering if I would have a chance to meet her," he said. "You see, if I could get someone to tell me yarns like that, I might make a start in literature without doing anything so ambitious as a novel."

"I am sorry," I said, "but she went away soon after leaving me. I could repeat some more of her stories if you like."

He lit a cigarette. "Don't let us waste this lovely afternoon. I don't suppose I could really do much at writing, anyway."

We smoked, packed up the basket, had another little walk, and then drove for twenty miles, chatting happily, till I turned about and regretfully headed for home.

Ten miles out, Mr. Mower seemed so interested in the car and my driving that I made a sudden resolution. "Do drive for a little," I said. "I am sure you are terribly good at it. Would you care to?"

"Love it," he said, "but I haven't got my driving licence with me."

I smiled. "That doesn't matter. I have never been asked for mine, and though I believe people are held up at times, I have never been."

So we changed seats, and as my intuition had told me, Mr. Mower was wonderfully expert for a beginner. But some men have the knack; just fall into it at once.

"Speak of angels," says the old proverb. I cannot say that I had seen any sign of angels in or near Lush Mellish, but Mr. Mower had hardly driven a mile before a policeman on a motor-cycle passed us, and then stopped us.

Mr. Mower looked uncomfortable, but I reassured him. "He may just have noticed that a wheel was wobbling or something."

I was wrong. The constable asked Mr. Mower if he might see his driving licence, and I said he had none with him, but I would take the responsibility. The man came from a village and I had never seen him before.

"I suppose, ma'am, you haven't forgotten yours too," he said, rather disagreeably.

"Save for a mile or so, I have been driving the car, and here is my driving licence," I said, producing it. "Duly signed, as you will see."

"Thank you, ma'am," he said, noting down the particulars. "But you have committed an offence in allowing an unlicensed driver to drive your car."

"I am not unlicensed," Mr. Mower said sturdily. "I can produce the licence within three days."

"Then I'll have to ask for your name and address, sir."

Mr. Mower handed him his card, and the constable said that it would be all right if the licence was produced within three days. He handed me back mine, and drove away. I turned to my companion.

"Silly red-tape," I said. "But I am so glad you were able to make him see reason."

As I said that, I suddenly realised what danger I had been in when I stayed down in Cornwall. Mercifully the police were few there, and not officious. All the time I was there, whether driving on the moorland roads, or sitting near the car, writing letters, or sketching pretty bits of scenery, I had never been approached by a policeman, or asked for my licence.

The most intelligent of us make errors, and I had taken the cottage under my *nom de guerre*, while my licence was, of course, in my own name. Luckily it had been taken out in London, and in that city no one inquires into his neighbour's business.

However, Mr. Mower assured me that the police could take no action against him, so we went home relieved, and I asked him in to sit in the garden for a few minutes before he went back to his lonely inn.

"I wish you would tell me something about your painting," he said, when we were under the copper beech again. "Or is it sketching?"

"I do sketch; just little fanciful things," I told him. "Impressions more than anything else."

"Pen or pencil?" he said.

"Mostly pencil for the impressions in haste," I told him. "Are you fond of art?"

"Rather! Just could kick myself for not taking it up seriously," he replied. "But I am afraid I don't know much about the impressionist method."

"Well, of course," I said, rising from my chair, "I do not claim to be in the front rank, but I can show you a few of my pencil sketches if you like. Look after Tiblits for a few minutes, will you?"

"Rather," he exclaimed. "Tiblits and I are great pals."

In my portfolio I had some sketches of the country round about Lush Mellish, a drawing of my dear cottage, and some bits done years before in Switzerland. Mr. Mower seemed very enthusiastic, and after looking at them all, and saying he had no idea anyone could do so much with so few lines, he wanted to know if I had ever tried a portrait.

Now it did happen that, long ago, I had tried a pastel portrait of my dear master, and I had it in my bedroom. All of us enjoy judicious praise, and as in censorious Lush Mellish one could not take him to see the pastel where it hung, I promised to get it for him, and again went indoors.

On my way I was detained by cook, who wanted to know if the gentleman was staying to dinner. For those she liked or admired, cook was willing to take any amount of trouble. But I was able to assure her that Mr. Mower was not staying that evening; perhaps another day.

I apologised for being so long, when I had returned to my guest. He was looking at one of my Swiss sketches when I rejoined him, and seemed to like it particularly. I offered to give it to him, but he refused to take it.

He admired the pastel, wondered at my versatility, then rose and said he must go.

"Now, I wonder if you would do me another favour?" he asked.

"Perhaps I may," I replied, feeling that we had got much closer to each other during the past few hours.

"Then will you lunch with me to-morrow at the Three Feathers," he said. "Do!"

That hotel was the newest, most expensive and fashionable in Lush Mellish. It was largely patronised by the county, the hunting set and their friends from London. The cuisine was exquisite, and I was, of course, delighted to accept.

I certainly did not let him down next day when we lunched at the Three Feathers and afterwards sat out in the riverside garden. I did not feel out of it, even among the town guests, some of them extremely chic, and I was amused to see even one of the local residents there, lunching with a very dowdy man, and staring at my companion from time to time.

Mr. Mower had the art of looking rightly dressed for whatever occasion. His lounge suit, as I believe men call this form of garment, was well cut, but did not look new. What a great deal there is in wearing clothes that have the apparent charm of newness, yet give you an impression that the wearer has just taken them up at random. There was a smartness and ease about my host that attracted general attention.

Of course, I was proud of him. Here, if blind Lush Mellish had only wanted to see, I thought, was proof positive that I had no need to seek for its wretched male society when I had a cavalier of this type at my disposal.

Mr. Mower had one peculiarity, though I did not think of it as a peculiarity at that time. He would not take anything without returning it in kind. If I asked him to tea, he asked me to tea or lunch, and as he had to pay for our entertainment, I thought it rather reckless of him.

"I should be quite content to stay in my garden and give you tea," I chided him. "Why waste your money on me?"

I remember his smile at that. "Oh, it isn't wasted," he said. "Quite the contrary, Miss Alice. I am getting to know all about you, and what that means to me, I dare not tell you."

I thought at the time that I had never had a nicer compliment paid to me.

Next day I heard nothing from him, and decided just to call at his inn to leave a copy of a book he had admired. The porter told me he had had to go to London by an early train, and would not be back that day.

So I was at a loose end again, and for the first time since Mr. Mower had come, I began to wonder what had been the effect of my last warnings.

They were to be my last. It seemed to me that I must have done some good, for I had been happy during the last few days, and even the wretched old woman next door seemed subdued and unprovocative since Mr. Mower had so wittily described her cat.

Soon I could forget the miserable dolts of police, the venal Chief Constable, his ineffective superintendent, and so-called detective. Their menace would have passed, but the good, at least some of the good, I had done, would have a permanently reforming effect. Lush Mellish had had its lesson, and even those who were too hardened to be improved by kindness had been deterred by fear from continuing their nefarious practices.

Of course, I would not remain in Lush Mellish. The coming of Mr. Mower had filled my mind with other plans, rosy plans perhaps, and castles in Spain.

My unpleasant experiences in the country, you see, had not changed my romantic temperament.

They had, I almost imagine, heightened it.

Curiously enough, on that one day when I was left to my own devices, I had news of at least one result of my efforts.

But you must not imagine that I am in favour of violence in any form, though times do come when children must be chastised, when the velvet glove must be reinforced by the iron hand.

CHAPTER XX

I DID not mean to end the last chapter on such a harsh note. When I spoke of the iron hand, it was metaphorically. Even chastisements should be gentle and not rough, and the person who inflicts the punishment must keep his temper, and moderate his possibly justifiable wrath.

There were a great many minxes in Lush Mellish, as I dare say you realise by now, but one of the most objectionable of them was a girl who was a professional pillionist, as I call it; always rushing about the country on the back of young men's cycles, and exhibiting her silk-clad legs, golden head, and fiercely coloured nails to the scandalised country people.

I had my attention first drawn to her during that disgraceful election. But it was not her part in it which moved me to wrath, only the knowledge that her father was a most respectable tradesman, obviously unaware that his daughter was rushing to ruin.

My duty had been clear enough there, and I had done it. I am sure I had not exaggerated anything. I am equally sure that her father would not have taken the course he did if he had not been convinced of the genuineness of the warning.

It was utterly absurd and mendacious to allege, as they did at the trial, that the young man on whose account her father had savagely thrashed the girl, was her fiancé. No doubt he said so when he found it convenient to do so.

It was equally unfair to blame me for the excuses into which his righteous rage had driven the father. I have always criticised the method of education in this country, and argued that the defects of the tradesman and artisan class are due to a lack of training in calm and restraint in their youth. If they had been taught to take trials, difficulties, unpleasantnesses, and even injuries, in a serene, untroubled spirit, it would have been an immense gain to the country at large.

To show you how grossly unfair and tendentious the evidence at the trial was, I may tell you that I was even blamed for a split in the tradesman's family! Lush Mellish would have blamed me for the prevailing drought that year, if they had found means to do so!

As often happens in these cases, the girl's mother was one of those soft, stupid people, who spoil their children. Mind you, I do not say that the father was free from blame in letting things go as far as they did, and then losing his head. But the mother was to blame for letting her daughter run about loose when she should have been helping in the house, or engaged in the shop.

At any rate, the woman took her daughter's part, actually turned on her husband, and went away for a week to her sister's, taking her daughter with her, and leaving her poor husband to make his own meals. This breach in the family was also put on me. I was told that I had separated husband and wife, when actually dozens of husbands and wives part for a week, and no one thinks anything about it.

This started the bees buzzing again, and I heard that the inspector had been seen coming out of Mr. Mower's hotel.

It occurred to me at once that this was the kind of new hare the Chief Constable *would* start. At his wits' end, and conscious that the whole town was aggrieved at his failure to do anything right, he must have heard that Mr. Mower had become a friend of mine, and plunged in desperation.

You see, it was thought at times that the writer of the letters might be someone who came from outside. That was when they gave up temporarily their idea that I must be the culprit. And here was Mr. Mower, apparently friendless save for me, a stranger, and with no obvious business in the place.

The joke of the thing struck me at once, though I was not anxious for my new friend to be worried or harassed by these nincompoops. Probably they would begin by counting his letters and seeing how many stamps he bought! Indeed, those sold to him might already be secretly marked with tiny crosses. Lush Mellish has no imagination.

Naturally I could not warn him, but on the other hand, since he would not write any letters which could be twisted against him, there was really no need for it.

Tiblits seemed to realise too that morning that he had lost his nice new friend for the time being, and would not keep away from me, but snuggled on to my lap whenever I sat down in the garden.

It was nearly noon when I remembered that I had forgotten to put a note in the book I had left at the inn for Mr. Mower. He was to return next day, and we had not made any arrangement to meet or have a picnic. I did not care to go back to the inn twice in one day, and I could not be sure that he would let me know what he wanted to do when he came back.

He might have felt a sort of diffidence about writing so soon, while I, as a local resident able to offer hospitality, could do it more easily. In any case I was not ashamed then, and did not see why I should be, to let him know that I valued his company and looked forward to our next meeting.

I went indoors hastily for a pad and an envelope, scribbled a short note, and went out to post it at the pillar-box. Two people in the road paused in their walk and looked at me as I posted my letter, but I took no notice of their impertinence now. For all I cared, they could rush off to the Chief Constable, and have the pillar-box cleared at once.

My housemaid told me about the new trouble that afternoon, and cook—who came in later to ask me if I wanted Sauce Tartare with the sole—was able to give me further details. I am afraid neither of them was very sympathetic about the girl. But that is not unusual, and may be explained in more than one way.

"They say her dad got another of them letters, mum," cook told me. "Anyway, the polis are making a fuss about it. Serve the young hussy right! That's what I says."

I shook my head. "I understand what you mean," I replied, "but that kind of excessive violence is likely to defeat its own ends. The man might have exercised greater surveillance over his daughter instead."

"Perhaps you're right, mum," cook admitted. "A bit of surveillance wouldn't do her no harm, I dare say."

"But surely," I went on, "it is not suggested that the poor man received a letter to-day, and thrashed his daughter so savagely at once?"

"Not that I heard, mum," she replied. "What I heard was that he got it some days ago, and started to ask about it before he made up his mind it was true."

Now that was a surprisingly long day. The days just before had passed like a flash, and it seemed ages before it was bedtime. Still, I had something to look forward to. Mr. Mower would be back, and I had suggested a long drive towards Fiksley Glen, where we could have lunch in the hotel, and take a picnic tea on our way home.

I got the car ready early next morning, and the housemaid came out good naturedly and polished the body for me, so that it looked very smart. Both the maids took quite an interest in us, and they are the only people in Lush Mellish for whom I still retain any respect.

The girl even took out the back squab and cleaned it, for when Mr. Mower was in the passenger's seat, I made Tiblits sit at the back, though he often volunteered to take the dear dog on his knee.

Mr. Mower, to my delight, turned up very punctually, and seemed pleased to go. He gave the girl five shillings, and smiled when he saw how helpful she had been.

"Tiblits moulting again?" he said to her delight and amusement. "I can give you a good tip for keeping his coat in condition. But you women always let your dogs get a bit fat," he added to me. "Kind, but unwise."

"The way these hairs get everywhere, sir; seem to creep!" she said, with a giggle, before she went in to get the picnic basket.

"Yes, Tiblits bestows his spare gold very liberally," he laughed. "Not a bit greedy with it."

He did not tell me what he had done in town, and did not appear either to have heard of our latest trouble. But this was the only time he mentioned our great Lush Mellish topic.

"Now what have I done?" he asked, when we were on our way. "A real live copper called on me yesterday. At least, called at my pub. And no less a person than a detective-inspector. Rather a shock to me when I got back. Surely they don't think I may be the Anonymous Terror of Lush Mellish!"

I smiled. "As the French say, Mr. Mower, they are *capable du tout*."

He grinned. "I must take your word for it. Do you think he will call again?"

Suddenly I saw it. My speculations and his joking theory were both at fault. The inspector had simply heard of the incident when I had allowed Mr. Mower to drive my car and we had been held up by the country traffic policeman.

I told him this, and he laughed again. "Gosh! That's better. Of course, that is what it was, and I took the precaution of bringing my driving licence with me from home yesterday."

"I wondered if you would."

He nodded. "I say, I suppose I ought to show it, just to prove that I was the cop's innocent victim?"

"You can go round to the police station when we return," I said. "One has to satisfy these officious jackanapes, I am afraid."

That day was delightful; the last really happy day I spent in Lush Mellish. Mr. Mower was full of fun, and I had to tell him more of Queenie's African stories. He said my way of telling these, as if I did not half believe them, was most artistic.

"What a waste of material, too!" he added. "Dozens of people in the colonies have experiences that would make a dozen books, and they never use 'em. This Miss—"

"Queenie Bostarby," I said. "But she *did* think of it. I expect she imagined I could do it better."

"That's more than likely," he said. "Even your little note to me, which I loved having, by the way, shows what a knack you have for writing."

"Oh, come," I said, smiling. "I don't profess to call my letters literature."

"That may be. You're modest and retiring about them," he returned. "Still, one can tell something of a person, even from their letters."

They gave us an excellent luncheon at the hotel, and then we walked down the glen, and I showed him various birds and country flowers, and things he seemed to know little about; even trout, which were large there, as the fishing was preserved, and stocked.

"The next time I go down into the west I shall take up fishing," he said. "Fancy me coming back in triumph to my hotel with a dozen fat creatures like these! That one you showed me just now was a perfect alderman."

"You won't have such luck there," I said. "Having been brought up in the country, I know something about fish as well as birds. They run small in the West Country; a three-quarter pounder is almost a giant."

"Ah, then I won't fish," he laughed. "I could catch tiddlers in the Round Pond in Kensington Gardens, and save a fare."

I never knew anyone to whom I could talk so freely on such short notice. When we stopped on our way home for our picnic tea, we had turned to favourite books again, and I told him about my old Scottish friend, and how she was a great devotee of Barrie.

"Same here," he said. "*Sentimental Tommy* and *My Lady Nicotine*, anyway."

"You aren't so keen on the others?" I asked. "I like the more romantic ones myself."

"What about *Mary Rose*, the play?" he asked.

"And *The Little Minister* is one of my favourites, too," I told him. "Don't you love it?"

He shook his head smilingly. "Not much, really. Lady Babbie always seemed to me a bit arch, and the minister a bit of a goof."

"You horrid man!" I cried. "Why, those contrasting characteristics seem to me to make the play."

"So you are really sentimental"—he turned to look at me—"and romantic?"

"Why not?" I asked.

"I am afraid I am not," he said. "Stern duty and the rigour of the game for me. Wouldn't think I could be hard-hearted, would you?"

"I know you are not," I said warmly.

"I think I know more of you than you do of me," he replied, almost seriously. "Am I mistaken?"

"I'll tell better when I have known you a little longer," I said, smiling. "You never told me what you are, by the way. But I think I can guess."

He looked at me quizzically. "I think not. You can try, if you like."

"Three guesses," I said. "The first is 'private means.'"

"Wrong! Try again. I'm really one of the world's workers."

I considered. "One of the Services—retired?"

He laughed. "Not military or naval. Last attempt!"

"A barrister, but not practising," I said.

"You are getting warmer, Miss. Alice," he told me, with a curious smile. "I am a solicitor."

"Not a practising one?" I said.

"Yes, of course," he said. "That never occurred to you, did it?"

"No," I replied. "I am rather surprised. What kind of work do you do—conveyancing, and business like that?"

He offered me a cigarette. "All sorts."

"Then I wish you had come here before," I said. "I am sure you would have helped me to discover the wretches who killed my three pets."

He shook his head. "Perhaps I might. I am rather good at that sort of thing."

I had to smile when I thought of it. Mr. Mower did not look the kind of man to tackle that sort of job at all. He seemed too frank, almost ingenuous. His handsome face and sunny disposition did not suggest a keen, remorseless sleuth.

"I know you men all like to pose as hard he-men," I remarked, "but I simply don't believe you. You're too kind-hearted."

"That's a veneer," he laughed. "Will you do me the kindness of dining with me to-night at the hotel where we lunched before?"

I humoured what I thought was his ingenuous anxiety to give cutlet for cutlet. "Thank you very much," I said, "but this must be the last time."

"I am afraid it may be," he said, rather regretfully, I thought. "I did not like to spoil to-day, but I was recalled to London this morning—had an urgent message, I mean. I must leave to-morrow by the first train."

"Really!" I cried. "But you will come back again?"

"Probably," he said, "but I can't fix the date yet. I may be called as a witness at the next assizes."

I know I stared. "At the assizes, Mr. Mower! What is the case?"

"I am not sure yet," he replied. "It may not get as far as that."

"Do let me know when you hear," I said.

"Oh, you'll hear all right," he said.

CHAPTER XXI

I MADE myself specially smart for our last dinner, and felt that I need not fear comparison with any of the other guests. Mr. Mower came in a dinner-jacket; the first time I had seen him in one, and he looked even more handsome and distinguished than usual.

In fact, after a cursory glance round the well-filled dining-room, I had no eyes for anyone else. He looked more serious than usual, so that I imagined I was seeing a new and not unattractive facet of his character.

Most naturally, too, I had an idea that his gravity was partly the result of our coming parting. I wished I could cheer him up openly, tell him that I could easily come up to town, and we might do the galleries and theatres together. But it was not really up to me to make the first advance. He would see for himself that this need be only a temporary break in our delightful friendship.

He half apologised presently for his seriousness, saying that he had a difficult case on his hands, and would have to settle it up when he returned to town.

A good many Londoners, who had no hunting-boxes locally, were staying in the hotel at the time.

There was to be a dance after dinner, and I confess that I looked forward to dancing with my handsome host, who was, I felt sure, as graceful a dancer as he was a charming friend.

We had just finished our coffee when a waiter came to our table with a message for Mr. Mower. He rose, apologised to me, and followed the waiter out of the room.

I lit another cigarette, and glanced about me. Among the smartly dressed women and men at the various tables, my eye fell on a young fellow who wore a badly fitting dinner-jacket and an obviously made-up tie. I seemed at first to remember his face, and then I felt sure that it must be a mistake. He was probably some counter-jumper, who had come into money, and ventured into society without even being aware how to dress correctly.

Mr. Mower was some ten minutes away, and then he came back, and told me that he had to go. "I am sorry, but I have settled with the waiter, and I can't get out of it," he said. "My partner wants to consult me at his own home about that case. I must bolt."

I went home. After all, I told myself bravely, this was only a break—an interlude. I could not expect Mr. Mower to neglect an important case to dangle round me. Then he would come back. Even if I did not see him before the assizes came on, the time would pass. I could go happily on with my interrupted novel.

What a lie it is to say that coming events cast their shadows before! What fools make our proverbs!

Next morning, I wondered when I could write a note to Mr. Mower. There was no reason to lose touch with him, even if he had returned to his office. Then I remembered that he had not given me his address. How foolish of me not to have asked him.

But I cheered up presently. After all, he was a lawyer in London. The town library had many reference books, and I went there and looked up the name. But his name was not to be found. Gloom again; then a saving reflection. Solicitors, more than other people, seem to promote long names not their own. "Slithers, Blow, Jack, Hardy & Ramble" is most likely a one-man firm conducted by a Mr. Nehemiah Smith.

I went home and wrote two notes to people with Mr. Mower's name and Christian name, very discreetly worded. There was no reply to one. From the other man to whom I had written I got a stuffy note of three lines, suggesting that I should keep an address-book. *Boor!*

So I must wait for a letter from Mr. Mower himself. I returned to my suspended novel, but admit that I was distrait, and did not get on very fast with it.

Then a thought occurred to me. There was a lawyer in Lush Mellish who was nominally in charge of my legal affairs. He was a dull, rather stupid man, who had a routine kind of practice, and kept very much to himself. This was all I had wanted from my legal adviser until then. I visited him and asked him if he knew what cases were coming on at the assizes.

"I have a friend, a solicitor, who may be a witness, and I have forgotten his address," I said. "A Mr. Mower."

That man was a fool. Beyond a case of trespass and assault he knew nothing about the cases to come on, and was not even aware that Mr. Mower had been staying at a local inn.

I was frankly disappointed when four days passed without a word from Mr. Mower.

On the fifth day came the dreadful blow; the culmination of all my troubles in Lush Mellish, and of the ruffianly campaign to drive me ignominiously from the town.

I was sitting in my drawing-room that afternoon, when a car drove up to the front door, and a moment afterwards, the house-maid told me that the inspector wished to see me. I told her to show him in, and he came in, looking like a funeral mute, and as restless as that hateful woman's black cat next door.

Then the blow fell, and for a few moments I was staggered and unable to speak. He had come to arrest me. *Me!* He gave me what he called a warning, and then read out what he called a charge, and wound up by suggesting that I should come quietly with him in a car he had brought.

That I should come quietly! Even at that terrible moment I had to laugh. Did he think I was a thug, or a rough, or a murderer, liable to resist arrest.

"Of course I will come," I told him, "and you shall hear more of this impertinent outrage; you and your Chief Constable, my man! But I hope you are not suggesting that I should come as I am."

"I will ring for your maid, mum, and get her to bring your things," he said.

"You will do nothing of the sort," I told him. "You will wait here while I go to change."

The charge was one of defamatory libel! Did he think I was likely to run away, or commit suicide in my bedroom? But the impertinent man said he had his instructions, and in the end, my hat and coat were brought down to me, and I put them on, and went in the car to the police station, where I interviewed the superintendent.

Of course, I gave him my frank opinion of his conduct, refused to make a statement, and demanded that my solicitor should be sent for. He was a poor stick, but at least he would know my rights.

When he came I had a short talk with him alone, and told him that I wished him to get in touch with Mr. Mower at once, to defend me.

"You are pleading not guilty, of course," he said.

"Of course," I replied, "but I want you to get Mr. Mower."

He did not seem to know what to say, and I reminded him that I was paying expenses. Surely it would not be difficult for him to get a clerk sent up to London to trace my friend.

"Well—er—" he said rather put about, "it may be difficult. I should have thought, Miss Alice, that you would have known his address."

"He only came recently here for a short stay," I told him. "He found my spaniel when it was lost, and came to see me."

I never saw the man so foolishly nervous as he was at that moment. "Where did he stay, Miss Alice?"

I told him, and added:—"That reminds me. Possibly they have his address at the inn where he stayed."

"He called himself Mr. Mower?" said my lawyer. "You are sure you have not made a mistake? I mean to say, it wasn't 'Power,' was it?"

I laughed. "Of course not."

"Was he a tall, fair man; rather good-looking?"

"Most distinguished-looking," I said impatiently; "but what has that got to do with it?"

I really began to wonder if the lawyer had not lost his reason. He shuffled his feet, grew very red in the face, and blurted out: "It must be Power. Someone told me this morning that they had got down a man called Power to investigate this—well, to put it briefly, in connection with this charge, Miss Alice."

I am afraid I lost my temper with him. "Don't be a fool!" I said. "My friend isn't a detective, he's a solicitor."

"Mr. Power is a solicitor," he said, redder than ever. "In fact, he did so well in a case he took up somewhere in the country that he rather specialises in criminal investigation—so they say. Rather like the man who did such marvels in that arson case some time ago."

I was furious. "I tell you Mr. Mower is nothing of the sort! He brought my dog back to me, and—"

"Just a moment," he said apologetically. "I don't have much to do with the affairs of Lush Mellish after business hours, Miss Alice, but I can't help hearing at times of certain incidents which—er—suggest—"

"Suggest what?" I snapped, as he paused.

"Your dog; your spaniel for instance," he went on nervously. "Were you troubled with dogs in your garden after that—er—loss?"

"I was, for a little. Why?"

"I—er—heard something about aniseed—didn't give much credence to it at the time, I'm afraid."

He must be mad. *Aniseed?* I said.

"Oil of aniseed, you know. It's attractive to dogs. That is to say, a few drops sprinkled in your garden—"

"Just a moment," I interrupted. "What have the dogs in my garden to do with the charge?"

He bit his lip. "Well, it just occurred to me, in the light of my present knowledge, so to speak, that someone might have attracted your dog away by means of a trail of aniseed."

"And then?"

"Well, I have an idea it may have been this Mower—Power. He took the dog, returned it . . . established confidence, so to speak, and—"

"Just listen to me," I said, for I saw that it was useless to reason with him. "You will get Mr. Mower's address, write, or telephone, to him, and tell him that I am anxious to have him defend me at the—"

"Before the magistrates, perhaps to-morrow," said the lawyer.

"Whenever it may be," I said firmly. "Then you will arrange for bail—"

"I am not so sure that they will grant it," he said in a tone of distress, "but I'll try my best."

"Nonsense!" I said. "I am not guilty, and I must have bail."

"You can't even apply for it yet," he said. "If the magistrates—" he faltered, and went on—"if they see fit to return you for trial to the assizes, I shall see what I can do."

"Mr. Mower is to be a witness in a case then. I told you that."

"You did. I remember. Well, I will do what I can. In the meantime, may I ask if you told—confided, that is to say, if you gave anything away to this Power—Mower?"

"What had I to give away?" I asked scornfully. "Mr. Mower and I were friends. I certainly did not regale him with titbits of local scandal, if that's what you mean."

"I am glad," he said. "I shall have to prepare your defence, I suppose. By the way, did this Mr. Mower know your neighbour—a lady with an—er—cat?"

I laughed. "I knew you were wrong," I said, and told him about the passage at arms over the fence. "But why do you ask?"

"Well, that was some of the gossip I heard this morning too, Miss Alice. There was a hint that he had been brought down by one of the complainants—the lady of whom I have spoken. Of course, it is on the cards that a clever fellow like this Power would pretend not to recognise her."

"My friend would not act in that underhand way," I said coldly.

He looked worried. "Very well. I will do what I can to get him. But here is the superintendent again, with his note-taker. He may want you to make a statement."

I refused categorically to make a statement. I was innocent, and I would plead "Not Guilty."

For fear you may read this, and think that I am flying in the face of facts, I must say that that idea is based on a misconception. I was to be prosecuted on a charge of *maliciously and falsely* libelling people. You have already observed that neither malice nor falsity had any part in my campaign, so, if I took their technical view and pleaded "Guilty," I should have been both guilty of *lying* and false to myself.

I need hardly labour the point for any intelligent reader.

Then I was horrified to learn that I could not go home that night. The bench of magistrates would sit next morning at a special court, and my lawyer either could, or would, do nothing to help me. I then asked that dear Tiblits should share my solitude. It was refused me. Lush Mellish came out openly in its hateful, brutal colours at last!

The evidence against me at the sitting next day was based on what the police called "Information received." Among the absurd pieces of "evidence" put in was an envelope, with a tiny fragment of golden hair still adhering to the gum! These savages were anxious to involve not only me but my innocent dog! My lawyer naturally remarked that Tiblits was not the only golden-haired dog in the world; also he stressed the fact that someone might have taken a hair from the dog—who had strayed one night—and endeavoured to incriminate me.

The superintendent replied that the letter had been received some time before the dog strayed, and other evidence of a most unconvincing kind was brought to show that I had been maliciously disposed towards a good many of those who were the complainants.

My lawyer made a good point there. He remarked dryly that people who complain of malice shown them are often maliciously disposed themselves. He added that he had proof that some of the complainants had induced the defendant to stand for a town council election, with the open and avowed purpose of bringing her into contempt. Was it not likely that they had planned to carry their campaign a step further by getting the object of their ill-will involved in a case of this kind?

"People who write anonymous letters," he added, "often address some missives to themselves. Miss Alice has not had anonymous letters addressed to her. Some of the complainants have admittedly received such missives."

But it was all in vain. The magistrates, while they must have been shaken by my steadfast bearing and the arguments of my lawyer, did not care to take the responsibility of discharging me. They returned me for trial at the assizes, and then came the struggle for bail.

It was touch-and-go, my lawyer said afterwards, but I was admitted to bail in two sureties of five hundred pounds each, and my own bail of a thousand pounds.

I was furious but undaunted. Then came the greatest blow of all. It was in the form of a letter from my false friend, that swinish hypocrite who had called himself Mower.

"DEAR MADAM,
"I am unable to undertake your defence, even if I felt anxious to do so. I am representing one of the complainants in the case.
"Yours faithfully,
WM. POWER."

"Yours faithfully"—*Faithfully!* What more ill-fitting word could that Machiavellian scoundrel have used than that?

But I did not break down. I was now more than ever determined to fight, to show that loathsome reptile that his underhand methods could not succeed. He had wormed his way into my house by stealing my dog; he had wormed his way into my confidence, but he had not heard anything from me which could help him to prove his case.

What instinct was it that had preserved me from telling him about my drives in Cornwall, the cottage where I had written my warnings, my earlier car, with that cunning little hiding-place in the rumble? Let that unworthy creature, who was not to be called a man, do his worst!

Tiblits was my only consolation then. I did not sit in the garden, for the old woman was abroad in hers at all hours, and wore a silly grin, as she carried her cat about, or encouraged it to walk on the fence.

My lawyer proved better than I thought he was, and did his best—hampered, of course, by the police ruffians—to get information as to the lines on which the prosecution would proceed. But they would not disclose everything, and he said there were certain things he could not legally ask for.

One afternoon, wearing a rather worried look, he came to tea with me, and asked me if I was prepared to spend a large sum for my defence.

"You see, Miss Alice, nothing but the best is good enough for us in a case like this. The prosecution has something up its sleeve, and has, I hear, collected a mass of evidence. They will most likely be represented by the famous J. Oviller, K.C., a most searching examiner, and a perfect terror to witnesses. I have tentatively approached Mr. Henry Chavel, K.C."

"Is he good?" I said.

"He is the best defender in the country," was the reply. "Juries seem to fall for him at once. I do not say that he is a brilliant lawyer. I do say that his combination of flattery and what they call 'human touch' has a marvellous effect on juries."

"Very well. Let us have him, if he will take the case," I said. "I have my all at stake. I am not only hounded by the law, but was subject to a sneaking, underhand, unmanly form of spying. I trust that, when the case comes on, Mr. Chavel will give that loathsome Power the scathing treatment he deserves."

My lawyer nodded. "If you will let me use your telephone, I will ring up his chambers, and see what he thinks of it."

"Do," I said, "and accept his terms, whatever they are."

He returned presently to me. "Good!" he said, beaming. "Mr. Chavel will represent us, and that is fifty per cent on our case to start with. But he will want to see you in town. You must tell him the whole story, and then he will know what line to take."

"When will this be?" I asked.

"To-morrow. He is a friend of my brother-in-law, and has consented to see us at his private house after dinner. We can travel up in the afternoon, and perhaps you will dine with me somewhere before we go on."

"Thank you," I said; "but will these fools here let me leave, even for a day?"

"I shall see to that," said my lawyer. "You will be with me."

CHAPTER XXII

IT MUST have been that gift of intuition again that made me feel that Mr. Chavel was more of a façade than a genius. He looked so like the famous pleader in a stage play that I could not believe in his real ability. That was to be my verdict in the end, too.

He wore a black ribbon round his neck, on which was hung a pair of pince-nez, which he swung from time to time in the conventional fashion. He was tall and handsome, with white hair and fine eyes, and one of those legal chins that you see on the films. I did not think that a great lawyer could look so like his part, if you know what I mean.

I was right. He might have got away with silly women, or fatuous juries. No doubt he did. But he let me down very badly, and had not the courage and tenacity that a case like mine required.

The lawyer and I dined at a quiet hotel, and reached Mr. Chavel's large house at Pelham Gate shortly after nine. We were taken by his butler into a spacious study, where the great man received us with a dramatic suavity.

"You will take coffee?" he asked, and gave an order to the butler. "You smoke, Miss Alice?" He passed me a box with three compartments, Egyptian, Turkish, Virginian. "A cigar, Layman?"

"Virginian, please," I said.

He smiled. "The smoke of common sense, Miss Alice. You prefer the Partagas, Layman? Mr. Layman, Miss Alice, is a good judge. He will be the greatest help to you—to us both."

He burbled on while we lit up, and the butler came in with the coffee. When the man had closed the door behind him, and gone away, he looked at me, smiled, put down his cigar, put on his pince-nez, removed them again, and put a question.

"Do you know anything about fishing?"

"To a certain extent, yes," I said, wondering when this amiable fooling was going to come to an end.

"Then you are aware that one uses a gut cast at the end of the line, and, if one is wise, tests it before venturing to cast. I knew a man once who did not. He was afraid he would break the cast by testing it. A—er—salmon broke that cast."

"I see," I said. "He lost more than he gained."

"You take my point exactly. It has some relevance to your case, and to the procedure in regard to it that I propose to adopt," he smiled. "That is, with your countenance and collaboration, but with a difference. In court you will be faced, not by a friend, but by counsel who will not spare your feelings, or hesitate to ask you questions which may be at once painful and dangerous to you."

"Go on!" I said rather impatiently.

"Mr. Layman here," he continued, "has been very successful in getting our friend the enemy to give him some details of the case against you. Remarkably successful, I may say. I congratulate him. Then I have read the account of the proceedings before the magistrates."

They seemed anxious to congratulate each other. "Yes," I said.

"In short," Mr. Chavel went on, "I propose to ask you questions with regard to your acquaintance with Mr. Power, to see if I can adduce from them any notion of the information he received from you—drew from you, shall I say?"

"I told him nothing," I said.

He smiled. "Power is, I imagine, a brilliant fellow—a man of brains."

"He is an oily scoundrel!" I cried.

Mr. Chavel put up his pince-nez. "Our views on such points are naturally relative and partial. But we must not underrate our opponents, Miss Alice. So far, the prosecution has not sufficient evidence, on the face of it, to convince a trained legal mind. On the face of it, I say advisedly, for the Public Prosecutor has apparently arranged that the case should come on. Obviously, there is some evidence as yet undisclosed to Mr. Layman and myself."

"Then I don't know how they got it," I said.

"Ah, that is another affair. If you had my experience in these matters, you would know that a witness in court, under examination, is often quite unaware that he is giving his case away all the time. The questions put to him are so framed that he is not always aware of their purport."

"And that is called justice?"

"We may leave that question aside, Miss Alice. We must face things as they are, and for a time you enjoyed the apparent friendship of a young man with great legal ability."

"*Enjoyed* his friendship?" I cried.

"At the time, Miss Alice, at the time," he said; "before he was discovered to be a serpent in your Eden. Later on, if you can search your memory, and tell me something about your chats with Mr. Power, I may be able to see what notions he may have drawn from your conversations. We must know something about this ace, you know; something of the surprise we fear the enemy will spring on us."

Mr. Layman, of course, bolstering up his fellow lawyer, said that that was essential. Mr. Chavel made a few more passes with his pince-nez, took my coffee-cup, offered me another cigarette, and sat down again.

"Let me see," he beamed. "As far as I can gather, the first suspicions about you—quite unsubstantiated, of course—seem to have arisen when you purchased ten shillings worth of stamps. Is that not so, Layman?"

"That is so, Chavel. I suppose the post office people had been told to be on the alert, and they noted that Miss Alice usually purchased a two-shilling book."

"Just so. I presume that they were keeping watch on a good many people, but that purchase, coupled with the posting of a mass of correspondence the same day, led to the regular clearing of the pillarbox in the road where Miss Alice lives. But I understand that none of these letters was other than harmless."

"Quite. Quite harmless," said Layman. "There was, however, another factor that they thought suspicious. I have a shrewd notion that the idea came from Power, later. He, or someone, seems to have suggested that Miss Alice suspected that she was being watched, and was having a game with the postal authorities in consequence."

"Ah, he's a clever fellow!" said Mr. Chavel, but added hastily: "Like so many clever fellows, he over-reached himself. Over-subtlety is a danger. Here, he argued, is a clever, intelligent woman. She will not write letters to herself; she will believe this a factor in her favour. Did you say that certain postage stamps were secretly marked, Layman?"

"So I hear. They were, of course, traced to letters, which were quite innocent epistles, Chavel. Great efforts were made to trace the paper used, and the machine too, but in vain. It was thought locally that a well-to-do woman would use cheap paper as a bluff, but the paper used was of the finest quality."

"Well, well," Mr. Chavel said as cheerfully as ever. "There was nothing but rather absurd suspicion, no proof, no evidence that a child would accept. Was there nothing but a vague prejudice against a newcomer in the minds of these Lush Mellish donkeys, do you think?"

"I gathered," Mr. Layman observed, "that one factor was the receipt of these missives by people who had offended, or been offended by, my client. That seems to have been their chief justification."

Mr. Chavel went on with his play-acting, but I could not interfere, as there was hardly time to get another counsel.

"After some fruitless investigation, Layman, the idea of Miss Alice's guilt was, if not abandoned, at least put aside for a time?"

"They found no evidence. Yes."

"And then an old lady, resident in a house next to Miss Alice, seems to have heard of this fellow Power, and wondered if she could get him to investigate for her? I see. It seems strange to employ a solicitor in a business of this kind, but I believe he did do something of the kind before. What was the old lady's complaint?"

"The receipt of an anonymous letter libelling her nephew, I hear."

"I see. She managed to get Power to take up the affair for her, and at his suggestion, he came down under another name—"

"As Mr. Mower," I said. "They ought to prosecute him for that."

"His ruse was possibly not cricket, Miss Alice, but it is also not actionable," observed Mr. Chavel. "If you don't mind, we shall not debate his moral responsibility in the matter, but just go forward with our analysis. Speaking generally, I see that Miss Alice's pet dogs had a good deal to do with the case. There was one, a cocker—"

"A golden spaniel," I corrected him. The fool of a man could not apparently distinguish between one dog and another.

"I stand corrected," he said with a bow. "A golden spaniel."

"Which that scoundrel stole, and returned to me," I said.

"Um—er—stealing in hope of a reward is a crime, Miss Alice, but his action, while underhand, would be a dubious cause for legal proceedings. One might make a point of it at the trial, with a view to discrediting the witness, but I should not advise it. He would not be forced to answer questions incriminating himself, and unless you have proof that he did steal the dog—"

"There was talk of aniseed," said Mr. Layman.

"Talk of aniseed, and no doubt aniseed itself! But we have no proof that Power bought or used the drug; granted that it was used by someone. A golden spaniel, a valuable dog, might be the object of some dog-stealer. How can we prove that one such did not entice the dog away with drops of the fluid, but did not succeed in catching the strayed dog? I think that would hardly help us."

"At any rate," said my lawyer, "Power did return the dog, and so ingratiated himself with Miss Alice here. It was a natural and grateful impulse to ask the young man in to sit for a little. He was not of the class to take a monetary reward."

"Ah," said Mr. Chavel, beaming at me again, "Miss Alice is generous, impulsive. We are often tripped up by our most agreeable qualities. Now let us see what happened. Mr. Power found himself *persona grata* with our client. He went to her house for tea, he asked her to lunch and to dine. He was driven by her in her car to certain picnics. Did you gather, from information supplied by you from the other side, that he abducted the dog for a specific purpose, other than ingratiating himself with its fond mistress?"

"Yes. It appeared that copies of the anonymous letters in the original envelopes were examined by him. Either because the police were careless, or insufficiently skilled, they had not noticed that under the gummed flap of one envelope, which had been slit open, there was a portion of a dog's hair. I understand that this was submitted, with a hair or two from Miss Alice's pet, to a scientific investigation, and it was decided that the hairs were identical."

I simply had to interrupt there. "If that is science, Mr. Layman, I do not understand the word! Hairs from golden spaniels are all the same. And even if it was a hair from my dog, what was there to prevent anyone from getting a hair? He often rubs himself on my gate-post, for example."

"An excellent point, and very well-reasoned," observed Mr. Chavel, and this was the first sensible observation I had heard him make. "We will make a note of that, Layman."

"You would think I was a murderess, the way these people have pursued and persecuted me!" I said indignantly.

Mr. Chavel smiled. "It is my experience, in this country at least, that there is great sympathy for murderers and murderesses; naturally, of course, where one is not a relative of the victim. People are stirred to the depths by the idea of the murderer suffering, but the victim is forgotten even before he is buried. We reserve our vindictiveness for pettier crimes."

Mr. Layman laughed. "Very true. But now, Chavel, I think you wanted to go over the ground with Miss Alice, following her meeting with Mr. Power. He showed great interest in the dog, and was subsequently invited to tea."

"Yes," I said. "We talked of authors. I really had the impression at first that he was a writer. He asked me if I wrote, and I told him I had started a novel."

Chavel nodded. "Did he ask to look at it? I have an idea that, in the first case he unravelled, there were some revealing points in a novel."

"You see, Miss Alice," said my lawyer, when I was puzzled by this remark, "people often, possibly unconsciously, use their own experiences for a first novel. He may have hoped that you gave something away."

"He certainly asked if he might see what I had done, and I showed it to him," I replied. "But it was not a realistic novel. When he was—or rather before he read it, the woman next door appeared with her cat, and Mr. Power made some cutting remark at her expense, or the cat's. I felt sure that he was on my side."

"Ah, he's very—very sly," said Mr. Chavel. "But what followed when he had read your manuscript?"

"He wondered if I found my inspiration in the country, or was like a friend of his, who could only write in town. I told him I preferred the country and its quiet."

Chavel swung his pince-nez, and looked at Mr. Layman, then turned to me. "You were doing your novel on a typewriter; what make?"

I told him, and he nodded. "I see. The letters, on the other hand, appear to have been done on a Cremona portable. I assume, Layman, that Power imagined that the letters were not written in Lush Mellish, but may have been in London or the country."

"I think so," said Mr. Layman. "If he imagined Miss Alice to be the culprit, he wanted to know where the typing was actually done."

"Another cigar, Layman?" said Mr. Chavel, and passed the box of cigarettes again to me. "Where it was actually done. Yes. Very clev—I mean to say, it falls in with what we have heard of his—ah—underhand methods. A dangerous fellow to come up against—Power."

CHAPTER XXIII

EVEN that night I could not help feeling doubts of Mr. Chavel's sincerity. I was to realise it later at the trial, when he walked out laughing and joking with the savage who conducted the prosecution. His professional admiration for sharp practices blinded him to the evil character of Power.

"It is rather a strain on your memory," he went on, "but can you remember what followed that fishing inquiry?"

Of course I could. I had thought the man my friend, and have no shame in admitting that in my innocence, in my ignorance of his character and aims, I had treasured every word he said.

"Yes, he represented himself to be a new motorist, and asked me if I drove. He said he knew Cumberland very well, and I took it that he came from the north originally. He wanted to see my car, and took an interest in the speedometer, which he said often flattered."

"Just a moment, please, Miss Alice," Mr. Chavel interrupted. "He took an interest in your speedometer? I think it is the last thing one looks at in a friend's car. What do you say, Layman?"

Layman nodded. "Quite. But if he took an interest in it, it means something. Now, what?"

Mr. Chavel reflected, puffing at his cigar, and looking wise. "Ha!" he said at last. "The speedometer is also a mileometer, isn't it? Registers the distance we go. Is it possible that Mr. Power was trying to discover if Miss Alice here made long journeys?"

"Excuse me," I said, "that could have told him nothing. It was practically a new car, and had not done many miles."

"Then the meaning of the manoeuvre eludes me," said Mr. Chavel. "Go on, please."

"After that," I told him, "he asked me if she was a good hill-climber."

"Ah, that's a common enough question," he commented. "A lot of this country is flat—round about Lush Mellish it is pretty flat, I think."

I did not understand what he was talking about, so continued. "We talked about hills, and I told him I had not driven in Cumberland. He spoke about the beauties of South Wales, and I told him I had never driven there."

"A process of elimination, Chavel," said my lawyer. "H'm. It has that appearance."

"I said I rather liked moors and heather," I went on, rather exasperated at their meaningless asides, "and he asked me—now what was it? Oh, I know; if I liked Derbyshire and Yorkshire. I said I had never been to either, and—"

"Excuse me," said Mr. Chavel, "it seems to me that he mentioned most of the English counties which are hilly and have moorland in some quantity. Let me see. There must be two or three more."

Mr. Layman put down his cigar. "Westmorland, Durham, and Northumberland," he murmured. "Decidedly."

Mr. Chavel put on his pince-nez. "Of course. Just a moment, Layman, while I look up my atlas."

"He never asked me about Westmorland," I told Mr. Layman, while the other man got out an atlas. "And what does it mean, anyway?"

Mr. Layman raised his eyebrows. "Rather like a game of animal, vegetable, or mineral, Miss Alice. Power seems to have been trying, by a process of elimination, to discover if you visited some particular part of England."

"Ah, I have refreshed my memory, and here we are!" said Mr. Chavel suddenly. "Roughly, Power mentioned all the hilly, moorland counties in England, save Cornwall and Devon."

"He asked me about Devon," I said; "then he talked about hill-climbing, and I said I had once climbed a hill supposed to have a gradient of one in five."

"You have heard of a brochure called 'Steep hills in England and Wales'—issued by one of the motoring organisations?" Mr. Layman asked me.

"No," I said. "Why?"

"Well, hills of the grade you mention are not very common," he replied. "One could trace some of the notable ones in that pamphlet, I think."

Mr. Chavel smiled. "Child's play, Layman! Your recollections are most informative, Miss Alice. Pray go on."

I have always boasted an excellent memory, and it was strange how, at this moment, every detail of my talks with that deceitful ruffian stood up clearly in my mind, and with it the sad realisation that he had found such an easy prey in my own unsuspicious, susceptible, and sensitive character.

"I remember he went on to talk of the country," I said; "he professed to know very little about it, not even about birds, or fish, or flowers. I shall never forget that part of it; for he made what seemed to me an absurd mistake for a clever, intelligent man—as at that time I took him to be—to perpetrate."

"What was that?"

"I said I had seen buzzards, and he said they used to be caught on Salisbury Plain, were good eating, but now extinct."

"I must consult my encyclopedia," Mr. Chavel murmured, and Mr. Layman looked at me, and put a question: "He probably meant bustards?"

"So he said," I returned, "though how he—"

Mr. Chavel had come back with a volume, and interrupted me. "But—Buv—Bux—Buz—Ah, here we are! Buzzard. Just a moment, please. Bird of prey of the falcon species—habitat—Ah, here we are! That accounts for South Wales—and North. Solitary places, hills, moorland. Here we are again! Devon and Cornwall. Thank you, Miss Alice. Did he ask you about any other birds?"

"I told him about the dipper—the water-ousel."

"No need to get your encyclopedia, Chavel," said Mr. Layman. "I can tell you about the water-ousel. It is often seen on moorland streams."

"I said I had seen ravens, too," I remarked.

This time Mr. Chavel had to get his encylopedia, and murmured once more: "Bird allied to the crow—hills, cliffs, moors."

"Animal, vegetable, or mineral?" Mr. Layman murmured again.

"Like plotting a position," said Mr. Chavel, beaming foolishly. "Draw a line which crosses moors and hills, intersecting ravens, buzzards and water-ousels, and there you are."

"What do you mean?" I said impatiently.

He looked more sober at that. "Well, evidently this fellow Power suspected you of visiting some remote place, and writing these epistles from it, Miss Alice. By fixing characteristic scenery, he could select some counties; by eliminating some counties, he could narrow the field to one or two. Left with one or two counties, and postulating moorland, hills, and streams, he would narrow the field still further by inquiries about the local flora and fauna."

"Grouse in the north, of course, but not in the south-west," said Mr. Layman.

"He mentioned grouse," I said.

"He would!" Mr. Layman agreed.

"He comes, at last, to a conjunction of buzzards, water-ousels, and ravens," Mr. Chavel remarked. "I see from my encyclopedia that that is a conjunction which might occur in several counties."

"With a gradient of one in five?" said Mr. Layman.

"As heather grows on high land," Mr. Chavel observed. "Yes, but we can cut out the counties in which Miss Alice says she never drove. I must say, Layman, that, had I been in Power's place, I should have plumped for Devon or Cornwall."

"I think I should have done the same," said Mr. Layman.

They both looked at me, but I did not reply. After all, they were no more acute than other men, though they thought they were, and I was not at all sure that either of them would understand the great difference between action with malice and action directed by good intentions.

As I did not speak, Mr. Chavel suggested that I should go on.

"I think I invited Mr. Power to come for a drive," I said. "We were to have a picnic. Yes, I am sure that came next. I told him about a friend of mine, from Rhodesia, who had stayed with me. She told me a lot of stories about animals and natives, and Mr. Power was much interested. She left to go back to Africa some time ago."

Mr. Chavel frowned. "I don't see the point of that, but go on," he said. "Had the drive any further significance?"

"No possible connection with the case," I told him, "but we were held up by a traffic policeman on our way home. I had let Mr. Power drive, and he had no licence with him. So the police-man asked for mine."

"But you were not driving the car? Were you proceeded against?"

"No; nor was Mr. Power."

"I wonder—" Mr. Layman began.

"Just a moment!" Chavel interrupted. "Let me see. Miss Alice's car speedometer showed that she had travelled x miles; not very many, on her admission. That might account for Power's interest in it, eh?"

"Jove, yes!" Mr. Layman cried. "Exactly what, I wondered."

"While the date of the licence—" Mr. Chavel began, when I cut him short.

"I am sure you gentlemen are being very clever," I said iron-ically, "but as I am chiefly concerned, I shall be glad if you will tell me clearly what all this means."

Mr. Chavel bowed. "Certainly. Layman here and I—having regard to Mr. Power's—Mr. Power's slyness, shall we say?—are wondering if he did not arrange for a policeman to see your licence, and get the date, without arousing your suspicions. You spoke to him of driving a good deal, and in country unlike that round Lush Mellish. Knowing the mileage recorded on your car, he may have—er—postulated the ownership of a previous car."

"And what of that?" I asked.

"Nothing, as far as we are concerned," said Mr. Chavel, "but he had already come to the conclusion that you had visited Devon or Cornwall by car, and was hoping to get something from that."

Mr. Layman nodded. "That was obviously his aim." They smiled at each other, though what they had to smile at, I do not know. Then Mr. Chavel asked me to proceed. "He visited your house again. What happened on that occasion?"

"Nothing, I am sure, which could have given Mr. Power the idea that I had written the letters," I said. "We talked about art, and I showed him some pencil sketches I had made in various places. Then I mentioned the fact that I had once done an excellent pastel portrait, and brought it down from my bedroom for him to see. He admired it, and left, after asking me to lunch with him next day at the Three Feathers Hotel."

"Apparently an unprofitable séance for him," Mr. Chavel murmured. "But these sketches now. Any subject you had done in—ah—Devon or Cornwall?"

"Only a sketch of a—a cottage in Cornwall," I said, "but I did not tell him where it was."

Mr. Layman sat up, and Mr. Chavel ran his finger over his chin. "You left him for a short time to get the pastel?"

"Yes, but not for long, though my cook did detain me for a few minutes on the way. He was looking at a Swiss sketch when I returned, and the sketch of the cottage had not been taken, if that is what you suggest."

"I should like to examine it, if you will forward it to me," said Mr. Chavel. "There is just the possibility—faint, though not impossible where a keen investigator like Power is concerned—that he seized the opportunity afforded by your absence to *trace* the sketch roughly. In that event your sketch would show faint indentations made by his pencil."

Do you know that he was right? Mr. Layman showed me this under a magnifying glass next day. But at the time I could not believe it.

"It sounds incredible," I told him. "Mr. Power went to London the next day and, as we had not made any arrangement to meet again, I wrote a note and sent it to his hotel by post."

Mr. Layman held up his hand. "Power sent that note to the local police. They say that there was a portion of a dog's golden hair stuck to the gum of the envelope, as on a former occasion."

"There may have been," I said. "It is a pure coincidence. Mr. Power will have to take a census of all the golden spaniels in the country, and then interrogate all their owners!"

"Ha, ha!" Mr. Chavel laughed. "Very good, that. Now we come to the day when Mr. Power returned from London. You lunched at a country hotel. Had Power's interest in art waned by that time?"

"We talked of books and plays," I said.

"Already," said Mr. Chavel, swinging his pince-nez maddeningly, "I see that Power generally turned the subject to something he thought would help him. Astonishingly relevant so far."

"Very much so," Mr. Layman remarked. "He appears to have gone straight to the point every time."

"Not 'straight,' Miss Alice would remind us," Chavel observed, with a smile at me. "Let us say, wasted no time on unproductive subjects. Plays and books? Now I wonder what that portended? Any particular play or book, Miss Alice?"

I considered. "Several," I said. "I think I mentioned my fondness for Barrie. My own novel, you see, was to be a fantasy."

Mr. Chavel shook his head. "I am in deep waters. Barrie? Does that name convey anything to you in this connection, Layman?"

"None, Chavel. May we have the substance of the conversation, as far as you can remember it?" he added to me.

I did my best, and they both shook their heads. *"Mary Rose?"* said Mr. Layman.

"The Little Minister?" Mr. Chavel murmured, and then they both shook their heads.

"We hardly discussed either," I said ironically, "so you are not likely to find anything significant in that."

"I am not so sure," Mr. Chavel replied. "By no means so sure. What did you say about *Mary Rose*?"

"I merely mentioned it," I returned. "As to the other play, Mr. Power did not like it very much. He thought Lady Babbie too arch."

"So it ended there?"

"Yes."

Mr. Chavel turned to Mr. Layman. "Make a note of that, please. We may see the relevance later."

I am aware that lawyers are adept in the art of making bricks without straw, but this seemed to me too absurd. "Even Mr. Power had to be honest and ordinary *at times*," I remarked acidly. "He asked me to dine the same night at the Three Feathers Hotel. He said he had been recalled to London, and might not be back again till the assizes."

Mr. Chavel beamed. "Extraordinary! That man Power"— here he caught my eye and had the grace to blush, for it was obvious again that even unscrupulous methods won his admiration if they were clever—"that man has no conscience!"

"But he seems to hold the cards, which is more important to us!" said Mr. Layman.

CHAPTER XXIV

WHEN you are dealing with people who have no fixed principles, and refuse to be bounded by the ordinary limits of decent conduct, it is useless to argue with them. Where there are no rules there is no argument.

But these two men, who had with difficulty hidden their admiration for the tricks, ruses, and underhand practices of the scoundrel Power, were the only two people on whom I could rely—on whom I had to rely.

So I had to put up with them, and a sorry business they made of it.

Mr. Chavel began again. "What took place at that hotel dinner?"

I told him how Mr. Power had been called out by a waiter, and had left after dinner. He said his partner wished to consult him about a case. I have not seen him since.

"Well," said Mr. Chavel, after a short pause, "I congratulate you on your memory, Miss Alice. There are one or two points about what we have heard which we must try to clear up—the significance of Barrie's plays, and Power's interest in your friend's African stories, for example—but generally, we can see how the fellow arrived at certain conclusions. I think I have you with me there, Layman?"

"Quite, Chavel, quite," replied my sycophantic lawyer. "We must try to screw a bit more out of the prosecution, and settle the questions you raise, though, indeed, one answer may do for both questions. We have an idea of the evidence we have to meet, but we do not know yet what explanation Miss Alice can furnish us for certain circumstances, from the actual facts."

It struck me at the time that those two men were a pair of nodding mandarins. Mr. Chavel nodded back, put up his pince-nez, and this time kept them on for five minutes on end.

"I was just going to suggest it," he said.

"Suggest what?" I demanded impatiently.

"Well, we are in the position of knowing more or less accurately what Power thinks you did. When we know what you did, we can decide on what to concentrate in rebuttal, and on what to concede a point, or slur it over."

"This may be clear to lawyers," I said, "but what does it mean?"

Mr. Chavel arched his eyebrows. "Your way of going straight to the point is wholly admirable, and makes the task of explaining to you much easier," he observed. "Let us begin with the possibility that a question is put to you by the prosecution. Say, that you are asked if you ever had a cottage in Cornwall. The question for the defence is: does the prosecution know that this was so? We are definitely unable to answer that question. Our defence may be based on the assumption that you have: (1) Never gone to Cornwall since you came to live in Lush Mellish. (2) That you have been in Cornwall since then, but did not live in a cottage. (3) That you have never been in Cornwall, and so had no residence, great or little, in the county."

I pondered rather anxiously. After all, these men were my legal advisers and I had to tell them something. Then Mr. Layman had undoubtedly heard from the other side, and the fact that I had been in Cornwall might be known to them. I decided to admit the cottage.

"Why, of course," I said. "But I do not see that a stay in a Cornish cottage is in any way relevant to the trumped-up case against me."

"It is just that trumped-up case that we have to destroy," said Mr. Chavel blandly. "We can assume then that you took a cottage in Cornwall for a longer or shorter period, and, as your residence is in Lush Mellish, and you did not take your maids with you, we may assume it to be a furnished cottage."

"It was a furnished cottage," I said.

"Thank you. This was during the period when you were being spied on and followed at Lush Mellish. Later, Mr. Power came down, and spent some time endeavouring to discover if you had gone into retirement, and, if so, where. We may assume from that that the local police did not know you had gone to Cornwall. I presume you went by car?"

Here again I did not know how much they knew. So I wisely admitted it.

Mr. Chavel smiled. "Thank you. From what you told us this evening, we may assume that it was a car you purchased prior to your present vehicle. We may infer that from Mr. Power's researches into the speedometer."

"Is it a crime to have been the possessor of two cars?" I asked.

"If so, it is a crime that many of us have committed," Mr. Chavel said laughingly. "But that, of course, involves another question. Power, no doubt, when he traced your sketch of the Cornish cottage, and was able by various cross references to fix roughly its position in Cornwall, made some inquiries with reference to the letting of furnished houses in that area."

"I rented it through a London agent," I said.

"You visited one to ask what he had on his books?"

"I saw a photograph of it in *The Times*. In the advertising columns," I told him.

"Power will take *The Times*; if only for the law reports," said Mr. Layman. "There is just the chance that he remembered the picture, or consulted a file of the paper."

"I think you are right," said Mr. Chavel. "I am well pleased with my house here, and my little place in Bucks, but I admit that I derive great pleasure from studying the photographs of houses in the better-class newspapers. If there is a fly in the ointment, it is the abuse of that loathsome phrase 'Choice little residence.'"

"From that," said Mr. Layman, "Power proceeds to trace the letting to Miss Alice."

"You are too clever by half," I reminded him. "As I was thinking of writing a book, I took my little cottage under a *nom de guerre*."

"*Touché!*" said Mr. Layman.

But Mr. Chavel started, stared at me, and spoke. "Moors, ravens, hills, ousels, buzzards, Barrie," he murmured. "Layman, we were right about the economy of Power's methods. He's an extra—a cunning fellow!"

"*Barrie!*" said Mr. Layman. "That's quite an idea, Chavel. But he must have known something! That didn't jump full-armed from his brain, what?"

"The agent, of course," said Mr. Chavel, while I stared impatiently at them in turn. "These snap-shots of his are marvellously effective."

"I need not make a mystery of the fact that I took my pseudonym from a Barrie play," I said with dignity.

"Babbie something, I am sure," said Mr. Chavel.

"Babbie Thrums," I informed him.

"A telling al—I mean, pseudonym," Mr. Chavel remarked. "But, of course, he linked you up with it after that conversation about Barrie's work. The agent probably gave him your description too. Was your licence ever examined in Cornwall?"

"Never."

"But no doubt Power had inquiries made the moment he got wind of the cottage," Mr. Layman remarked. "The locals, the garage people certainly, where Miss Alice got her petrol, would notice the number, and the presence of a golden spaniel in the car."

I raised my eyebrows. "Surely this is much ado about nothing, gentlemen? I bought a little car, took a furnished cottage in Cornwall, under my *nom de guerre*, and was accompanied by my dog. Even Mr. Belisha could find no fault with that."

Mr. Chavel agreed. "No. Of course, you may be asked how you spent your time down there."

"Sketching, writing, and lounging," I said. "I often sat up on some moorland height."

"A pleasant way of passing one's leisure moments, Miss Alice. As far as I can gather the manuscript you showed Mr. Power was typed?"

"I assume that he wanted to discover if the typing was similar to that on the letters in the case," I said. "The manuscript *was* typed. I do my literary work direct on the machine. My next door neighbours can tell you that," I added scornfully. "They were generally watching when I worked in my garden."

"So you took your typewriter down to Cornwall?"

I smiled. "I was not working on my novel in Cornwall."

Mr. Chavel nodded. "So your writing there took the form of—?"

"Naturally, I have always some correspondence," I said.

"You wrote that by hand?"

Possibly the man was trying to do his best for me in his foolish way, but it seemed to me unforgivable, his putting me in a corner like that. It would be unfair and disgusting if similar tactics were tried by the prosecuting counsel at the trial. But they might be, and that beast Power might conceivably have found some witness who had seen me typing in Cornwall. Even there, you cannot get absolutely away from everyone.

"Well," I said, "there is no harm in saying that I had a portable typewriter with me, that I found very useful."

"Quite," Mr. Layman said. "Is it at your house now?"

"No," I said. "I have my own big machine at home, and did not need it. I wanted a better car, so made an exchange, and about the same time I disposed of the machine."

"H'm," murmured Mr. Chavel. "If, by a coincidence, that machine happens to have been a Cremona, it may look awkward for us. Of course, it might be suggested from our side that Miss Alice, having been subjected to spying and annoyance locally, might have disposed of the machine, fearing that possession of it might deepen the unjust suspicions against her."

"That is what I am afraid it was," I said. "They are ready to believe anything against me."

"Come, we are getting on," Mr. Chavel remarked amiably. "We know our biggest snags. Power will have tried to trace the buying of that Cremona. Where did you get it?"

"It was a present to me from a friend," I said. "There is no harm in saying that my Rhodesian friend gave it to me, when she stayed with me at my house in Lush Mellish?"

Mr. Layman started. "The one whose tales Mr. Power was interested in?"

"Yes," I said. "Miss Bostarby."

"It is an odd name, and would be easily traced," said Mr. Chavel. "I imagine, too, that Rhodesia has a sparse white population. Did you tell Power that she had gone home?"

"Yes," I replied. "You think that was why he was interested?"

"It seems very likely, and a cable to the authorities there might bear fruit. But the possession of the machine alone may be got over. I am more anxious about the paper used. Layman here heard that it had been traced at last to a West End store. It was sold during a sale, and as there were some reams of it, it was sent to a hotel."

"There may have been a good many reams sent to hotels," I said.

"Very likely. We must just hope that there has been another coincidence, Miss Alice. They are not half so rare as many people imagine."

Mr. Layman cut in again, as I was digesting this unpleasant piece of news. "You say you disposed of the typewriter?"

"Yes."

"Does it seem likely to you that Mr. Power could trace the present possessor?"

"I don't think so," I said. "I disposed of it rather hurriedly, for the reasons you mentioned."

Mr. Chavel nodded. "I see. I see. But it will be necessary to know to whom you sold it, Miss Alice. You can supply us with that information?"

I was in a quandary, but my mind, as usual, responded to the stimulus of danger. "I am not sure that I can. It was something River—"

"A man called Rivers?" said Mr. Layman.

"We must hope that he has not run away," remarked Mr. Chavel, with his misplaced joviality. "Ha, ha! Yet it might be more of a handicap to the prosecution, eh, Layman?"

"The address, Miss Alice?" Mr. Layman asked, smiling at Mr. Chavel's poor witticism.

"Bridge something, or Bridge of something," I said hurriedly, "but surely there is no need to exchange names and addresses in buying or selling?"

"For cash; no, indeed," observed Mr. Chavel. "Sure the address was not Bridge of Allan?"

"I am sure I could not say," I replied. "I came across him quite by chance at—the side of the road."

To my relief (for in spite of the clever ruse I had adopted to short-circuit this inquiry, I was afraid they would want to know more) Mr. Chavel turned to my lawyer, and seemed to be conducting an unseen orchestra with his pince-nez.

"I am not quite happy, Layman, about that hotel dinner. We have no light on the significance of the conversation which took place there, and Power left soon after."

Mr. Layman assented. "Quite. Why the hotel again, too?"

Mr. Chavel looked at me. "I wonder if your feminine intuition can help us here? So far you will have noticed that every move of Power's had some point. Something which he might twist into evidence against you emerged from every single interview. Can you suggest why he invited you to dine at the hotel again?"

"No," I said, "I am afraid I cannot. But I am certain of one thing—that there was no trick too low, or lie too debased, to be used by that disgusting man."

"Naturally, you look at it from the point of view of a suspected but innocent person," said Mr. Chavel. "But we must all remember that most people regard anonymous letter-writing as a diabolical crime. Mr. Power may have considered that any method was justified in trying to catch someone who had already, indirectly, caused a suicide, and broken up some happy homes."

I had no time to reply, for at that moment Mr. Layman exclaimed sharply, and we turned to hear what he had to say.

CHAPTER XXV

"I WONDER if he had got someone down, Chavel?" Mr. Layman cried. "It seems to me quite likely."

"My dear Layman, why did I not think of it before? But, of course, he had! It is, or was, the obvious thing to do, once he had got so far. I wonder if we could get through on the telephone to the Three Feathers Hotel now?"

He jumped up, found a telephone directory, and began rapidly to turn over the leaves.

"What is the matter now?" I asked Mr. Layman.

"Did you see anyone in the room at dinner that evening—I mean, anyone you recognised?"

My thoughts flew to the loutish person with a made-up tie.

"How extraordinary! Why, Mr. Layman, there was a man at dinner whose face I could dimly remember—or thought I did."

Mr. Chavel looked up from his dialling, then went on.

"Can you not place him?" Mr. Layman asked.

"I am afraid not. I may be mistaken," I told him.

We both stopped talking, to listen to Mr. Chavel, who had taken up the receiver, and was listening intently. Presently he spoke:

"Is that the Three Feathers Hotel, Lush Mellish? Thank you—the reception clerk? Good! Mr. Chavel speaking."

To my surprise, he mentioned the date when I had dined with Mr. Power, and asked if one of the guests in the hotel that evening was a Mr. Simon from some place in Cornwall. A pause followed, then he spoke again:

"No, no; I said Simon, not Tregaskis. What? Oh, Mr. Tregaskis was the only visitor from Cornwall in the hotel that night? Just came for a night? I see. You are sure it was not a Mr. Simon. Sorry to trouble you, then. It is clear enough that Mr. Tregaskis from Porwen is not my friend Simon from Bodmin!"

He put down the receiver, and looked at me. "Now, Miss Alice; does the name Tregaskis, of Porwen, convey any meaning to you?"

"There is a farmer near Porwen, who also keeps paying guests," I said. "Now that I come to think of it, I believe I did once see that young man. But he was wearing breeches and a brown shirt, and carried a gun. I imagine he was rabbit shooting."

"He seems to have made a good shot this time," Mr. Chavel murmured. "So there you are, Layman. That fellow Power is the devil. He takes poor Miss Alice out to dinner, gets a fellow up from Cornwall to identify her, and then fades out. Amazing nerve!"

"We have a tough proposition before us," said Mr. Layman. "If the Cremona turns up, we shall have trouble in meeting that point."

"It may not turn up," replied Mr. Chavel, and put on his pince-nez to look at me. "Besides, my dear fellow, you forget that we have the resources of science at our disposal. They are not monopolised by the police."

"True, Chavel," said Mr. Layman, and turned to me. "Cheer up, Miss Alice. Our friend here is helpful, as usual. If this machine happens to be found, I will engage the services of—"

"Mr. Humphrey Settle—he's the best man," said Mr. Chavel.

"Of Mr. Humphrey Settle," Mr. Layman agreed.

"And who is Mr. Settle?" I asked impatiently.

Mr. Chavel appeared to be enthusiastic about the man. "Mr. Settle is one of the greatest modern experts on typewriting and the typewriter," he gushed. "He never makes a mistake, and the Bench pays the greatest attention to his evidence—a compliment it rarely pays to the expert witness."

"Yes, indeed," Layman chimed in. "He has some micro-photographic process, which is most ingenious, that enables him to tell at once if any piece of typing has been done on any particular machine."

"It's marvellous!" Mr. Chavel gushed again. "I remember one case, where two apparently identical machines from the same maker were used, and Settle unerringly picked out one piece of typing from the other."

Fortunately my withers were unwrung. I could see what would have happened if Mr. Settle had been able to inspect my Cremona, but, knowing that it was hidden from his sight, I was not at all put out.

"I am sure he would have been a great help," I said, and looked at my wrist-watch, "but it is getting late, and I forgot to book a room at an hotel. I can, of course, put up at my club."

"Allow me to ring them up for you," Mr. Chavel said, and did so when I had given him the number. "How time flies when one is engaged in interesting talk!"

It appeared that Mr. Layman was staying the night at his club, so he escorted me to mine, when we had said good-bye to Mr. Chavel, and arranged that we should travel back to Lush Mellish together next morning.

"Amazing fellow, Chavel," he said to me at parting. "I am glad he is not on the other side. Though, indeed, Oviller, if lacking in our friend's suavity and tact, is a perfect demon as an examiner."

Mr. Layman was right, as I had good cause to know.

I need hardly say that, on my return to Lush Mellish, and until I appeared at the assizes, I was treated as if I had already been found guilty.

But I appeared in a minor court before that, to give evidence against a band of local roughs who had made one night hideous in my road by assembling there, with various instruments, supplemented by tin cans and other kitchen utensils, and held an orgy of what they called "rough music."

Several of the ringleaders got off with small fines, but not one was sent to prison. Even the venal magistrates of Lush Mellish could not flout the law altogether, but they did their best to make it of small account.

The truth, of course, was that most of the magistrates sympathised with the brutes, and, for all I know, may have egged them on. One man's fine was, indeed, paid by a woman in court. She said it was because he was a cripple. But I knew the woman. Her nephew was one of my unjust accusers later.

In my later consultations with Mr. Layman, I found the lawyer very unresourceful. He did not seem to be able to make up his mind on our line of defence. It was very disturbing.

"You see," he said to me once, "Power may know something about your possession of that Cremona. If so, questions will be asked about it, and it might be wiser to admit it, and take measures to trace Mr. Rivers."

"I shall do nothing of the sort," I replied. "It is quite unlikely that the machine can be traced. Failing that, they would assume that I had used it to write these letters."

"Then we can only rest your case on a complete denial of the charge," he said. "Are you ready to go into the witness-box, if asked to do so?"

"Certainly, if it is necessary," I said. "I shall tell the court what I told you and Mr. Chavel. Thousands of Cremonas are in use; thousands of letters are written on them. Surely, in the absence of the machine, they cannot prove anything?"

"They dare not take it as a point for the prosecution only," he admitted. "I tell you what we must do. We must advertise, asking a Mr. Rivers, who was on a certain road at a certain time, to communicate with us. It need not be under either of our names. Otherwise we shall certainly be asked why we made no effort to trace the present owner of the machine."

I had to agree. After all, Mr. Rivers had passed under a good many bridges since I had come in touch with him. That little joke pleased me immensely.

"After that," went on Mr. Layman, "we must just do our best, see the line prosecuting counsel adopts, and try to counter it. Chavel is a perfect marvel when it comes to an impromptu defence. I have known him win a case of which he knew nothing when he got up in court."

"I hope your good opinion of him will be justified," I said.

After that interview I did not feel so hopeful. I was to be exposed to trial by jury, knowing that Mr. Chavel was able to convince juries, though he knew nothing about the case he was taking up. But I was also to be exposed to an examination by a counsel who put no decent limits to his questions.

If you went to visit at a house, and the maid said her mistress was "not at home," what would be thought of you if you refused to believe it, and insisted on saying that you had seen her mistress leave the drawing-room as you came in at the gate? What would they say if you asked her when and where her mistress had gone, and wanted to put her in a corner by unfair methods of questioning? I venture to say you would be, and would rightly be, ostracised.

Suppose this brute Mr. Oviller asked me where I had met Mr. Rivers, what he had paid me for the machine, and what was his description? I might refuse to reply, and say that it was a private transaction, and I did not think it fair to expose Mr. Rivers to the annoyance of being called as a witness.

Socially, a gentleman would, of course, take my word for it, but from what I had heard from Mr. Layman, Mr. Oviller was not a gentleman, but a pertinacious monster, without any ideas of the most rudimentary chivalry.

I like justice as well as anybody—more than most, I think—but I do demand common courtesy, which is apparently denied in our law courts, and its place taken by a ruthless desire, as lawyers say, to "get at the truth."

But I plucked up courage again before the assizes came on. I had the blood of my father in my veins, and he was a man who had never been intimidated by the farcical pomp of courts. Secure in his knowledge that he was right, he had held his head high, and fought venality from one of its high places to another.

My advisers were as feckless as before. True, they did make one attempt to have the venue changed, on the ground that I would not get a fair trial in a place where there was so much local prejudice. But that did not upset me. As I told them, a legal system that still allowed Power to practice after his exhibition of unfair spying and underhand trickery could not guarantee one a fair trial anywhere. In any case, my lawyers did not have their plea granted, and later I surrendered to my bail.

Just think of that phrase! Was I a beleaguered fortress, a wild tribe beaten to its knees after a career of terrorism, a mad dog, or something. I began to wonder if it could be that I was the only sane person in a world of fools.

Mr. Layman did not succeed in discovering much more about the intentions of the prosecution. He wouldn't. Like Mr. Chavel he was a fine talker, but a broken reed in action.

The day before the assizes began he actually asked me if I was still determined to plead not guilty!

"Why should I?" I asked him ironically. "It would be simpler and easier for you and Mr. Chavel if I admitted the crime. That, I presume, is why I arranged to pay his heavy fees?"

"Well, of course, if you have made up your mind," he said.

"I hope yours is as firmly made up," I replied.

Now wasn't that an encouraging champion for a woman to have when she was beset by all the forces of the law?

If my readers are interested in descriptions of the places where legal chicanery triumphs over innocence, they must read of them elsewhere. I had seen and heard too much of them in my early days to be interested. I shall only say that the court-house on the opening day of the trial could have been filled twenty times over with the morbid, scandal-mongering, and degenerate inhabitants of Lush Mellish.

I heard afterwards that they literally fought to get places in the queue. Animals will fight; monkeys, and tigers, and lions take their low pleasures in snarling and fighting. When I looked about the court that day, and saw the hot faces and eager eyes of the vulgar crowd, I gave up my last prejudices against Darwinism.

Even the lawyers, scratching their wigs, gave point to my feeling that I was alone in a wilderness of monkeys.

CHAPTER XXVI

THE JUDGE, with hypocritical courtesy, offered to allow me to sit in the dock. He was one of those old men who hide a hard and relentless heart under the guise of benevolence and paternal solicitude.

Before long I was to learn that he was a poisonous old fool, who had made up his mind about me before the case started.

As for the jury, it was composed of average Lush Mellishians, and I need say no more. My counsel challenged five jurors successfully, but at last the farce began, and I had the "pleasure" of hearing Mr. Oviller show some of the savage traits of which I had been warned.

It was at first difficult for me to believe that he referred to the letters I had written. From his version, it would have seemed to a stranger that someone living in the town had suddenly decided to invent a series of vicious lies, to spread them broadcast, and so cause the death of some, the agony of others, and the ruin of some two-score virtuous residents. Further than that, according to him, the letters had been written by a person whose venom bordered on frenzy, a vicious egotist, who had begun by setting the town by the ears, offended or affronted most of its inhabitants, and revenged herself for imaginary slights by starting a campaign which had separated husbands from wives, lovers from lovers, parents from children; had, in fact, plunged harmless Lush Mellish into panic and despair.

I looked at Mr. Chavel. He was smiling to himself and not in the least put out. His fees were safe! I said to myself bitterly.

I looked at the solicitors' table, and saw Mr. Power. He was leaning back with his hands in his pockets. There was no air of shame about him. But how could I expect it? Did I not realise that there were greater potential criminals down there among the lawyers than ever stood in the dock? For his was *legalised* wickedness.

I did not care what that degenerate audience thought, but turned to sweep a proud glance over them, and saw that the poor fools—those who were fools—wore a look of astonished reprobation, and scanned me in horror, as if I was some sort of monster.

"You are looking, my friends," I thought bitterly, "in one of those distorting mirrors one sees in fairs. You think you are looking at me there. But no! What you see is the reflection of your own prejudiced, vicious faces. As for the mouthing scoundrel to whom you listen, he knows only too well what fools and rogues you are. Otherwise he would not dare to put this rigmarole of lies, venom and deceit before you!"

Farce upon farce! I had been asked if I pleaded "Guilty," or "Not Guilty"! I made my views clear on that point in no uncertain voice.

Then came a succession of witnesses, those who received anonymous letters, who described the effect they said the letters had had upon their minds, or careers, or love affairs. Everything they said was exaggerated and multiplied and distorted a hundred-fold.

I must say that I thought Mr. Chavel's cross-examination of these witnesses, when Oviller turned them over to him, was extremely perfunctory. He asked them if they had any proof that I wrote the letters, and they replied in turn that I had some grudge against them.

I had, of course, elected to go into the witness-box and stand examination. Both my lawyers told me that we should have to admit the possession of a Cremona typewriter, and rely on the prosecution being unable to identify the letters as having been done on that machine.

The judge stared at me gravely as I took the oath, and the savage Mr. Oviller tucked his gown round his waist, and favoured me with a sardonic smile. I can only give you an account of some of our exchanges, and shall begin with a question of his with regard to my stay in Cornwall.

"Is it not a fact, Miss Alice," he began, "that you took a furnished cottage in Cornwall, and visited it for short periods during the past six months?"

"Yes," I said, and, determined to take the wind out of his sails, I added: "I took it under the name of 'Babbie Thrums.' I was writing a novel, and that was to be my *nom de guerre*."

"I see," he said. "Writing a novel. One understands that you are an imaginative woman. H'm. Were you working on that novel down in Cornwall?"

Mr. Layman had advised me to let them know the truth at once, as it would create a good impression.

"No," I said, "I took a little Cremona portable with me, the gift of a friend, and occasionally used it to write letters."

There was a stir in court, and Mr. Oviller glanced at the jury.

"Surely not the letters which are in question?" he demanded.

I did not deign to reply.

Mr. Oviller raised his eyebrows ironically. "Now, Miss Alice, you visited this furnished cottage for very short periods. Had you no other idea in your mind than that of taking a holiday, when you went there secretly—"

Mr. Chavel protested. Mr. Oviller went on:

"Let me put it in another way. You took care that no one in Lush Mellish should know—"

"Excuse me," I said, "Lush Mellish surely does not demand that it should be informed when residents take a holiday?"

"That is not the point, Miss Alice. You bought a second-hand car in London, kept it in a suburban garage, and—"

Mr. Chavel rose. "I submit, m'lud, that my learned brother is only beating the air. My client is ready to admit the possession of a car, the taking of a furnished cottage in Cornwall, and the gift to her of a Cremona portable, which she used for occasional correspondence. She is not ready to admit that the letters which figure in this case were written by her."

Mr. Oviller bowed. "Then the air is cleared to that extent." He took up a torn piece of typewriting paper and asked that it might be passed to me. "Do you recognise that paper?" he asked.

"No," I said truthfully, for how could I recognise a piece of paper with no writing on it?

"I am asking you if you used, for your occasional correspondence in Cornwall, paper of this expensive type?"

"I cannot say," I told him. "I am not an expert in papers."

"Would you be surprised to hear that this torn sheet was found by a Mr. Tregaskis near the spot where you once sat typing?" he said with a hateful smile.

"No," I said. "Personally, I can find anything I have put down myself."

"Put down yourself, Miss Alice?" the judge asked.

"Yes, my lord; in view of the methods of the prosecution," I told him, "I have little doubt that they were capable of placing objects where they could readily be found."

"I may have to recall Miss Alice later," Mr. Oviller said. "In the meantime, I must ask her to leave the box. I intend to call Mr. Tregaskis."

I felt that I had given the brute a nasty knock when I returned to my place and Tregaskis got into the witness-box and took the oath. He agreed that he was a farmer in Cornwall. He had been asked to come to Lush Mellish to identify a lady whom he had seen several times on his moorland farm. He had done so when dining at the Three Feathers Hotel.

"You saw her on three occasions?" Mr. Oviller asked him. "Did she see you on those occasions?"

"I cannot be sure," was the reply. "I know she saw me once. I was out with my gun. She was typing, and had a golden spaniel with her."

"And on the other two occasions?"

"I was at some distance, but I recognised the lady, and the dog, and the car."

"Apart from that, for we must be fair," said Mr. Oviller, "were you able, readily, to identify her after one close look at her?"

"Yes, sir. I was."

"She was typing, Mr. Tregaskis. Did anything strike you about that?"

"I thought she must be one of those authors," said the farmer. "Now and then we get them. I saw she had a lot of pages done."

"Oh, that," said Mr. Oviller, "was the lady's *occasional* correspondence."

Mr. Chavel rose to protest. They could not be sure that Mr. Tregaskis would be able to see all that as he passed with his gun. Miss Alice had already admitted that she typed letters on the moor. He submitted that this evidence was irrelevant, if Mr. Oviller bowed again. "That is, I think, a matter for the jury to decide. Now, Mr. Tregaskis, look at the reverse side of this sheet of typewriting paper."

Tregaskis examined it. "Looks as if a dog had stepped on it."

"Will you tell the Court what you once observed Miss Alice's dog to do?"

"He was playing with a bit of paper the time I went shooting," was the reply. "Had one end in his teeth, and his foot on the other, sir."

"I see. A playful animal. What else?"

"As I turned away, sir, I saw him nose it under a rock."

"As dogs do with a bone?"

"Yes."

"Thank you, Mr. Tregaskis," said Oviller. "That will do. Call Constable Morfus, of the Bodmin Constabulary."

Constable Morfus took the oath in a gabble, and Mr. Oviller smiled at him.

"Now, constable, acting on instructions, you were taken some time ago to a spot on the moor near the cottage occupied by Miss Alice?"

"Yes, sir. I was taken by Mr. Tregaskis."

"You were shown a rock with a sort of cleft in it?"

"Yes, sir, I was."

"You found there a piece of torn paper, a piece of expensive paper, with an ivory-finished surface?"

"Yes, sir. It was under the rock."

"Take this piece of paper in your hand—thank you. To the best of your knowledge and belief, is that the torn paper you found?"

"It is, sir, and here's the mark of the dog's foot that was on it when I picked it up."

"Now here, constable, is a piece of paper from a lot sold earlier in the year by a London store."

"Well, sir, I must say they look alike."

Mr. Chavel rose. "I object. The constable is not an expert, and the finding of a torn piece of paper—however it got under the rock—is no proof that my client wrote the letters complained of."

You will not be surprised to hear that Mr. Chavel was not at all cross with my accuser. They kept on bowing to each other, which showed what humbug the whole thing was. And Mr. Chavel did not cross-examine the witness, who was told to stand down. Mr. Oviller then recalled me.

"Now, Miss Alice, the prosecution alleges that you purchased a car in London—a car which was never seen in Lush Mellish—for the purpose of stealing down secretly to Cornwall. Is that true?"

"I went down openly by day, sometimes," I said.

"May I ask why you travelled such a long way by car?"

"I prefer to travel by car. It is more comfortable," I said.

"Yet you used to return from London by train—a considerable distance."

"I hope I am entitled to use my judgment," I said.

"Quite. Did your judgment suggest that, when you returned from Cornwall, it was quicker to return via London, rather than save a hundred miles and drive straight to Lush Mellish?"

"It seems rather beside the point," I said.

"Very well. The jury will have to use their common sense about that," he said, with a smarmy smile at the twelve Lush Mellishians. "A friend who came from Rhodesia, and stayed with you, made you a gift of a typewriter?"

"A criminal proceeding, surely!" I said coldly.

"A generous one. Curiously enough, that machine was a Cremona portable."

"Are Rhodesians forbidden to use Cremonas?" I asked scornfully.

"Not as far as I am aware," he replied. "She handed it over to you—where?"

"In my house."

"In your house. Your maids are aware that you type?"

"Of course."

"But they were unaware that you had a second machine?"

"They are not so inquisitive as some people," I told him.

"Yours is not a large house," he said. "It would seem strange that your maids did not see the machine in the course of their duties."

"The explanation is simple," I informed him. "I had no use for it at home, where I had my large machine. I put it in a trunk."

"I see. You took it to London in a trunk, and transferred it there to the car you had bought?"

"Obviously, since I had it with me in Cornwall," I said.

"Thank you," he said sarcastically, "but the car was much oftener in this lock-up at the Ealing garage than it was in your cottage in Cornwall. I understand that machines of the kind are liable to damage through neglect, or exposure to damp."

"The rumble of my car was quite dry," I said.

"Oh, you kept it in there, did you?"

"I do not see the point of that question, Mr. Oviller," said the judge.

"I submit, m'lud, that it goes to prove the secrecy with which these journeys were carried out—the secrecy which surrounded Miss Alice's journeys to Cornwall."

"We do not admit the secrecy," Mr. Chavel interposed.

Mr. Oviller bowed. "I should hardly expect the defence to do so," he said. "Now, Miss Alice, you are aware that work done on typewriters can be identified by experts as done on a particular machine?"

"I must take your word for it," I said.

"You may. There is no harm in possessing a portable Cremona, no harm even in having some reams of ivory-surfaced paper, originally bought at a sale by a visitor from Rhodesia, and sent by the store to her hotel—"

"M'lud"—Mr. Chavel got up—"counsel for the prosecution is either examining the witness, or making a speech."

The judge instructed Mr. Oviller, who bowed to him, and went on: "But, having a Cremona, witness will be only too glad to have her machine examined, and the question settled, one way or the other."

"If you can trace it for me, certainly," I said. "My legal adviser has advertised for the present possessor, but without success."

"I was not officially informed of that. May I ask the name?"

Mr. Chavel got up. "The name was Rivers. Miss Alice was not very clear what address he gave, but it was something Bridge."

"A curious conjunction!" Mr. Oviller said. "Rivers are a wandering race, if his lordship will allow me a small witticism. You are sure his name was not River Bridge, Miss Alice?"

CHAPTER XXVII

FOR A moment I was staggered; then I recovered myself, and smiled ironically. "A fondness for punning feebly may be an asset in a legal career, Mr. Oviller, but it seems out of place here."

You see, I felt sure he was fishing. How could they have discovered that I had disposed of the machine so cleverly?

"Then you cannot supply us with an accurate description of the purchaser, or the place of meeting, or how you came to suggest selling a typewriter to a complete stranger?"

"I refuse to be made the butt of your feeble jokes," I told him. "If you can trace the machine for me, I shall be ready to answer further questions."

"I shall not inflict any more of them upon you." He bowed to me this time. "Stand down, please."

I smiled at Mr. Chavel. I thought that I had neatly disposed of the clumsy brute. I resumed my place in the dock, and the wretched inspector who had interviewed me before got into the witness-box.

Now I began to see that the coward Power would not be called at all. He hid behind his wretched police tools!

But the hand was the hand of Esau.

"Acting under instructions," he began, when Mr. Oviller asked him a question, "I was driven from Cornwall to London—"

"By what route, inspector?" Mr. Oviller interrupted.

"By three different routes, sir," the inspector replied.

"Three different routes? For what reason?"

"I understood, sir, that Miss Alice had taken these routes on different journeys from her cottage in Cornwall."

"You mean that inquiries showed that she had travelled by these three routes?"

"It seems to me that that is what the inspector has told us, Mr. Oviller," said the judge. "Go on, please."

"I followed a schedule given to me," said the inspector.

"I see. You had other special instructions?"

"I had, sir. I was to notice what rivers, streams, or water-courses were crossed while travelling by these three routes."

Mr. Chavel rose hastily. "We have no proof that Miss Alice did travel by any, or all, of these routes."

"You will have your opportunity to cross-examine the witness later, Mr. Chavel," said the judge.

The inspector smiled faintly, and I wrote a note and had it passed to Mr. Chavel. I did not wish him to contest the point, since I felt sure now that the fiend Power had gone over every inch of the ground, and secured witnesses who had seen me, or the car, *en route.*

"What was the meaning of this instruction about rivers and watercourses?" Mr. Oviller asked, with a smile for the jury.

"I was told to trace the typewriting machine, sir."

"I hope you were not misled by the fact that the machine was supposed to have been transferred to Mr. River Bridge—I beg your pardon, to Mr. Rivers."

There was a snigger in court at this, and the judge, with what I am sure was *mock* severity, told Mr. Oviller he must keep to the point.

"I bow to your ludship's ruling," said Mr. Oviller. "You had information to the effect that the machine might have been thrown into a river where it was crossed by a bridge?"

"That is so, sir."

"Were you successful in your quest, inspector?"

"I was, sir," said the man, and there was a gasp in court once more, and some noise which the judge subdued.

"Just tell the Court your *modus operandi*," said Mr. Oviller, and the wretched inspector beamed, as if he had found out something for himself. I was horrified, but not without hope. Immersion for such a period in the river might have rusted the type face, and made it impossible for the expert to say what had once been written on that machine.

"I stopped at each bridge," the inspector went on, "and examined the water above and below it. In some cases it was too shallow; in other cases—"

"Come, come!" said the judge testily. "You examined various pools. You found the machine. Where did you find it?"

"I found a portable Cremona typewriter under a narrow bridge that passes over the River Grimble, adjacent to the hamlet of Clay Grimble, North Dorset, me lord," the inspector said in a breath.

"Do not address me; address yourself to the jury!" said the judge, as if that mattered.

"Is the machine in court?" Mr. Oviller asked.

"It is, sir."

"I want it produced at once, and possibly Miss Alice may be able to identify it as hers," the brute observed.

Of course, I was unable to identify it. I had never taken a note of the number which, I believe, is impressed on all machines of a series, and, of course, one Cremona looks just like another to the amateur. It is true that it might have been my discarded machine, but I was not going to swear to the identity of one which might (with the deceitful Power at the back of the inquiries) have been substituted for mine.

"But I can safely leave that to the jury," said Mr. Oviller, when I had spoken. "We have witnesses to prove that she drove her car from London to Cornwall by that route on her last journey from the cottage. I think it is safe to assume that this machine belonged to her, and was thrown into the river pool in the course of that journey."

"If we are to try this case on assumptions—" said Mr. Chavel.

Mr. Oviller bowed to him. "You can now cross-examine the witness," he said.

Mr. Chavel refused. "I have heard what he has said. My client does not identify the machine as hers."

Mr. Oviller made a gesture. "You can leave the box, inspector. I am going to call Mr. Humphrey Settle."

I saw a little ginger-haired man go into the witness-box. This was the famous expert of whom Mr. Layman had spoken. I listened as in a dream while he took the oath, and then explained how he had examined the machine, cleaned it carefully, and conducted a series of microphotographic experiments which proved, he said, that the letters received by various persons in Lush Mellish had been written on it. Various photographs and documents were handed over for the inspection of the jury, together with three magnifying glasses, and twenty minutes was wasted in this farce.

When Mr. Oviller had done with the witness, Mr. Chavel rose.

"Tell me, Mr. Settle," he said. "It was necessary to clean the machine after its immersion?"

"Certainly."

"I suggest that a letter written on it, after this necessary cleaning, would differ in some points from one written when the type face was new, unrusted, and uncleaned?"

Mr. Settle shook his head. "There was not much rust on the type face. My cleaning was done with a view to preserving that as far as possible—"

"But only as far as possible?"

"In its original condition," said Mr. Settle. "Having regard, however, to the possibility you suggest, that microscopic portions of the type face might have been damaged by the immersion and subsequent cleaning, I concentrated in my experiments on finding similarities not directly concerned with the type face itself."

"Such as?"

"A tendency of the type-spacing bar to stick."

"That might be due to rust," said Mr. Chavel.

"A fact which was proved by the letters, which were admittedly received prior to the machine's immersion," said Mr. Settle. "So we may rule out the effects of rust."

"And is that your sole proof?" Mr. Chavel asked scornfully.

"It is one of many points," said Mr. Settle. "I compared the matter of several letters, written by Miss Alice to various people months ago, with that of the anonymous letters. In both, there was a succession of mistakes. In both, the letter 'o' was often written where the letter 'i' was intended. Where hyphens were required there was a tendency to put the dash which goes under a letter on a line to indicate that italics are intended. I could multiply examples, most of which have already been shown to the jury."

Mr. Chavel sat down. He was a poor specimen compared with the witness, who obviously had brains—if they were enlisted in an unworthy cause.

Mr. Oviller took over the witness again. "With your experience as an expert in these matters, extending over twenty-five years, Mr. Settle, you are confident that the machine in court was that used in typing the series of disgusting and scurrilous epistles, the receipt of which has been testified to in this court?"

"I am. I have no doubt about it whatever," said Mr. Settle.

I looked at the judge, the jury, the wretched, morbid fools who crowded the court, as Mr. Settle left the box. I glanced at my miserable counsel, and knew that the die was cast against me. From that moment I ceased to take any interest in the proceedings, which droned on for three more long hours.

Of counsels' speeches I will say little. Mr. Oviller was as brutal, as unfair, and illogical, as even I had been led to expect. Mr. Chavel transcended my most pessimistic expectations. I consider that he was a disgrace to the Bar.

I had to interrupt him a dozen times. I made what is called "a scene." I was threatened by that unjust judge. Afterwards, Mr. Layman tried to excuse the man by saying that our case had not a leg to stand on, and he was pleading in mitigation of the sentence, or some fusty phrase like that. But what right had the man, paid by me at extortionate rates, to suggest that I was not in my right mind at the time?

But that was what he told the jury. He told them that I was in some measure the victim of heredity, and a tendency to regard hostility to myself as evidence of local persecution. He remarked that I was self-centred, and the victim of a temperament inclined to megalomania. Then I was intensely humanitarian, and losses of successive dogs, to which I was deeply attached ("My client's devotion to the canine creation may be held by some to be so excessive and exaggerated as to amount to a species of mania; though I myself could hardly subscribe to that view"), had upset the normal balance of my brain.

"There is no doubt," he added, after the last scene which I had felt compelled to provoke, "that my client was subjected to snubs and slights in Lush Mellish. I plead this in mitigation of her offence, and suggest that any expert in these temporary mental disorders will agree with me that what was done by her—and I am not trying to suggest that the offence is a slight one—was done when she was not in a condition to appreciate the harm that might ensue. Alternatively, the very fact that her letters were directed at what she obviously thought to be moral lapses, or unsocial conduct, hints that a form of religious mania may be at the bottom of the affair."

I need say no more about the vapourings of that treacherous scoundrel. I protested. I assured the Court that I did not, and did not intend to, plead guilty. I begged the judge to have the two local parsons put into the witness-box to give evidence. But all to no purpose.

When quiet had been restored, the judge summed up. He summarised, that is to say, the lies, the twisted evidence, the silly speculations of the expert, the local prejudices of Lush Mellish. He had even the impertinence to suggest that my conduct in court proved that I was unbalanced, violent, and irresponsible. He had "even had thought of postponing the trial so that I should be examined by an alienist"! He had concluded, however, that pride, malice, egocentricity, and a very revengeful nature were at the back of my "scandalous, cruel, and loathsome" letters.

And so I make an end. The jury retired, and came back to find me guilty.

I went to jail, refused even in my misery the consolation of the society of my dear Tiblits. The rest you know.

Now I am free again, and have finished my task.

I hear that Mr. Power has just become engaged. They say that she is a charming girl. I am sorry for her. I should like to be able to help her; to save her, before it is too late, from linking her fate with one of the most clever and slimy scoundrels it was ever my lot to meet.

Well, now that my book is done, I am going abroad. To do good by stealth—just one last good deed—I shall send her a copy of this book.

THE END

Printed in Great Britain
by Amazon